CITIES OF WEATHER

D1714229

CITIES OF WEATHER

STORIES

MATTHEW FOX

Riverbank Press
an imprint of Cormorant Books Inc.

OTTAWA PUBLIC LIBRARY
BIBLIOTHEQUE PUBLIQUE D'OTTAWA

Copyright © 2005 Matthew Fox

No part of this publication may be reproduced, stored in a retrieval system
or transmitted, in any form or by any means, without the prior
written consent of the publisher or a licence from
The Canadian Copyright Licensing Agency (Access Copyright).
For an Access Copyright licence, visit www.accesscopyright.ca
or call toll free 1.800.893.5777.

Canada Council   Conseil des Arts
for the Arts   du Canada

ONTARIO ARTS COUNCIL
CONSEIL DES ARTS DE L'ONTARIO

The publisher gratefully acknowledges the support of the
Canada Council for the Arts and the Ontario Arts Council
for its publishing program. We acknowledge the financial support
of the Government of Canada through the Book Publishing
Industry Development Program (BPIDP) for our publishing activities.

Printed and bound in Canada

LIBRARY AND ARCHIVES CANADA CATALOGUING IN PUBLICATION

Fox, Matthew, 1977 –
Cities of weather / Matthew Fox.

ISBN 1-896332-20-X

1. Title.

PS8611.O9C48 2005   C813 .6   C2004-906521-1

Cover design: John Terauds & Tannice Goddard
Cover illustration: *Evening Hour* by tomolennon
Text design: Tannice Goddard, Soul Oasis Networking

THE RIVERBANK PRESS, AN IMPRINT OF CORMORANT BOOKS INC.
215 SPADINA AVENUE, STUDIO 230, TORONTO, ON CANADA M5T 2C7
www.cormorantbooks.com

For my parents.

contents

city of weather

Janey saw her life as two worlds connected by ugly tunnels. There was her apartment — three clothes-strewn rooms that smelled of clay — and there was the office. Between them were the Metro, its gaudy stations, its long tiled tubes, and the Underground City snaking beneath the snowy streets of downtown Montreal. In this last leg of the journey, Janey had to keep herself from staring at the people around her: the dream-yanked faces, the winter-white skin framed by fuzzy scarves, the wet morning eyes with crust trapped in the corners. The office workers walked at the same speed between the shiny, tiled walls, with the same queer ignorance of one another, the same urgency robbed of bustle. Even at twenty-five, Janey ploughed through the wet tunnels like a seasoned veteran. It was so much simpler to remain caught in the tide of bobbing heads than to turn back to her bed. But she still wondered how they all managed to produce transit fare, find the right train, the right tunnel. Wasn't it remarkable that so many people could handle the tasks of life and not get derailed? Not get distracted by each other? By designs on the gritty, wet floor? By the city's frenzy of tiny beauties?

The company she worked for was good at compartmentalizing. The front door of the CyberSmart office opened to a field of dividers that, with an intricacy she found marvellous and unnecessary, sectioned off cells for each of the employees. She made her way down the carpeted paths to her desk, giving token nods to co-workers and running a hand along the tweed partitions. In her cubicle, she turned on the computer and sat in her ErgonoMaster chair. For $24,500 per year, Janey recorded art's presence on the Internet, cataloguing the names and styles of artists into various categories: abstract, figurative; Renaissance, Victorian; French, Canadian, French-Canadian. She dealt with paintings by Monet reduced to colourful smudges and Miros that only the Internet could render lifeless and uninteresting. Sentences like "The presence of Cubism on the Web is negligible," were typical of her summary reports, copyedited in the next cubicle by her smoking partner, Debbie, and proofread by Toby, the assistant manager. They then came back to Janey's desk and she attached a catalogue sheet, photocopied the stack, and placed them in various boxes in the mailroom.

But really she spent most of her time staring at her hands,

amazed that such minute movements could create language. By five o'clock, she found herself fixated on the collection of characters on the keyboard itself, her tapered fingers hovering above them. On Thursdays, a memorandum from Toby was batch emailed to the staff: bend your wrists, sit with wide shoulders, take microbreaks. Janey lived for her microbreaks, during which she crafted tiny figures out of metal paper clips. Last Christmas, she had created a nativity scene for Debbie using only office supplies. Debbie had stared at it, lifted one of the masking tape sheep and said, "I don't think I get it." Now Janey was working on a chess set: wire bishops holding wire staffs topped with wire crosses.

Janey was watching her computer screen come to life — *loading personal settings, finding network connection* — when Toby appeared at her cubicle. "Miss Forsythe?" he said. He was a puffy man, but always looked puffiest in the mornings in a still-crisp white shirt and flaccid tie outlining the curve of his gut. "A word?"

His office had a door, windows, walls that went all the way to the ceiling.

"Do you like it here?" Toby said, sitting down, his chair squealing in pain.

"Yes," she lied. "Do you?"

He smiled but for a second. "Yes, Miss Forsythe, I like it very much. So it would make sense to you that I'd be uncomfortable when one of my employees is not working up to her potential, wouldn't it?"

"Sure," she said.

"And have you noticed that your numbers are not what they were when you first started here? They started slipping in September."

"OK."

"You know why we have quotas, right?" he folded a squadron of thick fingers over his stomach. "Our users depend on us to tell them what's out there on the Net. It can't be good for them if our information is out of date, can it?"

"I guess not," Janey said, thinking it unlikely that Picasso was going to paint anything new. But professional life, she had discovered when she got out of art school, was ruled by a pressuring logic unrelated to reality. All questions had been asked and answered an eternity ago, and it was up to every employee to make sure those answers continued to be correct.

"Well, I can understand that the thrill of a job can wear off a little a year into things, but we have to persevere," he said, "don't we?"

"I've been having some problems. In my personal life."

He looked across the desk at her, seemingly baffled by the concept of a personal life. "This is just a warning," he said. "But I want you to ask yourself, seriously, every day — is this job for me?"

"OK."

He gave her an unconvinced smile, then stood to extend a thick hand. Its fat was closing in on the fingernails, reducing them to little islands. She took it, squeezed, felt its give and thickness. "Glad to hear it."

‡

Janey was a sculptor. She lived on the second floor of a triplex on Coloniale Street, across from a deaf couple that always waved at her, and above a rabbi who, like her parents, spent most of the winter in the United States. Once the door clicked shut behind her, Janey felt like she was finally outside the realm of work-time necessity and reason. Unlike her cubicle, the world of Janey's home was sealed up and private. It was a railroad apartment, with rooms flowing one into the next like in an art gallery, and walls the colour and texture of eggshells. The place became progressively dirtier — and more exciting — as she moved from the front door through the unused living room, through the chaos of the bedroom, to the kitchen. There were rags everywhere. All the drawer knobs were darkened by clusters of grubby fingerprints and the linoleum was spotted with clay-brown footsteps that converged near her sculpting table.

After work, she marched straight to the counter to look at her Big Project. At the moment, it was three hands reaching up from forearms, the fingers curved as though gripping at invisible objects. In her mind, though, she could see the completed sculpture: a clutch of hands — strong, old, young, bony, cratered, smooth, veined — coming up from nowhere and covering every inch of a body, a hidden woman, whose nose and breasts and knees and muscles were denoted by curves in the smothering fingers.

Janey took off her coat and wrapped it around the back of a chair. From her bag, she pulled out her sketchbook and began to flip through, past drawings of lumpy bodies and pinkies and furniture. Next to each, she had written lists of adjectives — flashwords that could prompt inspiration when she confronted a fresh brick of clay. Sometimes she went to a café to observe the patrons. Tonight she stopped at a page titled "Toby" and stared at a sketch she had made earlier, at work: her boss's right hand, flat on his desk. Next to it, she had written, "turgid, grotesque, puffy, fat, busy, self-important, like ten tubes of marzipan." Arrows took each word to an appropriate place on the fingers.

Janey filled a wide metal bowl with steaming tap water. From the fridge, she unearthed a small piece of clay, removed the limp Saran Wrap, and rolled up the sleeves of her blouse. She began pounding the brick with wet hands. At first, the clay was cold. "Come on," she said to it, "resistance is futile." Moving from it to the hot water, her hands became tingly and self-possessed, barely obedient as she harassed the stiff angles of the block into a tube that expanded at one end. The shapes were there, under her fingers, she could see them — the hump of Toby's strained tendon, the bloated cliff of his cuticle. As the form appeared, she had to rock forward and back to see all its angles, to pull the edge of a fork along the wide end to proportion the fingers. Tonight's sculpture will go over the eyes, she thought as she slid a butter knife underneath the clay. Each of the digits needed be curved accordingly and the wrist required a dramatic bend. The surface of Toby's arm was now sloppy with water and its base conformed to the table when upturned. She worked from underneath, creating lines on the palm, as brown tears tickled down her skin toward her elbow. The whole room was participating now, the fridge humming its compliance, the window whistling, the yellowed cupboards reaching up to the ceiling, cheering her on like spectators at a marathon.

When she was satisfied with the result, she sat next to the sculpture and lit a cigarette, the filter wet and brown from her hand. She was exhausted, and leaned into the wooden back of the chair, legs apart. She avoided looking at the creation itself, it would get her excited again and she'd be unable to sleep. Moonlight was intensifying through the prisms of frost on the windowpane. She didn't know what time it was, but her neighbours' light was still glowing across the courtyard.

She loved spying on the deaf couple's routines. They were moving around now, preparing for bed — Janey could see their shadows. They were a cute couple, Janey's age, whose faces lit up whenever they saw her in the street. The wife seemed pert and he was a gangly man, tall, with attentive eyes and a slightly bucktoothed smile. They both nodded a great deal, encouraging conversation. Yet, Janey thought, the couple appeared to share a silent, ongoing communication that was so intimate that no one would ever be able to join in. She came close once, when she caught sight of them having sex on the couch. He was on top of her, pushing himself up and down with the tops of his feet, his buttocks clenching and unclenching in the blue tint from the TV. Sitting in her darkened kitchen that night, Janey had felt sneaky and aroused. But as she kept watching her neighbours, she began to feel distanced from them. She was not accessing intimacy at all. She was stalking. While everyone else was fucking, she was in her little kingdom squeezing clay and talking to herself and picking her nose.

She pushed her cigarette butt into a chunk of wet clay. It hissed. The light below went out and Janey felt a pang of relief. She left her sculpture on the table to dry and walked to the shower, sneaking a peek at the Big Project on her way out of the kitchen. With the water hot and stinging on her neck and back, she lowered herself onto the floor. Lately, she had been showering cross-legged, eyes closed. She pictured the Big Project, its intricacy and busy hands, and felt the hot water run down her body. From that far down, the drops of water sounded louder, felt fatter, harder.

‡

Nearly three months had passed since Mike left Janey alone with her clay.

When they first met at a bar on Crescent Street, she had been happy that he spoke English and had a job. His shoulders were square and muscular, tugging creases into the front of his shirt. Janey was jealous, admiring. She longed for a dramatic shape of her own. She hated being tall and pale, though everyone told her she was beautiful. He bought her four drinks and she folded the stirring straws into a tiny windmill for him. That night, and many nights afterward, Janey would sit in a corner of her room, smoking and watching his form under the sheets — lumpy, soft, unmoving. They were an immediate couple. He routinely showed up at her apartment after leaving the gym — in an Adidas tracksuit, Nikes, and gold watch — with some misbegotten gift, something he must have thought artsy: an instrumental CD titled *Sounds of Inspiration*; a tin case of paints intended for a child; an enormous Loreena McKennitt poster that Janey tacked to the wall even though the singer looked psychotic. Most nights, they ordered take out and watched TV. Janey always found some way to hold and examine his hairy fingers. He tensed when laughing at *Will & Grace* or *This Hour Has 22 Minutes*. "You don't think that's funny?" he would ask, and she would admire him for being so earnest.

They went on one trip together — to visit Mike's parents on a farm near Toronto. Mike insisted on long walks through the fields, family board-game sessions and group cooking at mealtimes. Janey was restless the whole weekend, grabbed moments to escape for cigarettes.

"Don't they look happy?" Mike asked, more than once.

"Sure," she said. But they didn't. To Janey, his parents

seemed downright miserable and bored, shiftless, hiding their hands under their folded arms because of drafts they refused to acknowledge. The mother asked about a transfer Mike had been considering to the Royal Bank's head office in Toronto. "It would be nice to have you so close, Michael" or "There's so much more money in this part of the country" or, to Janey, "Doesn't it just make so much more sense?"

Back in Montreal, early autumn was heavy with awkward discussions over chipped beer mugs at Café Parallèle. He talked about the future, using words like "security" and "convenience" and "Mississauga." Janey would nod at the window, smoking. These were the calling cards of normality. She had been waiting for them, and yet it was like he was talking around her, like she was overhearing the conversation from another table. One night in October, Mike said that he had accepted the transfer to Toronto. "I had to. My boss told me that they couldn't wait any longer."

"Why?" Janey asked. She was sitting at her kitchen table, arms crossed over her chest. "Is it the money?"

"Yes, in part. We've been through this. Think about the future. My position here has no opportunities for movement."

"There's nothing for me in Toronto."

"Oh, except your boyfriend." He nodded his head ironically.

"Do you think that you can just move me around? Is that it?"

"I've been waiting for you to make a decision for weeks now," he said. "I think I've been very patient."

"You would say that."

"Why do you have to be so difficult, Jane?" He was stand-ing now, looking down at her. "Why do you want to stay?"

She stared at the tabletop. "I don't know."

"Well, I'm doing it," he said, sliding his arms into his coat. "If you want to be alone, go right ahead."

In the silence after he slammed the door, Janey's eyes started burning with tears — she'd imagined more screaming, toasters being thrown, an explosion. She rose and walked to the fridge. Near the back was an old brick of clay she had kept after taking a night class in sculpting. It bore the imprint of the wire shelf, like a grilled piece of meat. She filled a wide metal mixing bowl with warm water and placed it on the kitchen chair, still warm from Mike's body.

She was up all night reproducing Mike's hand from below the wrist, with slightly curled and fatty fingers, self-manicured nails and thick knuckle hair. This felt new. There was no unfinished work staring at her from a computer screen. Unlike when she was at the office, she didn't have to toss her creation in a drawer when people passed by. No one passed by; the space she worked in was all hers.

At dawn she was sleepless and exhilarated. She washed the clay from her hands, dressed, and headed for the Metro. Walking through the tunnels toward CyberSmart, instead of thinking about Mike and her range of girlfriendly inadequacies, she just watched her fellow commuters' heads moving up and down, looking like a swarm of knuckles,

11

curving and kneading. That was when she got the idea for her Big Project — it just popped into her head. She could see it perfectly. In her cubicle, she did no work, just spent the morning sketching. She stepped out periodically to smoke with Debbie and to attend the weekly business development meeting.

"That meeting was so pointless," said Janey. She and Debbie were standing by the building's emergency exit. Janey pulled the smoke into her chest with such force that the filter tapped against her teeth. The building also housed a moving company, but this was October, not the season for Montrealers to move. Most of the grey, heavy trucks sat in the parking lot like sleeping pets.

"Like a Sartre play," Debbie deadpanned. "A bad one. One of the ones he wrote in school." Janey loved Debbie's bitterness. Thirty-two and twice divorced, fond of pink and tan, she was a beacon in a pantsuit, waving her hands and poking her cigarette at the world. She suffered from rheumatoid arthritis that was often painful; her left hand was so swollen that the wedding ring from her last marriage was stuck there for eternity. Debbie held her hands in one another when she wasn't typing or smoking, fingers in italics, all gnarled and bent in the same direction. As the condition worsened, Debbie was frequently away from the office and even more frequently vowed to quit working with her hands altogether and become a medical test subject.

"Why do editors have to be involved in business development meetings?" Debbie said. "Isn't that that the point of
having de*part*ments?"

"Everyone knows what everybody else is doing this way.
It's innovative managing or something."

"Yeah, well, sometimes this company is so cutting edge, I
just want to throw up." Debbie sighed, disgusted at even talking about the meeting. "You look like *you* could throw up. Did
you get *any* sleep last night?"

"No," Janey said.

"Another fight with Mike, then? I can't even hear you
typing in there."

"Oh right," Janey said, surprised suddenly that she had not
told Debbie about what had happened. "Mike stormed out."

"*What?* The bastard. I'll kill him," and Debbie made a
move to hug her friend. "I'm so, so sorry." Janey had always
shared with her the details of her love life. She wanted badly
to tell Debbie that it was OK, that out of the breakup had
come the Big Project. But then Janey thought better of it.
Men and work, it seemed, were Debbie's only touchstones.
Once, Janey had brought pictures to the office of a sculpture
she had made in a studio class — the bust of a melting snowman. The eyes of the figure were bulging from its decaying
face and the carrot nose had curved with rot. Debbie's sole
comment was to ask what Mike thought of it.

"But he came back," Janey said and shifted her weight.

This was a lie, but Janey thought maybe if she spoke of the Big Project as if it were Mike, she could trick Debbie into understanding. "He came back and I grabbed him. I spent the rest of the night with him."

"He changed his mind? Just like that? That sounds dodgy."

"But Deb, it felt new. After last night, I think I can finally see a future there. It was like he had crossed into something completely different and exciting."

"That's the dodgier side of love." Debbie looked concerned.

Janey laughed. Her lie felt like truth, her words had the cool release of honesty. "I just feel like I've been spooked. He was so apologetic; I think I can mould him into whatever I want. Like I can make something totally new. That's what it feels like."

"I know that feeling. You feel passionate now, but it doesn't last. It's risky. And you can tell him that if he lets you down," Debbie put one gnarly finger in the air, "I will kill him."

‡

"Hi, Dad," Janey said into the cordless phone. "It's your daughter."

"Which one?"

"The one you like." Janey was an only child. This was their game.

"Oh, right!" and he chuckled. "How's work?"

"Great, great. How's Florida?" She hated the idea that her

parents had joined the leagues of other ageing Montrealers in the southern U.S. She had always viewed them as more original than that.

"Too many old people," he said. "How's that Mike?"

"That Mike couldn't be better. He's right here," Janey said, walking through the empty apartment toward the drafty kitchen, where the Big Project sat on the counter. "The weather?"

"Your mother's burnt to a crisp. I see in the paper that the snow keeps piling up on Quebec. A real Quebec winter!"

"It's quite beautiful, Dad. You're missing it." Outside her kitchen window, snowflakes circled wildly. She sat in her sculpting chair watching breath escape from her mouth. The room reeked of wet earth. Across the courtyard, she could see the deaf couple eating chicken and carrots in front of the TV, drinking glasses of wine, as was their Saturday afternoon habit.

"My legs could never take it. Do you still make those faces in the snow?" His voice trailed off. "Remember those faces Janey used to make in the snow?"

She could picture Mom in her teal kitchen, listening in, scratching painfully pink fingers against the pockets of her apron.

"Busts, Dad."

"Sure. Full of talent, you were. Still are! Did you read in the paper that thing about the National Film Board?" Last Christmas Janey arranged an international subscription to

La Presse for her father so he could keep up his French. She had since started regretting the gift. "It's a good time down there. Government office and all."

"Work is fine, Dad." But he did not hear her. His voice was pulled away from the phone again as he spoke to her mother:

"She says things are super. But she's still in the dingy apartment. It's a far cry from Westmount. Janey," his voice still raised, "it's a far cry from Westmount."

"You don't have to keep yelling when you come back on the phone."

"You call these NFB people. It's all artsy stuff down there now. Right up your alley."

Janey lit a cigarette. She loved her father. Loved his concern. She could not blame him for dreaming big dreams for her.

"Are you smoking?"

"I'm actually up for a promotion at CyberSmart."

"She says she's up for a promotion. Big Money. Janey, your mother and I just want you to be happy." Janey choked back a guffaw, but she felt she owed him a response. By happy, he meant something else. He meant comfortable. She poked mindlessly at hard piece of clay on the tabletop.

"I am. I am happy, Dad."

‡

The Big Project grew. After finishing Toby's hand, Janey had moved on to pulling images from memory — completing hands belonging to her mother and father, their fingers bent into fists, gripping invisible ankles. She was particularly proud of how she denoted the feet of the sculpture — a series of baby's hands, with fingers like larvae, holding onto each toe. By mid-December, there were so many hands that Janey moved the Big Project to the floor of her room. She took down the giant Loreena McKennitt poster and laid it face down on the floor, then sat on the white rectangle and traced out her body. She sketched in the relief of a woman's features: kneecaps, navel, hip bone, clavicle. It looked like a topographical map. She brought the arms in from the kitchen and laid them out in their intended places on the poster so that she could gain perspective on how the final product would look. She stood on her bed and looked down at the Project. Everything fit. There were barely a dozen hands in place, but her imagination filled in the white areas. It had never been so clear to her. Janey could see all the arms and fingers, but also feel the clammy smothering and picture the face of a mysterious woman: scared, shadowy, resigned.

She was too excited to sleep. Warm and buzzing, she left the apartment without a coat, sketchbook in hand, hoping that a walk in the cold would calm her down, tire her out. As soon as she stepped out on Coloniale Street, she knew that this was impossible. She had brought her private little world out into the city. Snow covered everything. The sidewalks were gritty with traction pebbles dotting the whiteness like chocolate chips on ice cream. Tires had cut parallel paths down the centre of the road. Janey moved north through the winter; the cold wrapped around her, pinching her nostrils. At the corner of Pine Avenue, she stood for ten minutes watching a man brush the snow from his car, changing it from a blanketed monster to an automobile — hard corners of metal and glass. Janey watched his green mittens move back and forth, gripping the brush, and imagined the hands inside: chapped, dry, prickly with hangnails.

She turned left, moving quickly now, down to the all-night café on the Main. She found a seat by the sweaty window and looked for a blank page in her sketchbook, the sheets falling from under her thumb, each giving away "Debbie," "Dad," "Stranger 7." When she found a fresh page, she sketched the hand of the car owner, both with the mitten and without, making the fingernails well bitten and putting calluses where the fingers met the palm.

It was well after midnight, but Café Parallèle was still packed with McGill and UQAM students cramming for December finals. In thoughtful moments, searching for an idea or a word, she stared into the glass, then caught two gay boys flirting at a nearby table — a redhead and a brunette — their images reflected in the dark glass. She studied their movements as they sipped from a mug and a tiny cup of espresso. Oh, how she loved the closeness of people in winter, when tables and chairs were pushed up against each other. The boys wore scarves and had wet pant cuffs marbled with salt. She studied their faces — the ample skin near the eye, or the gentle loft of a nostril's edge. The downward brush of facial hairs. Their differing smiles. Her sculptor's heart bubbled with the life around her, so much laughing, so much variety of nuance and humdrum beauty.

"Utilitarian!" she said and banged on the table, her demi-tasse spoon rattling in its saucer, then wrote it down next to her drawing of the car owner's hand. She linked the word to the calluses with a bent arrow. When she looked back up at the window, she saw that she had an audience — the eyes of the boys were on her. The brunette was chuckling. She wilted. She felt a cold breeze on her ankle. She picked up her sketchbook and walked out of the café, being careful not to draw any more attention to herself. She felt the cold now, shivering as the wind blew past her up the Main. She turned toward the warmth of home, but took a final glimpse into the Parallèle. The interior, framed by the window, glowed with an orange light that looked warm and inviting — like a painting of a Parisian café hanging in a Parisian café. The redheaded boy looked up at her. Don't slip on the ice, she told herself as she started walking. She crossed her arms across her chest. Don't give them a reason to laugh.

‡

CyberSmart installed new cataloguing software on the same day that the managers handed out the Christmas bonuses. Janey staggered out of Toby's office with a two-volume user's manual in her arms and an envelope in her teeth. The new system was intended to cut down on paper, but in order to activate it, each employee had to print out a sheet of installation codes. And, of course, this was the day Janey crippled the central printer by cramming the wrong paper into its tray. She was drowsy and distracted, like she had been in the early days with Mike: oversexed, euphoric, and stupid. "I was carrying too much," she said to the co-workers lined up behind her. "These stupid manuals."

While the printer was being repaired, employees drifted down the corridors, gossiped, coagulated in the kitchenette, rearranged their cubicles. Embarrassed, Janey hid at her desk and skimmed the manuals — there was a whole new language there, full of periods and hyphens and acronyms. It reminded her of a disabling force she felt with Mike. He had expected her to treat their moments together with reverence. At first, she had tried to remember all the details of their togetherness, but soon they became a soup of movies and dinner parties and small bars on St-Denis Street. Janey had to admit one day that she did not remember which video they rented on their two-week anniversary. Mike was angered by such lapses. Although Janey thought him quite petty, she'd participated. She came to live in a constant state of apology.

"There's printer trouble," Janey said, looking down at the salt-stained moving trucks.

"There will always be printer trouble," Debbie said, raising a finger. "They turn on you. They are very much like men."

"Boy, when you put your finger up like that that you almost look like you know what you're talking about."

"Oh, I never know what I'm talking about," Debbie said, diseased finger still in the air. "That is why I'm always right. That is why I'm a copy editor. I am the solver of superficial problems."

Janey considered this. Corporate culture produced armies of people like Debbie — bitter but functional, ready to smile in spite of a hangover.

"Mike's nothing like a printer."

"He'll run out of toner one day soon."

"Last night he made me this huge dinner," Janey lied. "Carrots and breaded chicken — oh, and he bought this incredible Peruvian wine. And afterward we went to St-Louis Square and built a snowman. We were drunk, so it looked sort of lopsided. I should have taken pictures." Janey sighed and looked wistfully into the grey sky.

"No wonder you look like hell," Deb said. "Up half the night playing in the snow."

"Neither of us wanted to sleep, so we went to this little all-night café on the Main for hot chocolate, and he asked me if I would quit my job. He says we can just be together. He's worth enough for both of us."

"Is there a ring in there somewhere?"

"Maybe."

"Maybe?" Debbie shook her head and put on a world-weary face. "Jane, what do you want from him?"

"Happiness. That's all I've ever wanted from him, from everything, really."

"Then let me tell you something," Deb said, squinting. "You're young. Hold onto him real tight. The most important moment of my life was when everyone stopped telling me I could have whatever I wanted and started telling me I could have nothing I wanted." And then she reached over and touched Janey's face, pushing up the corners of her mouth with her thumb and forefinger. "Smile, bitch. You're not there yet."

‡

Janey slept lightly during the week before Christmas. Every morning she was woken by a falling icicle or a nightmare she couldn't remember. On Thursday — she thought it was Thursday — she woke up on the floor, rows of shadowy poles filling her field of vision. At first, she thought she was still dreaming — this was a forest, dense with slick-barked trees — but when she lifted her head she saw that she had merely fallen asleep next to the Project.

When she turned on the kitchen light and looked outside, all she saw was her own image in the windowpane. She was trapped inside by a wall of night and morning felt aeons away. The slamming of a cupboard door and the rush of tap water abraded the silence. She circled the table near the window as the mixing bowl filled in the sink. She pulled out two chairs, one for the bowl and one for herself. Within minutes she was working the mound of clay. The material was stiff and clammy under its plastic wrapping. It was good clay, expensive. Janey pushed into it with the heels of her palms. Slowly, the earth turned to dough; she rocked, feeling the paste come off onto her skin. Then she saw a shape — a ring, a wedding band, throttling the base of a finger. It became Debbie's sad, arthritic hand, gnarly and curved, like the exposed roots of a tree.

The phone rang — a shrill slice through the silence. Suddenly, the world was there. The clouds were lightening. The fridge hummed. Below, the couple were eating bagels in their housecoats.

The answering machine picked up the call: "Janey? I thought I'd catch you before you went to work. Are you there?"

It was her father. She leaned back in her chair, resting without moving.

"OK then. You know, we haven't spoken to you all week and we'd like to know what time your plane gets into Orlando on Christmas. Did you call the Film Board? You'd better get on that. They'll all be gone for the holidays soon. Give us a call back and let us know when we're going to see our favourite daughter."

Her mind raced; she didn't want to be distracted from the Project. She could see it there, through the door of the kitchen, spread out over the floor of her room. She had to see it through. Maybe this was a naïve dream, but it was a good dream — to have beauty at the tips of her fingers. So specific, so detailed was Janey's vision that she believed failure was impossible. Life always made allowances for creation.

23

Somewhere, though, the smooth realization of this got jammed, like the paper in the printer. In unconfused moments, alone in her dirty space, she knew that it was not fair to have spent so much time focussed on the Project, only now to spend so much energy typing reports and cursing at a printer.

‡

That morning, Janey didn't have time to shower. She arrived at CyberSmart with brown nails, smelling of earth. Feeling unsteady, Janey dropped into her ErgonoMaster chair. She sat motionless before the dead monitor, looking at her warped face in its matte emptiness. What a funny cube of machinery, she thought, so sleek and heavy. Everything interesting about a computer is hidden. Janey felt like it may explode, it was so desperate to reveal its insides.

"Let me at least *try* to understand you," she said, but the glass gave her nothing but empty desperation. From her bag, she produced the sketchbook and pencil. She drew a square within another square and began to shade the left half to represent the gentle bend of the screen. As she moved the pencil around the page, she could hear the slow carpet-shuffle of her co-workers and the muted chug of the photocopier. Near the drawing she jotted down random adjectives. "Utilitarian!" she yelled and banged on the desktop.

When the phone rang, Janey jumped.

"Hello?"

"Late again, I knew it."

"Oh, Deb, I didn't get much sleep."

"In that case, I have no sympathy."

"I know," Janey said. "But what can I say? Mike's demanding. We went all night long."

"I joke, but it is good to see you finally getting a grip on things. You've seemed happier."

"Where are you?"

"Home," Debbie said. "I'm making this a long weekend. My poor joints couldn't take a day in the office."

"A long weekend? It's Thursday."

"No, it's Friday," Debbie said. "All that sex is rotting your brain."

"Do you need anything?"

"No. My mother is here. She's making me a lasagne."

"Poor you," Janey said. "Are you ok?"

"I'll live, but I may kill her." Janey pictured her friend sitting on the edge of her bed, gripping the phone with white, crippled knuckles. "What are you doing this weekend?"

"I've decided to spend the entire weekend locked in the apartment with Mike."

"You make me sick. You know that, right?"

"Yes," Janey said, rubbing a hand along the coarse tweed of her cubicle. She felt desolate and philosophical. She picked up one of her little paper-clip pawns by its head. "You know, Deb, I hate this place. It was smart of them to pad the walls in advance."

"Stop it. I think I'm starting to rub off on you."

"That's OK," Janey said "There are worse people in this world."

"I should hope so," Debbie said. "Are you OK, Jane? Has he done something?"

"I'm fine. Finer than I've ever been," she replied. "But you're wrong, you know. I don't have a grip on anything."

"Are you sure it's not Mike?"

"Mike is not everything." Janey placed the pawn on top of the monitor, its thin paper-clip arm waved at her. "He's gone, you know. Long gone."

There was a pause. "What do you mean?"

"I haven't seen him since the fall, since he walked out. It's pathetic when you think about it."

"You've been lying all this time?"

"Something like that." Janey stared into the computer screen. It was like looking at herself through a peephole. "You know what? It doesn't matter."

"Of course it bloody matters. I'm your best friend." Debbie sounded frustrated. "What the fuck have you been talking about all this time?"

"Hands, fingers, arms." Janey laughed. "A lot of things."

"Jane, stop laughing. I don't understand."

"I know you don't."

Toby appeared at the cubicle and waved. Janey was shaking with laughter. "But it doesn't matter any more, I don't think. I have to go. Toby's standing here."

She hung up without a goodbye and followed her boss into his private office, closing the door behind her.

‡

Turgid, grotesque, puffy, knobby, fat, busy, and self-important. Like ten tubes of marzipan. They jabbed. They were to-the-point.

Janey said nothing.

‡

Janey left the building via the emergency exit to avoid her co-workers and lit a cigarette. She held a small box containing nineteen wire chess pieces and a dozen stolen pencils. It was only three-thirty, but Friday had already surrendered itself to evening. December crept toward its merciful end; even the street lights couldn't keep up with the darkness. Wind from the St. Lawrence River blew up the narrow street and the orange ember of Janey's cigarette strengthened with it. She exhaled a plume smoke indiscernible from her breath.

She walked home. The cars on the Main were smoky in the cold, rammed against each other on the slow Friday crawl north towards Laval. The sidewalk rose to skirt the snowy face of Mount Royal. Behind her, the skyline bristled with steeples and bridge tops. Janey pushed strands of hair from her mouth with her tongue and felt buoyant and alone.

Approaching home, she could see the rabbi unloading boxes from his car onto her stairway. She did not want to talk to anyone, so she ducked down the alley, hoping she could enter from the back. From there, she was level with her ground-floor neighbours. Behind her reflection in the glass she saw a man, pasty white, motioning to someone in another room, fingers gracefully poking the air. In his face there was something thrilling, not angry. Like violence subdued. It was sign language. Janey was intoxicated with the motions, with the strength of his hands. She watched the digits — agile and sleek, like a series of tiny swimmers — and tried to memorize them. They would be a perfect finishing touch for the Project.

She assumed that he was signalling to his wife. Janey imagined her lying naked and prone on their bed, breasts flat on the sheets. The small curve of her back was graceful and perfect, a crest of windblown snow. She is lucky, Janey thought. She can listen without breaking the silence.

prove that you're infected

I'm not OK.

I'm sorry I left Montreal without telling you. But there didn't seem to be enough time. Besides, leaving wouldn't have been spontaneous then.

I'm not trying to hurt you. Or maybe I am. I don't know. Am I being ambiguous again? You tell me. You know me better than anyone. You know I am not a betting man. But tonight I took a big gamble. I had to do something dramatic. Something random. I love the fact that I did it, too. Left, just like that. It's so unlike me.

I'm in Toronto, sitting on the window ledge of room 442 of the Waverley Hotel, putting my thoughts on paper for you. It's February, but there's a thaw on and the city smells like autumn. Last's years leaves are showing under the melting snow and look like wet dead mice. The streets are splashy and colourful, reflecting the traffic lights in squiggly lines down Spadina Avenue. The sidewalks have people on them even now, at 2 am, shouting, drunk. Canadians know to take advantage of the warmth — it won't last long. But I think I prefer the bitter, bitter cold. It has guts. It doesn't pussyfoot around. There's something concrete about it. Is it still cold in Montreal?

I don't know what it was about today that made me run. It was a day like any other: pills, espresso allongé. Worked on my nemesis, the thesis. Smoked. Talked to my mother. Woke you up (*Will you leave me four cigarettes?*). Went to class, went to work. Came home and went to the bathroom. Blood again, but that's normal.

Sometimes I'm sure that I'm going to die. Standing there, I look down at the redness creeping across the toilet bowl. It's like the illness is evacuating all my body's important fluids in one shot. I have this image of one of my roommates opening the door and finding me there, exposed, lifeless on the cold bathroom floor, pants twisted awkwardly around my thighs. My last memory is that of my belt buckle clanging against the tile. *Shit, man, are you ok?*

But then I am ok. I leave and sit with you and the roommates on the futons in that tiny living room, being quiet and aloof, in my shell. *Don't coax him out! Don't open the floodgates!* And when you don't, I wrap myself in self-pity. I go to bed early and wait for you to join me so I can hear you breathing, grinding your teeth. I feel you flopping about and I hope that somehow, inadvertently, you'll touch me.

But that's not what I did tonight. I took off. I ran.

The receptionist didn't even flinch when I asked her for this specific room. I started writing on the bed, but it smells rancid and the sheets are spotted. From here I can stare at half a woman's face sketched on the opposite wall. She is stark grey under the fluorescent light, and looks almost animated when it buzzes and flickers. Her skin is drooping, lived-in, and has been unintentionally blemished by squashed bugs and cracks in the bloated plaster. She has a half-set of teeth, crudely sketched, covered by full lips, pinched at the corner into a sort of understanding, motherly smile. She was probably some sickly whore, drawn by someone in love with her. She seems unimpressed with the likeness. She looks a little uneasy, like she doesn't trust me, sitting here in the window. *Don't fall.* I name her Linda.

This is the room where I lost my virginity to Beth. She was stout and solemn when we were teenagers. In spite of an occasional sobby telephone call — *I could never be what you want* — we were just confidants; we knew each other's histories, like siblings; prom dates on acid, many years ago, when I wasn't gay. We danced, ate and left the prom early to get drunk on a bench along Philosopher's Walk. While she was peeing in the bushes, a group of Engineering frat boys called me faggot and beat me with orange, prickly sticks from a snow fence. They tore my suit, bashed my face, kicked my weak kidneys. I saw Beth running towards us from the shrubs, lacy sleeves flailing in the air. A final swing of that splintered wood as I pulled away. It sliced down my face, splitting my eyebrow, eyelid, and the top of my cheek, then breaking my nose. I could feel the cut on my face and a warm rivulet of blood tickling around my nostril.

No hospital; we were on drugs. Beth checked us into the Waverly, the receptionist not asking any questions (it's that kind of neighbourhood). We got into room 442 and Beth stopped the bleeding with a pillowcase that eventually gave me scabies. *Life is a series of tests*, Beth said, *and this is just one of them*. But she was wrong, at least in part. Life is the disease, I told her. The tests just prove whether or not you're infected. She laughed and called me melodramatic. We ended out numb, giggling, still drunk and high, making pounding, mechanical love on these rusty bedsprings under Linda's watchful eye, *IloveyouIloveyouIloveyou* coming out as loud, wet whispers in the slurpy proximity of sex. *IknowIknow*. That night was a gamble, too, one that didn't pay off. I barely spoke to Beth after that. Our relationship had become something else, something muddy and maimed by sex.

I have never understood why you were interested in my sickly, gangly body and M-shaped hairline. And yet you never wanted to fuck me, or even kiss me. I dream of your index finger probing my arm, pressing into my chicken-pox craters and making circles with the hair. I've explained to you every mark, every imperfection of my body, and yet you wouldn't let me get into your shorts. Not once. I always felt jealous of those men who'd grope past me at the club to put their hands up your shirt and pinch you. You'd smile coyly and pull away from them. *How do you know you're gay if you don't sleep with other men?* We laughed at them. But what if I had done that? I feel as though I have so little time left anyway, why didn't I? No sex: your single proviso for entering into boyfriendship with you. The words still resonate in my head.

I like sex. Sex is reliable, a security, a certainty — there are no two ways about sex (no pun intended): we are fucking or we are not fucking. Part of me wonders if I want you because I can blame everything on our sexlessness. Yet I can't be sure of that. When it comes to you, there is too much ambiguity. Your power is to disarm me, turning all anger and sadness inward, towards yourself; not wanting to solve it, but to save it and savour it. You've never had any use for blame or forgiveness or guilt. I don't want that. When we clash, I want you to feel guilty, like you owe me something, some affection, some term of endearment. That is, until you curl up on our bed, brooding. When I finally have you feeling guilty, I can't stand it. I pull away and take with me the reason for remorse. I am disarmed. I can never be what you want.

On my way to the bus station, I saw two women fighting on the platform of the Charlevoix metro stop. One kept screaming *You bitch!* And the other, with a line of blood on her neck, was retorting *Laisses-moi tranquille!* They were pulling at each other's hair, screeching, slapping each other's

33

ears — only understanding one another with these passionate actions. Aggression, attack: these are things everyone understands. It was one of life's little tests. I just sat there, and let the subway doors open and shut mechanically. What would you have done? Stopped them? Translate the screaming? The anger? I'm taking action now, I think. I may be running away, but at least I'm acting.

There is an unsettledness to Montreal that I can no longer stand. The city's foundations are old and unstable. I feel the instability everywhere — in cafés, in streets, at political rallies. There is always some citizen who says something out of place, yet ironically appropriate. People unveil their fears in public, acknowledge them. In that kind of place, randomness is impossible to ignore. Some like to be reminded of it — like you. You thrive off the freedom. But the city takes its toll on people like me. I need a point of reference. After I moved there, my initial defences gave way to masochism — throwing myself into what scares me the most. The Quebecois, they cut their losses with passion — religion years ago, and now sovereignty. The English learn how to be barbed, to fight off the madness by becoming a small part of it. The rest of us shout obscenities to passersby and don't come in out of the snow. Or run. Run towards something solid. Montreal does not pretend that there is balance — and relishes the void. That is why I am here. Toronto pretends. Toronto is safe.

God. Listen to me. All I have to do is write about important things, academic things — but I can't seem to get over myself. Everything I write seems to be half mash-note and half manifesto. It's like there is a conversation in my head between me and the self-righteousness of every person I've known. I never know who to listen to, but always feel as though I'm wrong. Am I wasting your time? I assure you there's a purpose to this letter and I will write until I find it. You know, I was always jealous of your ability to express yourself in an instant — blot your thoughts onto paper. I'm not as practised as you. Your raw thoughts are far more eloquent than mine. I'm trying to learn from how you think.

There is a pain in my side; stinging, swelling, like a thousand tiny fish hooks pulling on my kidneys. What I hate about my sickness is that it's not even one of those valiant diseases that have their own telethon, like AIDS or cancer. I also hate its name, unpronounceable and obscure: IGA nephropathy. It's not terminal enough for Jerry Lewis, that flamboyant bastard. What I think I hate most about my disease is its ambiguity, the *I don't know*, the *I'm not sure*. Doctors are stupid, I hate them all. *The tests are more detrimental than the disease itself.* The attacks are random. I can't see them coming. I'm powerless to stop them.

Do you remember that commercial on the CBC for the "Ice Storm '98" mail-order video? That's the slogan: *We were powerless to stop it!* But you weren't powerless. The electricity was out, no heat, no drinkable water. Under your command, we wrapped ourselves up like children at winter recess and walked around the Plateau with your rusty shovel to dig cars

35

and people out of the snow. I fell in love with Montreal that day — its languages and its beauty, its trees dipped in glass in the silence of the silver ice storm. One woman leaped from her driver's seat with a cigarette pinched between her fingers and hugged us both in the middle of Marianne Street. She kissed us on both cheeks. *God bless you queer boys!*

I fell in love with you then, too. Your kindness, your love of people. I thought maybe you could take away, at least in part, some of the randomness of the world. And in a way you did. But in the moist cringe-worthy air of this mouldy hotel room, straddling its window ledge, I'm more scared of the randomness than ever before. There you sit (probably thinking I've completely lost it) and my kidney is still throbbing; every breath is a test, every word is a gamble. *You're completely unable to make a decision*, you tell me. You call me passive, you call me crazy — maybe I am crazy, just sitting here, lost.

So here's something decisive for you: I can't stand the waiting anymore, the threat of a bad outcome. The randomness of the world is far more apparent when you're sick. What if I died right now? What if I had an attack and fell from this window? What if I jumped? What if I just took off to yet another city? What if I ran? The "what if" factor. I've tried before to make it work for me, but alone I can't seem to find any way to turn the tables on the scattered, arbitrary way destiny takes over our lives. And, right now, in this window, looking at Linda on one side and down Spadina Avenue on the other, I feel inspired to act.

So here's the gamble I propose: come with me. Let's take off. Let's go somewhere else. Run with me is all I ask. Let's widen the gap between me and my disease, between us and the icy sidewalks, and school and work and friends and family and the rest of the boring necessities of life. Let's gobble up the black space in front of us and listen to mix tapes and blow smoke out the windows. Let's speed towards Mardi Gras on Bourbon Street, through greasy spoons with horrible food, past speed traps and weather-beaten New England homes. Let's make cousin-marrying and hurricane jokes. *Where the fuck did they go?* Or maybe we should head east, through homey, winter-loving towns named after saints and speak French and pick up hitchhikers with thick Quebecois-black eyebrows weighing down their French/Native/Irish eyes. We can argue with them about beer and poutine and sovereignty. Then we can stop at a café named after some Acadian hero and drive along the shores and talk to the fishermen and laugh and get as laid back as them, look at their nets and pottery and pewter before sliding down the cobblestone streets of St. John, toward the harbour. We can buy American cigarettes and smoke them on the ferry and swim in the ocean and have fights with the mucky red sand, then watch the tide come in and pull together under an afghan to fight off the chill. *This is so not like them.* Maybe we could go west, and pass through small Ontario logging towns and eat bad fish and chips out of newspapers in the front seat of our car. We can count the number of pickup trucks and take bets on the population of the next town. We can park for the night and buy a bottle of gin and drink it with our feet hanging off the ledge of a lock, then run through the forest, chasing each other, screaming into the night, and then pass out together in the backseat, wrapped in a blanket, draining the car battery by playing David Bowie on the stereo and not caring.

What if we just disappeared?

advanced soaring

Almost every night for a month, Mark and Luke had been drinking tea in the same café on the Main. Initially, they agreed they came for the music — the night girl always played the same rockabilly tape and they enjoyed predicting when the harmonica would come in by raising their hands to match the harmonic intensity. But by the time she switched to *The Very Best of Santana*, they had no need to find excuses for meeting. They had discovered how easy it was to be bored together, to be mundane and ridiculous. Winter was dying and they watched the activities on the street, cars and people pushing through the dark, between bluffs of snow that were heavy from melting, the clouds over downtown Montreal lit white by the skyscrapers. Luke spoke of the Toronto girls he'd left behind, about his guitar strings and recording projects. Other times, he moved his chair around to Mark's side of the table so they could share the *Globe and Mail* crossword. Mark loved Luke's excitement when they found the right word — Luke would point, giggle out the syllables, say, "See, I told you I was a genius," and playfully slap Mark's knee.

They sat in the window. Mark made sure of this, arriving early at Café Parallèle and pouncing on a prime table as soon as patrons left, a coffee-house predator. Luke's arrival would put Mark's nerves on edge, but in an exciting, anticipatory way, with one particularly electrifying factor: an audience. All those passing by could look in and see them there together, night after night: *oh, those two!*

Luke was raised in some forgettable Toronto suburb — Thornhill, Richmond Hill, some brand of hill — but had moved to Montreal to study literary theory at McGill, "but really to escape my folks." He was always galvanized by passing ambulances as they flew up the Main in a blur of light and furious noise. "Poor man," he said as the siren faded. "Suffered from a bizarre disorder where the goatee tries to consume the face. Nastiest case of pretentia I've ever seen."

"I've seen worse," Mark retorted. "He's lucky he didn't have ponytail cancer." Luke laughed, throwing his head back a little, his big teeth shiny with tea.

"I love cancer," Luke said and, after a guilty pause, they laughed together. "OK, OK. No more cancer humour."

"I love cancer humour."

"Me too." And they roared again, without guilt this time.

It was not uncommon for them to part at dawn, exchanging goodbyes in front of Café Parallèle with the confidence that they would see each either again the next night. Mark sauntered home slowly, eastward through Parc Lafontaine, the celestial, silent blue of dawn amplified around him by the white, white snow. On these wordless mornings Mark would often sit on a park bench and stare out between the bare branches at the brightening sky, his brain clicking anxiously with thoughts of Luke. They came and dissolved before they were full, like the colourful flashes of dreams during a fever. Luke the musician, Luke the sex god. Later on, Mark could never remember these images exactly, but knew he was fond of them.

‡

Mark was sure he'd be flying by now. As a child, he'd insisted it was within his power. "I'm learning to fly, you know," he announced at recess one day, only to be thoroughly mocked. People cannot fly. It's as simple as that. So Mark invented details: his mother drove him to flying school every Saturday afternoon, out to Mirabel Airport, where his teacher, Mr. Crisp (actually his scout leader), gave him lessons in tilting his body a certain way, in forcing his toes into balls under the canvas of special shoes, and getting him off the ground. "I'm just at the Hovering Level," he explained once to a small group of kids, "I can only get a few inches off the ground. But you just wait." Luke nodded his head when Mark told him the story.

"How far did you get?" Luke said.

"Pretty far. You'd be surprised how quickly I went through the fictional ranks." He paused for effect, sipped his tea. "Up and up, to the Advanced Soaring Level, even."

"The kids at your school must have been pretty dumb. We would have demanded a demonstration. I probably would have beat you up." Luke changed the angle of his cigarette and the smoke crawled up one side of his face, casting a shadow of on his cheek.

"Oh, they did. I feigned exasperation. 'You can't just do it anywhere,' I told them. 'Only at the airport. The law says so.' I even told them how insufferable they all were for not knowing about the school. I was a pretty big geek, really. My school life was a mess. Whenever I got beat up, I'd say, 'I wish I could do it right now and fly away from all you losers.'"

"I wonder how many parents were coaxed into calling the airport just to shut their kids up about your flying school."

"I was pretty convincing."

"I believe it." And Luke lifted his head up, looking at Mark from the bottoms of his eyes, seductively, lids slightly weighted, charging Mark's brain with excitement. It was the same rush he'd imagined would materialize when the school-yard disappeared below him and his enemies shrank into dots, looking up at him, knowing that he was chosen, spectacular and free.

‡

Mark had dated two men before he met Luke.

His first boyfriend was a young francophone he had found online: 'Desperateanglo' meets 'esprit_blessé_69.' The boy's real name was Fred — Fred-air-*ique*. On their first date, they ate sandwiches on the terrace at Café Santropol and Fred told Mark about his current project: an album of songs about defunct comic book characters, the ones that never sold well and disappeared when their series were cancelled. "What happens to all those people?" In the long stretches they spent in Mark's studio near Parc Lafontaine, they talked about body art and folk music, spat grape seeds at each other, came up with ways to kill Fred's CEGEP teachers. Sex sometimes began with tallying the new cuts Fred had sliced into his own arms, but always ended in crying, Mark rubbing Fred's back, sometimes crying himself from the intensity. Mark threw himself on Fred like he would throw himself on a grenade: defended the relationship to his friends at work, read *Maclean's* in the waiting room while Fred was with his therapist, told Fred he was normal. This is how it ended:

"I could never be with an anglophone," Fred said, arms folded, election imminent.

"But don't I make you happy?"

"I've never been happy."

The second boyfriend, Christian, spun records at a gay club on alternative night. Studded belts, fishnets, cocaine,

The Cure. They spoke often about sex: "I'd like to get right in there," Christan said one night, pulling a flattened hand up the inside of Mark's thigh. They were standing in the elevated DJ booth, eating the tuna fish sandwiches Mark had prepared. "Get in there and cause some damage." But the follow-through was consistently underwhelming. After the club closed, the pair would head to Christian's basement apartment — one drunk, one high — with a collection of screaming friends, adorned in vicious metal accessories, ears pierced with dowels of steel; boots; sparkles; hair pink or black or green, unwashed and wild, like cotton plants gone to seed.

"Come on and do it," Mark said, hours later, among the smiling, sleeping faces of friends passed out on the basement floor. "Fuck me silly. You promised."

"Can't. Too much sniffy sniffy."

When the basement flooded last spring, Chistian called Mark immediately. "I'm up to my tits here." Mark arrived and found Christian and two friends sitting in their underwear on the kitchen counter. Christian smoked as Mark swept the water out the front door. It was inches deep near the middle of the apartment because of an uneven floor, but in most places it was just the carpet that was damp. Eventually, Christian did help, tying twine across the room to hang his wet clothing, the wrinkled black T-shirts blaring out their messages: The Cramps, The Ramones, Masturbation is Not a Crime.

"Thank God you came. What would I have done without you?" And he never called again.

‡

Spring. It flashed momentarily in mid-March and then it was immediately winter again — a wetter, sloppier winter than the one that had just mercifully ended. There was much overflowing of sewer grates and jumping over lakes of slush at street corners. Mark treaded tenuously along the Prince Arthur *pietonnier*, avoiding puddles of water and frozen splashes of vomit left by the previous night's revellers. He swung north up the Main, increasing his pace along the plowed sidewalk. The drizzle put everything out of focus by landing on his eyelashes and diffusing the glare of the streetlamps. The wet from the slush had found its way through the leather of his boots, through his socks, through his skin, it seemed, right to his little toe bones.

At last he found himself at the Parallèle, wrapped in tobacco smoke, sitting in the window with a *tisane aux fruits de champs*. He stared through the glass for a moment, unlit cigarette between his lips. He loved the way the reflection of the nicotine-stained rainbows from the café's walls superimposed themselves on the bustling street, like an exposure error at the photomat. And there was his own face, soft and freckled, red curls spiralling out from under his toque as though they wanted to escape.

Luke did not arrive at his usual hour. I enjoy solitude,

thought Mark, watching the ash fall off his cigarette as he rolled it against the edge of the ashtray. But I am still worried. Before Luke, Mark had been in the habit of sizing up every man who entered the café and attaching to him — his bag, his wallet, the shape of his lips — a sense of intimate familiarity, the kind appropriate only to a mate. He would think, "Could I get so used to those shoes that I would no longer notice them?" Sometimes, if the Parallèle was dead, he'd spend his time drawing the Main's buildings on napkins, altering their pediments and windows to suit his own taste.

At two-thirty, the night girl dimmed the lights and fluttered from table to table with a tray of shot glasses that contained lit candles, placing one on each surface. She is still very beautiful, Mark thought, admiring the way the fragile little flames appeared to dance in her face and eyes. When he had first seen her, many months before, he had been struck by her beauty. While taking a break, she had been slouched forward, androgynous, with black hair, pallid skin, biting off her split ends. Who is *that*? But once settled at a table with his tea, he had looked a little closer at her fine features, those treacherous mounds on her chest. Her name tag said "Catherine." Damn, he'd thought. Damn damn damn.

She lingered very close to the patrons — she was good at it. Mark often admired the way she operated. Men, sitting alone, would find her nearby, industriously wiping tables, chest jiggling. "*Je t'amuse?*" she would ask. She flirted indiscriminately, as though this is what they paid her for, as though at any minute she would climb atop the serving bar and begin to strip and gyrate with a coy look on her face.

She slid a candle onto his table. "*Ou est ton copain?*"

"He's not really my *copain*," Mark said, in English. "I don't know where he is."

"Aren't you gay?"

"Oh yes," Mark replied. "I'm tre*men*dously gay."

"What about him?"

"Well, I don't know," Mark said and lifted his glass mug of cold purple tea. "Here's hoping."

‡

Work: a vile necessity, Mark thought. At least Montreal was cheap enough to live in and work part-time, spend nights in cafés. He was employed at a call centre on the southern fringe of downtown — just before the city drops off toward the Old Port — way up in the Sun Life Building, with a view of Place Ville Marie and down the St. Lawrence River, over the Victoria Bridge and the steeples of Verdun, all the way to Ontario on a clear day, or so Mark convinced himself. He had started working there two years ago, to put himself through architecture school. When he was not accepted at McGill University, he gave up on that dream, but stayed on at the call centre. He was good at his job and his desk-with-a-view was his prize for being Teleplus's top seller the previous year. His performance evaluation had read: *Mark genuinely cares that customers get top-notch long distance service.* On his less

47

enthusiastic days he would slouch down in his high-backed chair and look out the other way, at the other view: a regiment of earpiece-laden heads propped up behind desks, and think: at least here I am in a privileged place. I'm the best.

"Hi, this is Judy from Teleplus and I'm calling you with some exciting news from America's oldest and most reliable phone company." This from Mark's boss, who was not named Judy at all. She was named Marlene but had been dubbed Judy by the staff at Teleplus during an initiation ritual as old as the three-year-old company itself, whereby the staff assigns a pseudonym to newcomers based on their resemblance to a famous person. Marlene looked like Judy Garland. Mark, a young Bob Barker. They were in the elevator together, at the end of a shift. "We are about to revolutionize the way long distance calling is made in America. Aren't you interested in saving money, goddammit?"

"Yeah," said Mark. "What the fuck is wrong with you?"

"Don't hang up the phone!" she continued. "That's right, stay on and let me bully you into a ridiculous calling plan where you pay in arms and legs."

"You must be horrendously lonely to have stayed on the phone with me so long."

"Not to mention ugly."

"Why don't you ever get out of the house?" he said. "I mean other than to grab another case of Schlitz? I don't know why I'm even trying to sell you long distance — nobody likes you. Who the fuck are *you* going to call, anyway?"

‡

Luke had not materialized the previous night. Mark felt somehow betrayed and foolish. After returning to his apartment, he had hung his jeans over the back of a chair to dry their cuffs and spent the hour after work staring at them, listening to the cars splash by on the icy street. It was Friday. He was restless, keyed up and self-sorry. He wanted to go out, but not to the Parallèle. Someplace gay, he thought. Someplace faggy. He stood, tapping his foot. I just wanna dance.

Mark prepared his room before leaving. He matched the top of his sheet — the side with the wide hem — to the top of the comforter and, ensuring that the covers were aligned, whipped them away from his body until they were flat against each other. He guided the bedclothes gently to his futon, making sure the sides hung evenly. He then folded every pair of pants he owned — four of them — and put them away in the bottom drawer of his dresser. Shirts were harder to fold, so he bunched them into the closet. The sweaters, which he cherished, were draped carefully on the back of his rolling chair. He whipped all the other floor-bound articles into a precarious pile above a hamper that hadn't had its lid closed in months.

Mark stood in the doorway to examine the result of his efforts. He took a practice walk to the futon to ensure that whomever he brought home would not see a stray sock or a bank-machine receipt or a forgotten penny. He tried the walk with a swagger, imitating Luke strutting down the Main towards the Parallèle, all hips. He kept his feet just ahead of the rest of his body, taking long strides, longer than one would expect, considering he was shorter than Mark.

"My father taught me how to walk like that," Luke had explained once. "Indirectly."

"Indirectly?"

"Well, my mother always called my walk squirrelly. 'Stop that squirrelly strutting about and set the table.' So, I changed the way I walked, and modelled it after my father. But he is 6′3″, see, and so now I walk like I'm on a mission." After that, Mark, alone in bed, had imagined missions for him. Luke entering through the window with an urgent warning, some reason to take Mark away; spying on the informal bohemian artists' meeting that seemed to be ongoing in the back corner of the Parallèle; rushing to headline some rock show on the other side of the planet. Luke and some other English majors had formed a ska-inspired cover band named Margaret Atwood. They rehearsed in Luke's living room and played small shows that Luke would describe in detail. "Thank God you were not there, the band wasn't with me the whole time" or "Everyone there was there to see me" or "You should have been there — we kicked ass." And he would make two fists, place them thumb-to-thumb, raise the pinkies, and say, "It was too much rock for one hand."

‡

This was a bad idea, Mark thought. He was standing near the cushioned benches in the lounge area of the club, waiting for a seat to be vacated. He shifted his weight onto his left foot from his right. Before him was a flock of boys who all seemed twelve-years old mixed with older, muscular men. In any other setting he would have assumed it was a father-son event. Everyone was gyrating and impeccably dressed, regardless of their actual style. Hair had been frozen into place; clothes were tight, ribbed, highly intentional. Colour abounded. There was a pervasive energy in seeing all those gay men in one place created such energy, which somehow mixed disgust in with his excitement. The effect made the beer he had drunk sit like a solid block in his gut. Tonight is the kind of night where I need to find either my soulmate or a moronic slut, Mark thought.

Madonna came on — "Ray of Light" — and many of the patrons abandoned the lounge for the dance floor. Amid the migration, he saw Luke. Mark's muscles tightened. *Here's hoping.* He felt four years old, as though he had just run into Santa Claus shopping at Eaton's. Luke commanded the most prized position in the club, up on one of the raised couches, looking out over all the spiked, gelled, pommaded, combed over, bleached, shaved, bobbing to the beat, giddy with liquor heads. Luke seemed almost intentionally mysterious, in a carelessly chosen Harley-Davidson shirt with the sleeves torn off and an old studded belt, its lustre long lost.

"What are you doing here?" Mark asked, shouting over the beat.

"I come here sometimes," he said. "I know the DJ."

"Funny. So do I."

"Any luck yet?" Luke said. "Any play?"

"Not really. I don't think anyone's interested." This was new territory for them. "Everyone has so much confidence." After an awkward silence during which Luke shook his shoulders to the beat, Mark said, "You alone?"

"I'm here with everybody."

"Of all the gin joints in all the world — why did you walk into this one?"

"You mean a gay one?"

"Yeah."

"Look at all these people," Luke said. He was drunk: speech slurred and eyelids heavy. He pointed out at the crowd, randomly singling out men. "They all turn and look. They are amazed that I am here all alone, thrilled that I'm pointing at them."

"I'm here all alone."

"But you need to know how to work it. You have to sit here and let them stare."

"You just look aloof."

"Well, *you* fell for it," Luke said. "You should try it. It would make you feel better about yourself. Guaranteed." Luke started laughing, high and loud, letting out beer fumes. It made Mark wince. He had never heard Luke laugh like that before; it sounded evil, inspired, like Vincent Price. After a few minutes, Luke excused himself to the bathroom and never returned. Four beers later, Mark went home with a Vancouverite named Chad who reeked of Barbicide.

‡

Mark could see the weather coming from his desk. Off in the distance, far beyond the steely grey bridges and smoke stacks and the strings of suburban light posts, he watched the silent approach of low springtime clouds rolling up above the river. They were grey at first, like a sheet of slate laid flat above the horizon, and then grew into texture: curled webs, heavy with rain or sleet or snow, expanding towards the city, billowing like exhaust into the innocent blue of the sky that framed them. Why didn't I bring an umbrella? Mark asked himself, assessing the inevitable downpour, hoping that his shift would end before it arrived, or that he could use his flying techniques to deke the storm and get to his apartment above it, where the sun was captive, as more sleet and ice was dumped on Montreal. He considered jumping out the window and gliding over the Old Port and the river, the human density tapering off below him into huge yards and swimming pools and hockey rinks, to the edge of the storm. He could save the city by negotiating with the weather as he would with an unsuspecting phone-customer in Wichita or Junction City or Helena: you only *think* you've got it right.

Marlene had warned Mark twice that his sales were dropping off. The evaluation for March had listed his performance as average: *Mark seems to be in a lull.* But Mark didn't feel like he was in a lull — he just found himself more concerned with the long-distance view than the long-distance savings. He wasted time by chatting up the housewives and secretaries, straying wildly from the assigned script, making jokes.

"Can you see the middle of nowhere from your window?" he asked a woman in Augusta, Georgia.

"I don't have time for this right now, I'm afraid," she said. "I'm in the middle of making dinner. My husband's due any second."

"Gee, sorry," Mark said. "I wouldn't want to get you in Dutch with your cousin."

‡

Fame found Luke, without warning to anyone, least of all Mark who gulped an extra breath at the image of Luke in the *Montreal Mirror*. Within a week there were features about the band in the *Montreal Gazette* and the *Globe and Mail*. But it was when Mark read the piece about Margaret Atwood in *La Presse* that he knew Luke had broken through since the French newspapers typically ignored the English music scene. This was an accomplishment.

Nearly a month had passed since they had seen each other at the club. Mark bought the Margaret Atwood album, which featured fifteen cover songs, from "Deeper and Deeper" to "Alfie." Mark only listened to it once. Each track was driven by a hard thump on the upbeat, and to him each one sounded like the next. The cover photo showed the band members crammed into a car with a bunch of beautiful women in gauzy dresses, faces pushed up to the windows. Luke's mug took pride of place against the driver's-side door, cheek flat and round where it was pressed up to the glass between his two muscular hands.

Mark propped the CD case open on his night table, and looked up at the image each night before turning off his lamp. He imagined the day of the photo shoot, imagined himself as the producer, ordering around the women and tilting Luke's head just so against the glass, one hand on his hair, the other under his chin, the rough rub of stubble against his palm. One hard tug and Mark could snap the singer's neck.

‡

The part in Chad's hair started low because his forehead was small. So small, in fact, that Mark's eyes easily made a line from the white streak of scalp down the boy's face, divvying up his features: eyes, nostrils, ears and teeth fell into opposing groups, begging comparison. The left side was weaker. Chad winked with his right eye and his smirk came from nervously raising of the right corner of his mouth, poking up over and over again as though he could not decide if he was happy.

Propelled by the vigour of sex, Chad's hair would flare at the tips, like a blonde bell, its base circling his neck.

Afterward, he would sit on top of Mark, naked, leaning back on his partner's knees.

"Sorry, but is this OK? Can I sit like this?"

"Sure," Mark said, pushing the division further, separating Chad's nipples and the slight crescent shadows under his chest muscles, like a pair of young moons. "You don't have to ask every time."

"Sorry," and the lopsided smile would appear.

"Don't apologize." Mark wondered where his underwear might be. They were black and, in the morning light, they were usually easy to find: a dark blotch on the hardwood floor. During the weeks they had been seeing each other, Chad had taken to pitching the boxers out of reach or stuffing them somewhere unlikely after they were done. Looking up at him, Mark faced Chad's curious post-coital state: wide crystal blue eyes frosted with nearly imperceptible blonde eyebrows — a look of young, precious vacancy, topping a winter-white torso punctuated by tiny nipples. He was hairless down to the crotch, where he had shaved a blonde halo of hair. His bent legs forced his knees apart, and his feet — veinless, white, and creamy — were planted firmly on either side of Mark's torso, just below the armpits.

"I have a surprise for you," Chad said, lip raised.

"Oh, dear."

"This is a good one." His previous surprise had appeared on their first date: a dozen blue roses — blue because Mark had stated (he couldn't remember when) this to be his favourite colour. Mark had carried the bouquet around all night, to dinner at L'Express and then to the movies. He felt like he was advertising his date with this young, blonde thing. But he had felt obliged. After all, it was their first date and the flowers included an earnestly written card: "I think I like you," or some such crap.

"You'll like this surprise," Chad said and raised himself to stand above Mark for a moment, bouncing, staring down, a twink Colossus, before jumping to the floor. With Chad off the bed, Mark could see his boxers rolled under the sheets at the base of the futon. He slid them on, then reached over to get his jeans from the chair. He was in no mood for further affection or to be forced to compare his body to Chad's. Morning sex always revealed too much, anyway: bad breath, wild hair, drool lines, skin blemishes.

"Why do you always get dressed?" Chad said, turning from his bag and skipping to Mark who was standing beside the bed, now merely topless. "I like you naked."

"Well, that makes one of you."

"ok, you ready?" Chad said and tilted his head a little, dimple deep now and expectant. Mark was prepared for disappointment. "Ta-da!" He whipped his hands out from behind his back. Wedged between his thumb and fingers, like a hand of cards, were two cardboard passes for the Jailhouse — a rock bar on the Main.

"Holy Christ," Mark said, snatching them.

"I did good?" Friday, April 12. Margaret Atwood. Backstage admittance.

"I can't do this," Mark said. "Don't get me wrong. I totally appreciate it. But we can't go."

"Why not?" Chad crossed his arms over his bare chest. "The lead singer is a friend of yours, you told me so. The album is right there on your nightstand. They are like the biggest thing to come out of Montreal since poutine."

"And look how well that caught on."

"ok, I'm sorry," Chad said, snatching the passes back. "It's too much. I should have known."

"No, for the love of God, don't apologize."

"I just thought it was something you'd like. He's *your* friend. I really am sorry."

"It is, he is."

"Besides, rumour has it they suck live."

"Really?" Mark said. "You know what? Let's go anyway."

The lips turned up. "Great."

‡

Luke kept the microphone low, pointed up at his clavicle. To sing into it, he had to bend his knees, guitar banging off his thighs, hand pumping wildly against the strings. The stage lights caught the front of the instrument in an alluring way, as well as all the skin of his face and the saliva coating his mouth as he screamed into the head of the microphone.

When you know the notes to sing,
You can sing most anything.
That's what my mama told me.

When the words ran out, he bounced away from the mike stand and threw his head into violent, thrashing little circles that Mark would have thought impossible of any human being. This wasn't the Luke who could pour himself into a café chair, who had mastered the fluid motions of raising his cigarette, his pen, his leg to cross over his knee.

Chad and Mark were sitting on a loveseat placed on a riser against a window. From their position, they could see into the crowd: punks, students and a handful of local weirdoes, all androgynous under the criss-crossing cylinders of light, dancing and swarming around the tables and heavy couches the club had purchased in lieu of easily throwable chairs. Black walls stretched out on either side, hugging the stage at the back.

"This is fun. Isn't this fun?" Chad said. "But I don't think I understand all this music. And I'm a *dancer.*"

"It's ska," Mark said. "It's like punk, only different."

"It's very angry."

On stage, the band had moved onto their last song, a children's song, "There's a Hippo in My Tub." Luke was shaking his beer, thumb covering the opening, building up the suds. Then he popped it, foaming the heads of the closest revellers.

"It's not." Mark sighed. "It's Anne fucking Murray." Mark looked at Chad's bleak white face and big vulnerable features. Mark was drunk. The hard beats of the music seemed to be pushing Chad away, deeper into the couch.

The crowd cheered as Luke left the stage, raising his hands above his head, absorbing all the applause. Just off to the side was a familiar body, not instantly recognizable because her excited hands were in front of her face. But when she dropped them to kiss Luke — passionately, deeply — Mark knew her: Catherine.

"I better get more drinks," Mark said.

The patrons began to circulate more aggressively now that the show was over, running to the washroom or to say hello to friends. At the bar, Mark was caught in a cluster of people waiting for the band members to come out from backstage. When he finally appeared, Luke was grabbed and prodded, people were hooting. His face was a huge smile as he nodded to each of his fans. "Thanks. Thank you. Were we any good?"

Mark ignored him, staring up at the bottles of liquor, shouting his order to the bartender in French.

"Hey Mark," and Mark turned, noticing right away that Luke's body was more substantial than he'd remembered; it filled his clothes like a turgid leaf fills its thin skin. Oval sweat stains bit the pits of his arms. Mark just looked into Luke's proud, proud smile, a white patch against his sweaty face.

"I'm so glad you finally came," Luke said.

I heard you sucked live, Mark thought, but just smiled.

"You stopped coming to the café." Luke touched Mark's arm. "Didn't you miss me?"

"I've been busy."

"With the blonde?" Luke's eyes shot over to the loveseat, where Chad was perched, back straight like a frightened cat.

"Sure."

"I don't know," said Luke disapprovingly. "He may be cute, but he doesn't look very spontaneous. I saw you guys from the stage and you know what I thought?"

Mark looked away.

"I thought, I bet that kid doesn't do anything. I bet he doesn't even act out little scenes when he's alone in an elevator." Luke was shoved closer to Mark by the crowd. He was hot and wet, moving his hand up Mark's shoulder, under the lip of his T-shirt sleeve. An undertow of desperation clenched Mark's stomach, a volatility. If I faint, he thought, Luke would have to catch me. Luke was right. Chad didn't act out scenes. He probably didn't even sing in the shower. The shower was for washing only.

"You don't know the first thing about him."

"He's too young for you. He's, like, twelve," Luke said. "What are you going to do? Save him from his youth? You need a real man."

"Like you?"

"For lack of a better example."

61

"You know, your girlfriend is right there." Mark waved at Catherine, who waved back from her position in front of the stage, still ecstatic. "I didn't even know you were into dating the Catherines of the world anymore."

"Yes you did," Luke said. "And admit it, you loved it."

"I don't know what you're talking about."

"Admit it."

"Why?"

"It would make me feel better."

You're an asshole, Mark wanted to say, but decided he should offer no encouragement. Mark just wanted to save himself — he was tired from the drink, tired from this conversation. Tired of Luke. Mark smiled and shook his head as he placed money on the bar. He turned away and started for the loveseat behind a stream of punks heading for the exit. They were too slow. Luke followed, laughing, high and loud. Vincent Price. Mark's walk was precarious from the alcohol, but he was pushed forward by his determination to let the laughing meet his back, unacknowledged.

"Sorry that took so long. I got stuck behind the straight pride parade," Mark said as he approached the couch. He placed the drinks on the low table, then nestled himself into the corner farthest from his date and stared out at the traffic in the street. Chad looked at him, lips going up and down, undecided.

Luke's voice started an introduction, but Mark didn't care. He didn't even turn around. In his mind Mark was gone, out the window and over the rooftops, up the Main, looking down at all the beautiful buildings, cutting through the drizzle, over the oceans of grey slushy sleet. Gone, gone, gone.

the strike

Over breakfast, the three of us tried to talk about anything but the teachers' strike. Mom mentioned the weekly shopping, dinner, how fall was particularly glorious this year. She was right, too. On other side of the patio doors, I could see the depleted early October sunshine come through the leaves, making them an outrageous, almost radioactive, yellow. Fat squirrels leapt and played in the branches, shaking chestnuts onto the porch from high, high above.

"Did you finish that sign?" Mom asked, bowing to the conversational pressure. I nodded. I left the table and returned with a bristol-board rectangle haphazardly staple-gunned to a one-by-two. It read: MAKE LEARNING POSSIBLE. "Good stuff." Mom turned to my brother. "Rob, keep an eye on him. Don't let him hang out with those Goofballs."

"I'm not spending another day watching him."

"Yes you are. He'll be good." She looked sceptically at my grin.

"Always good, Ma."

"I mean it. Behave. And don't call me that. And don't leave the yard. And maybe it's you who should keep an eye on Robby. Don't let him impregnate that girlfriend."

Rob rolled his eyes and his cheeks turned pink. He was a teenager now and had grown out of being my bright, older playmate. He stayed out late, locked his bedroom door, took off his shirt at every opportunity. All summer he had worked at the nearby GM plant, driving the shiny new minivans around to various lots. On the phone one night, I heard him say he wanted to have sex with his girlfriend, Nicole, in every model before Labour Day.

Mom stood, adjusted her bathrobe, and looked down at us. "My men."

"Mom, stop *say*ing that." Rob's face had gone from pink to red.

"Well, you guys have been great during all this. Things will be back on track soon, I promise." She looked at the clock. "I'm going to be late. Better run and put my face on." She left the kitchen, chewing on the crust from her toast. Rob and I sat, listening to Peter Gzowski's voice ramble out of the radio on top of the fridge, waiting to hear the car pull out.

Rob, adhering to our striketime routine, disappeared instantly after Mom. "Don't let me see you with those faggots," he said, before pressing play on his Walkman and slamming the front door.

Adrian lived across the street and, because he was scared of Rob, watched for my brother's departure before abandoning his living room window to come over. I was an inch taller than him and fancied myself stronger. As he sauntered into the mudroom he had an apprehensive look on his face — the same one everyone in town had adopted. It was an autumn without authority, as if summer had been extended despite the changing weather. The teachers' strike had permeated everything and knocked the world out of whack. Breakfast was at nine-thirty instead of seven and Mom was on the TV news sighing about the Minister of Education. I saw the school bully on Maple Street holding the hand of a grey-haired aunt or grandmother. He looked at me, disarmed, unfamiliar with being in the street on a weekday in mid-afternoon.

"You gonna bring pop for them again?" Adrian asked.

"Yeah." I walked toward the pantry where Mom kept the decks of soda cans.

Every couple of months, my family would go to the Price Club, me sitting in the huge cart pushed by my brother, my head hanging upside down over its edge, looking up at colossal, inverted buckets of mayonnaise, giant cigarette cartons, and office desks hanging from the walls on makeshift platforms. Massive labels and brand names hovered every-where, and I dizzily followed them with my eyes as if I was floating through a catalogue in the World of the Huge. I would pick out nine cases of pop — three Dr. Pepper for Robby, three Pepsi for Mom and three Crush Variety Packs for me.

"Stuff your pockets," I instructed, and Adrian dutifully shoved two cans of orange pop — my least favourite — in his jacket and two in his pants.

We exited to the deck, where we dangled our feet over the side. We could see the rooftops of the subdivisions below. Beyond them were the cylindrical stacks belonging to the factories along Highway 21, then the omnipresent General Motors water tower set on high metal girders, seemingly weightless against the sky.

We waited for the three Goofballs, our fellow members of the World of the Small. Adrian and I had forged a surprisingly easy bond with them during that strange autumn, the five of us united in our hate for the World of the Big (adults). The other Worlds consisted of the Huge (cars and trucks) and the Enormous (like trees). As Small People we were the sworn enemies of the Big. We hated them for making us go to school, and hated them even more for taking it away. The rivalry, when we discussed it, took on a mystical air. It was a predestined enmity.

Adrian and I slurped on our cans of pop, enjoying the fizzy rush against our lips as we strained to cover the openings with as much mouth as possible, and we talked about climbing the impossibly tall metal ladder to the top of the GM water tower. Such an excursion would be made possible, Adrian and I decided, because the tower belonged to the World of the Enormous. To us it was logical that if the Big and the Huge were allies, then we, the Small, were friends of the Enormous.

We talked about the strike, about the Goofballs and TV — *Family Matters, You Can't Do That on Television*, and *The Simpsons*.

"I like Lisa," I said.

"I like Millhouse," replied Adrian and I sighed.

"Nobody likes Millhouse," I said. "Nobody's sup*posed* to like Millhouse." Then we sat in silence, listening to squirrels jump branches above us and scanning the base of the ravine for the other Small People breaking through the fringe of tall grass that separated our property from theirs.

Once we spotted them, we slithered through the gate pickets into the ravine. I didn't feel like I had lied to Mom. My theory was that the ravine that lay behind our house could still be considered "the yard" because neither the properties at the top nor bottom had any backyard to speak of.

I slid down the leaf-covered slope ahead of Adrian, gripping exposed tree roots for support. I had mastered moving on the layers of decomposing leaves, but Adrian, his pockets heavy with cans, toppled into me a few times. I reluctantly supported him with my shoulder, knowing the eyes of the others were on us. We arrived at the bottom of the ravine in a messy package: breathless, clothes twisted, Adrian gripping my forearm. The other boys looked at us and I yanked my arm to my side and straightened out my jeans and hooded sweatshirt. I could feel the dirt and twigs between my white socks and greying canvas Keds.

"Did you bring the pop?" asked Lou. Adrian silently distributed the cans to the others, who cracked them open, with loud hisses and foamy spray.

"We already drank ours," I said, to no one in particular.

Mom called them the Goofballs. They lived at the bottom of the ravine, in the newest homes in town. Their parents worked at GM and, like us, they were abandoned each day of the strike with an indifferent sibling or overly trusting grandparent. Lou was the tallest, with orange springs of hair adding to his height. Bannon was easygoing and overweight, with a body like a pillow. He wore red Converse high-tops with dirty laces and a grey sweater printed with a faded Canadian Auto Workers logo. The last Goofball, Paley, was short, with blonde hair, no lips and a conspicuously chipped front tooth. I liked him for his bluntness. "This hill is so *boring*," he said.

"Let's play nicky-nicky nine doors," said Lou.

"*All* the kids are doing that," said Paley. "Nobody even answers anymore."

We all pretended to think of a new activity. I was thinking about the cherry table in the breakfast nook, about peeling away the plastic mats on humid days, and the loud, satisfying noise they made as the bond broke. Adrian, I figured, was thinking about *The Simpsons*. I could tell from the unfocussed look in his eyes. Really, we were waiting for Paley to produce an idea, as he usually vetoed other suggestions. Paley, the rest of us joked, was the biggest of the Small People.

"Men, we need to go on a mission," he announced finally. Dull grins all around. "But I can't say it out loud." Larger grins. Larger because we were familiar enough with Paley's secret missions to know it would be captivating, at least for the afternoon. Now Paley grinned too, and I could see his tongue poking at the chip in his tooth.

We rummaged in the ravine for walking sticks and throwable ammunition — green chestnuts, prematurely fallen, with their thorny shells still intact. Clouds began to crowd out the weakening sun and the wind picked up a little, rustling the bright leaves as we lined up along the tall grass before the mission. Paley informed us that he knew where he was going and that we should keep quiet. He didn't want to attract any other kids along the way.

And then we began, marching single file along the base of the ravine. Our steps turned up the smell of wet, rotting leaves — the smell of autumn. To our left, the trees grew out of the slanted ground like umbrellas, with long trunks that were bare until the very top, where rusty leaves with curling edges branched out in domes. We quickly became dirty. Slashes of mud and small reddish cuts appeared across our cheeks from branches flung back at us by the Small Person we were following. Lips were sticky from the soda and we poked orange tongues out at one another as we marched.

Periodically, Paley spoke from the front of the group. "Freckles, you OK?"

"Yeah," Lou replied.

"Bannon?"

"Yeah."

We passed backyards: rusting bikes, tool sheds, canoe racks, basketball hoops. A few other Small People were playing on the other side of fences. We looked at them as though they were animals in a zoo, and they looked at us with somewhat dazzled faces as they, like us, imagined possible destinations.

The path and the ravine eventually opened into a ditch and the pebbled edge of Highway 21. Without the shelter of the trees, the breeze blew stronger against our faces. Across the highway was one of the GM lots. Hundreds of minivans, lined up in rows as though farm-grown, waited to be shipped away to dealerships across the country. Above it all, the water tower loomed, weathered and grey, so much like the clouds that the logo became one with the skyscape.

As we filed along the shoulder, cars and trucks came up from behind us, sounding like wasps flying dangerously close to our ears. With each one, Adrian's head snapped around. His skin was pale and his eyes were huge. I couldn't tell if he was looking at me or at the traffic.

"OK, stop," Paley said, looking up and down the highway. "We have to cross over."

"We do?" Adrian said. Everyone appeared surprised to hear his voice — even Adrian himself, who looked up at me as though he'd just accidentally smashed my favourite toy.

"Why?" I said.

"Because that's where we're going," Paley said.

"It might rain," I said. "Why don't we just go back?"

"Pussies."

Before I had a chance to respond, there was a break in the traffic. Paley ran. Bannon and Lou followed. I could feel Adrian waiting for me, as I watched the others climb over the guardrail on the other side of the highway. I slapped him on the back and started across, forcing myself to walk instead of run, hoping I looked fearless. Adrian was right behind me.

Beyond the guardrail, there was another, steeper ravine with fewer trees and a yellow, boxy structure built into its slope. The others were already halfway down. I started my descent with wobbly legs, unfamiliar with the incline. Adrian gripped my shoulder from behind and didn't let go until we were on the roof of the yellow building. From there, I could see that we were on top of the public washrooms in Exhibition Park, looking out over its baseball diamond and playground: a slide, monkey bars, and a sandbox. A worn path led diagonally from the parking lot to the door of the men's lavatory. Another path led around the building and turned away, disappearing through a hole cut out of the chain-link fence that surrounded the playground.

"From there," said Paley knowledgeably, his finger out toward the opening. "They'll come from there. See, that's a secret passageway. To another *world*." We watched, silently. It was indeed another world. Beyond the fence was where the highway curved towards downtown, lined on both sides by car dealerships and fast-food franchises: the World of the Big and the Huge. "Anyone coming from there is the worst of the Big People."

Paley waved us back towards the retaining wall at the base of the ravine so that were obscured by overhanging tree branches. I was aware of everyone's hands moving into their pockets to feel the prickly bulges of chestnuts. We squatted, ready to pounce, staring squarely at Paley's back. Nothing happened. I leaned back against the retaining wall to give my ankles a rest. Traffic passed above my head, in beats. The rooftop was desolate except for Paley, a few puddles and, in the far corner, a mangled grey umbrella with spokes reaching up like the wing of a half-flattened pigeon. Behind me, a missing chunk of the retaining wall provided a perfect place to rest my head, with my eyes cast upward, catching glimpses of the sky between the leaves. The clouds passed silently in those gaps, layering the shades of grey like the exhaust of billions of cars.

Before the strike, all the parental worry in town was focussed on this bathroom. No matter how badly I need to pee during a Little League game, Mom would insist on walking me to the McDonald's or the Esso station. When asked why, she alluded to non-specific, unspeakable things. I pictured monsters behind the doors of the stalls, or some other visceral wickedness escaping in pipes of light, like the ghosts exploding out of the roof in *Ghostbusters*. I imagined Mom materializing on this rooftop with a disappointed frown. "See what my boy does when he's not in school?" she said to imaginary news cameras. For some reason, I pictured her holding her picketing sign and wearing her patchy terry-cloth housecoat, tied loosely just below her breasts. "Send us back to work now and put an end to all this madness."

Lost in the image, I missed Paley's command to attack, but looked up in time to see the other boys' backs as they ran away from me towards the roof's edge, spiked green weapons in hand. Adrian was with them at first, but noticed my absence and turned to me. Distracted, he stepped too far and a look of shock changed his face. He lost his balance and toppled over the edge.

The others started to laugh at him. I had the urge to run across the roof myself, just to see if Adrian was hurt — but I'd been called enough names by the Goofballs that day. Distracted by this new and harmless prey, the boys made an impulsive decision to strike Adrian with the chestnuts instead of their original target. I stared at the umbrella for a moment, listening to his muffled protests breaking through the laughter, then lifted my head again to the fast-moving clouds far, far above me.

go home lake

"I didn't think that was possible," Sal said.

"I know," Rick said. "We haven't done anything that wild in months."

This was the night of their first-year anniversary. They had gone to see *Les Misérables*, followed by a late dinner. Then, still warm from the wine, they walked back to Sal's house, the one he shared with Nonna, his grandmother. Sal's room was in the basement; it was large, with a low ceiling and a series of squat, book-packed shelves that lined the walls like wainscotting. The mattress was soft and old — it had belonged to Sal's mother before she died — and the frame squeaked under duress. A single window, half-below ground, looked out onto the driveway. The sting and throb of aggressive sex was evaporating from Rick's body in the calm of the night.

Sal's wrists were still bound together and he had thrown them over his boyfriend's head. Rick could see that Sal's eyelids were heavy.

"Tomorrow, all those bored teenagers will be looking up at me, waiting for insights about *The Merchant of Venice*, and all I'll be thinking about is your body," Sal said.

Rick laughed. He tried to keep himself hard and healthy. Previously, he'd slack off from working out once he had snared a boyfriend, and since his relationships tended to fizzle out after three months, his body had never slid too far into flabbiness. But Sal made such appreciative comments about his body's power and beauty that Rick kept going to the Y even now that they had been together for a year. The strength served them well in bed. Sex was the only realm where Sal gave himself over to Rick — and he did it with the giddiness of a child riding a Tilt-A-Whirl. They had developed their own pattern of intimacy: quiet meals and light jokes (usually with Nonna) working up to insane sex after she had gone to sleep. Sal practiced a submission that dared Rick to go further, to get rougher, to lash his boyfriend's ankles to the bed or make a gag from the necktie Sal had worn to teach that morning. Rick's forte, as far as he was concerned, was getting Sal to beg. "Do you want it? Do you like that, bitch?" And his rush always came then, withholding some touch, some thrust — and listening to Sal squeal his desperation as his body shook in Rick's grip. For Rick, who was usually willing to do whatever Sal had in mind, sex was a chance to prove that he too was worldly in certain ways, and that he could be entrusted with the responsibilities that came along with domination. He made sure that the whole act was full of surprise and thrill, was rough but safe, safe but never unrealised.

There was a tapping on the ceiling.

"Shit," Rick said. "Do you think you woke Nonna with all that screaming?"

"I don't know." Sal's eyes opened fully and flicked from Rick to the ceiling and back again. Rick began to feel uneasy — he could sense the romance dissipating, Sal getting wound up. The tapping resumed. "Untie me."

Slowly, Rick ducked out of the bound embrace and began unravelling the leather ribbon from his boyfriend's arms. Before he could finish, Sal got distracted and stood up. Rick felt absurd, following him around the room, naked, as the old woman knocked on the ceiling. They moved frantically from the door to the closet to the dresser, until finally Sal was free and hopping out of the room, pulling on a sock, the long leather cord trailing after him. It was a strange sight for Rick to see. Sal was only like this in an emergency, when he felt threatened. Usually Sal assumed a sophisticated control over the aspects of his life: administering the high-school English department, the daily care of his diabetic grandmother, or supervising the student debating club. Rick had grown to count on Sal to always be on time and then make light of Rick's tardiness. Sal laughed at sarcastic comments — he roared, in fact, in a joyful staccato way — but always asked afterward if Rick was kidding, just to be safe.

Soon, Rick could hear the urgent patter of feet above him and the authority coming through in Sal's voice.

"Oh my God, let me help you." Sal said. "Why did you knock? Why didn't you just yell?"

"I didn't want to interrupt you and the *frosholino*," Nonna replied.

Rick stood and pulled on his cargo pants as the two voices rose and fell; Sal authoritative, Nonna compliant. Rick imagined his boyfriend up there, an anxious party hostess: putting on his coat, getting Nonna's medications, paging her specialist. Even after a year, Rick tended to stay out of Nonna's medical affairs. He forgave himself for not helping because she was Sal's cross to bear and Sal seemed to want it that way.

But this time was different. Sexual control was still on Rick's mind, and it occurred to him that he could take over this emergency, if only to calm Sal down. Before Rick could even climb the stairs, though, the headlights of Sal's Volkswagen shot down the driveway and through the window of the bedroom. Rick watched the dramatic shadows shrink back into darkness as the car backed out onto Euclid Avenue.

Still determined, Rick went up the stairs, past the familiar side entrance, and headed into the kitchen. It was warm and tidy, softly lit under low-wattage incandescent bulbs. There was a single set of dishes resting clean in the rack next to the sink and in the air were the lingering smells of Nonna's dinner — onions, tomatoes, seared meat. The leather cord squiggled across the tiles. Rick picked up the phone and dialled Sal's cell.

"Rick?" Sal was flustered and shouting over the traffic.

"Who else would it be, Beautiful?" It was important to sound calm, reassuring.

"Sorry," Sal said. "I'm driving Nonna over to Saint Simon's Hospital."

"You should go to Toronto Western, there's a bigger emergency staff there. Do you need me to call her specialist?"

"Could you?" Sal said. "The number's on the fridge. She's having abdominal pain on the left side."

"Don't worry," Rick said. "I'll take care of everything. I'm sure it will be fine." But Sal was already gone.

Rick dialled the number for Dr. Rosa, leaving a message and his own cellphone number. He lit a cigarette and started boiling espresso in the battered silver pot Nonna had brought from Italy — it was the only coffee Sal would drink. In the corner next to the telephone, under a small iron crucifix, was a short table covered in candles melted into gold-rimmed saucers, each emblazoned with the name of a saint. As the espresso brewed, Rick ashed his cigarette into the sink and examined the framed photos on the shrine. Having no hard evidence of his own family history, Rick had fallen in love with these old images: Nonna's late husband, a stout, thick-haired man in a suit standing in front of the house; two young women, Sal's aunt and mother, caught in mid-laugh, both with the same horsey teeth; and Nonna herself, in her younger days, sitting at the edge of a dock with a cigarette, feet disappearing into the water, ripples like halos expanding away from her legs.

An hour later, at Toronto Western Hospital, Rick emerged from the elevator with the coffee poured into two travel mugs and a bouquet of daisies in the pit of his arm. Sal was surprised to see him.

"There's a growth," Sal said. "They have to operate."

"I'm sure everything will be fine."

"I think I'm going to be here all night," Sal said. "At least all night."

"Here," Rick said, extending one of the beverages. "Happy anniversary."

Sal focussed on the mug and his face filled with happy disbelief. "Christ," he said. "Will you marry me?"

Rick laughed, the sound echoing down the sterile hall. They spent the duration of Nonna's colostomy operation joking about marriage, about Rick moving into Sal's base-ment room, about who would wear the dress and whether or not it would be white. And Rick made sure that they never mentioned it again.

‡

They are all dead now, the people in the pictures: Papa, Nonna, Ma, Aunt Valencia. Papa was taken by a heart attack the year Sal was born. Ma and her sister had both succumbed to cancer. They managed to spend a few years in Toronto with Sal before they succumbed to the disease. Three summers passed after the colon removal before Nonna finally died: peacefully, wearing a dress with a wild print of overlapping paisley tears, sitting on a dock bobbing off the shore of Go Home Lake. She was eighty-one.

It comforts Sal that she died there. She loved the lake — had even asked him and Rick to take her up for "one last summer" at the cabin before she resigned herself to professional care and her smelly colostomy bag. She had bought the place just prior to Sal's birth and, in his mind, it existed only in the summertime: bathed in sun and moist, clean breezes off the lake. Each Dominion Day, when Sal was finished with school, he and his grandmother would pack up a few toys, swimsuits, and summer clothes, then climb onto a lumbering Ontario Northland bus, with its logo of white and green that, to this day, makes Sal's gut bubble with anticipation. When Sal turned sixteen, he and Nonna split the cost of a car and they drove to the cabin each year. Her last three summers were tough: fingers curling up, eyes failing, every movement requiring a bigger sacrifice. Rick had joined them, taking the passenger seat as Nonna dozed in the back. He helped out and Sal was thankful.

Now, nearly a year after her death, they head to the cabin alone. Without Nonna and her colostomy bag in tow, the vw is refreshingly pleasant. The boys can run the air conditioning instead of having the windows open to circulate the air. The mere idea of the cabin excites Sal as they head out of

Toronto along Highway 400 — but the real physical anticipation (the jumpy stomach and goofy grin and whistling
through his teeth) begins when the highway narrows north of
Crooked Bay. Sunshiney lakes wink through the trees as the
black Central-Ontario dirt edges closer to the car. The other
vehicles on the road are clearly headed towards similar destinations, their interiors packed to the brim with snorkelling
gear and minnow nets and cooler bags, kids up against the
windows, either sleeping or making faces.

Sal often looks over at Rick. In profile, his boyfriend's nose
rises far from his cheeks to a curvaceous little nub and his stubble is just long enough to grow in a swirl out of the column
of his neck, like Corinthian leaves. A minivan full of summer
equipment pulls up behind them and Sal moves the vw into
another lane, slowing to run parallel with the family. Rick
turns and waves at the kids in the back seat. Sal smiles. With
Nonna having died at the cabin, this trip could be so awkward,
so sad, but Rick's childlike enthusiasm saves it from gravity.

Sal considers Rick to be the ideal English student, even
if Rick is nearly thirty. He reads the books Sal recommends
and listens without the need for scholastic threats. He also
performs little acts of infatuation. Rick still brings roses to
Euclid Avenue (he used to bring two bunches — one for Sal
and one for Nonna) and they still fuck regularly, with shock-
ing, fantastic creativity. In the bedroom, Sal feels like Rick's
student, allowing himself to be flipped over and tied up. This
is enough to assure Sal that those things that are usually so

temporary — the flowers, the sex, the romance — are here to stay.

In the right-hand mirror, Sal can see Rick crossing his eyes and pulling his mouth at the corners to stick out his tongue. Sal tries to imagine what it would be like to be alone at this northbound moment: the CBC and the road and whatever pops into his head. Then at the cabin there would be long days of other people's laughter coming over the water. He'd rearrange the *National Geographic*s. Clean every inch of the place. In the silence, every little sound would tap him on the shoulder, and he'd turn to see no one, no family. There would be just the musty monuments to fun summers, now long gone.

Rick feels a scared hand on his bare knee, squeezing tenderly but too tightly. He notices that Sal is speeding up, weaving a little, flicking his eyes at all the mirrors. To calm him, Rick places his own hand on Sal's, weaving their fingers together to break the grip.

"This book you told me about is deadly," Rick says, motioning to the copy of *Swann's Way* sitting on the dash. The lake signs begin to appear on the side of the road: Lake Joseph, Lake Muskoka, Balsam Lake. "So far it's all about sleep."

"It picks up, don't worry," Sal says.

"It picks up? Really? How?"

"They start walking around. They have tea. There's a garden. You'll love it." Sal lets go of the wheel for a moment and flicks a finger from his head into the air. "It's all about how you remember things."

"Remembering things is overrated," Rick says with a smile. He likes when Sal tells the story of some book or another; *Beautiful Losers* or *Naked Lunch* or *Crime and Punishment* — titles Sal could never teach in his high-school English class. Rick gets excited by the summaries and pulls the book from Sal's shelf and reads it, slowly, over several months. In the end, Rick always believes Sal's synopses and gestures and passionate intonations are better than anything Dostoevsky wrote, or Burroughs, or Cohen, or anyone.

"Madame Octave, she turns out to be a real dizzy cunt. Sheer brilliance."

"But 740 pages?" Rick says. "That's a hefty commitment."

"And this is just Volume One."

The paving ends when they turn onto Go Home Lake Road, a dirt passage that winds around the water. This is where Nonna usually woke up, when gravel crunched under the tires and the car began dipping over the potholes.

"So close I can smell it," Sal says, using Nonna's annual post-nap declaration. Rick remembers, too, and smiles; he has worried for the whole drive that maybe this year's trip was doomed. The rest of the year, their lives were full of distractions — Sal consumed with school and students, Rick running to fashion shows and meetings with photographers. When they were alone together, they often had talked about Nonna — prescriptions, supplies, and diagnoses all rushed in to fill gaps in conversation. Now Rick imagines four weeks of Sal's mournful calm, finding one of Nonna's pill casings unvacuumed in a corner and then disappearing into silence, sitting on the dock and staring out at the lake, as he had last year after Nonna died. Rick could still hear the provincial police ambulance lumbering down the driveway, siren off, branches slapping against its girth, when he caught sight of Sal through the picture window. He was standing on the dock, head bowed towards one of the empty chairs. People die, Rick thought. At least she got what she wanted.

"Yep," Rick says, "I can smell it too." The vw slows and then turns down a private driveway. Sal is breathing heavier — each year at that turn, he worries that the cabin is no longer there, that they will twist around the trees to find only the sheet of rock sloping down towards the water.

But here it is, in its tired pine skin, survivor of another winter. The tall triangular roof cascades down to wide troughs choked with leaves and young, fresh saplings — foolish saplings that will be removed by Sal before the week is over. Windows look out from every wall, seemingly dirty because of the dust-clogged screens. The front door opens into a wide, long room with a pine table. The wood panels around the living room and kitchen glow yellow in the sunlight and disappear at night, seemingly absorbing the moonlight, or deferring it to Nonna's prints and posters: the Group of Seven, Modigliani, Hopper. Pollock, even. All the furniture has the same soft, damp, broken-in quality and is arranged around a picture window cut out of the rear wall, to frame the northern view: a pulled-up dock being kissed by the lake water at the end of a narrow path that crawls up to the back door under a canopy of pine branches. To Sal, the room has a sense of eternity — at least as eternal as the forest or the lake — as though it has always existed, as though, on the seventh day, this is where God had come to rest.

"Let's go swimming," Rick says, already rummaging through his gym bag for his trunks. "I'm all icky from the car. This year, I want to see if I can reach the other side by the time we leave."

"No, let's bring in the stuff first, do the dusting."

"The dust will still be here when we get back," Rick says. He is standing now, turquoise lycra bunched in his fist. He begins shimmying out of his shorts, leaning on Sal's shoulder for support as he lifts each leg. "And if it's not, all the better."

Sal stands firm to keep him from toppling, looking at the floor sprinkled with expired wasps and the curls of dust dancing through the beams of sunlight. He and Nonna had a game — they would arrive and place the bags on the stripped mattresses in their separate bedrooms. Then they would clean, saving the swimming for afterward, letting the excitement of it build up in Sal as he vacuumed, mopped, stood on the table with a broom to wipe out the cobwebs, anticipating the jump from the dockside and the freezing, bubbly rush of the water against his body.

Rick is already gone, flip-flops snapping against the stone pathway. The crazy geometry of the pine branches divides the sunbeams into shapes of yellow light against the ground. He can smell the fishy odour of the water and hear the roar of a boat motor carried over the vastness of the lake. At the shoreline, he encounters the dock, which has been pulled most of the way onto dry land for the off-season, its huge empty plastic barrels exposed. Rick bends and starts pushing. Within minutes it is floating, pointing north across the lake like a finger, providing the perfect length Rick needs to run and jump, extremities flailing, into the water, knowing that Sal will hear the splash way up in the cabin.

‡

The summer after Nonna's operation was the first time Rick had joined them at the cabin. His co-workers at the fashion design studio tried to convince him that he was crazy to stay such a long time in the middle of nowhere, especially with Sal's ailing Italian grandmother. The possibility of aborting the trip was always there, he told them. Sal had a car and had promised to drive him back to Toronto if Rick could no longer handle the situation: the smell of her colostomy bag, the abject isolation, the blackflies.

Once he was at the cabin, Rick began to think that the co-workers were right. The cabin reeked, and he grew to be terrified of the zipping sound coming from Nonna's room —

it meant her colostomy bag was full and she was going into her supplies sack for a fresh one. There was a shrine there, too, just to the left of the back door where the same pictures had been rubber-cemented to the outside wall of the cabin next to corresponding obituaries clipped from *The Toronto Star*. One night, as she lit the candles, Nonna grinned and told him the stories of her family members through the filter of her grandson, how each one had contributed to and dropped out of Sal's life.

"This is like a foreign language to me, all this family," Rick said. "I haven't spoken to my parents since I was eighteen."

"What happened to them?"

"Oh, nothing. They live in Calgary and they're Mormons. We never really got along."

"Family is key," Nonna said and ran a single shaky finger down the side of her husband's picture.

"Tell me, what happened to Sal's father?"

"Flew the coop," she said. "For Sally, I'm it. I'm old, you know, but that is why God let me stay." When she looked up at him, her smile had dissolved. Through her glasses, her pupils were huge, forceful discs. All the better to judge you with my dear, Rick thought. "And He won't let me go until someone else can take care of Sally."

He did not sleep well for the rest of the week. While his boyfriend slept, Rick developed an elaborate lie in which his next-door neighbour, a geezer named Mr. Shoreditch, had died and for some crazy old-man reason, had chosen Rick to be one of the pallbearers. During the day, however, there were ample distractions from the fear that he was being groomed to inherit Sal. He worked together with Sal to accommodate Nonna, preparing two shots of insulin, lighting the candles at the shrine, helping her up and down the sloping path to the dock, over-boiling the vegetables so that she could chew them more easily. He told stories. He told jokes. Rick also found many small chores in the service of odour control. Each morning, while Sal tended to his grandmother's dressing, Rick passed by each window, lifting the panes to let air in off the lake, through the cabin, and out towards the driveway, taking Nonna's smell with it. On the mantle, he placed some old soup bowls topped with mountains of potpourri. He had even driven into Crooked Bay once, bought two young but expansive lilac bushes, and planted them on either side of Nonna's bedroom window. And he smoked. Sal was very careful about the geography of his boyfriend's habit and made sure that ashtrays were only placed near the windows. But he couldn't deny that the burning tobacco cut Nonna's stench. During rainstorms, when the windows were closed, Rick smoked his cigarettes on a lawn chair outside, next to the photos, under the lip of the roof, and stared up at the wet trees.

He sits there now, smoking, drying from his swim, listening to Sal whistling off key in the kitchen. With Nonna gone, the largest draw to Go Home Lake is the setting. Rick often closes his eyes and dreams of the massive changes the environment suffers each year. The seasons must be dramatic this far north: autumn lighting the maples on the perimeter of the lake into a ring of fire, the winter ravaging the roads and roofs with compressions of snow, and the spring bringing impromptu rivers and maple keys spinning down to the dirt. Rick only imagines these changes. He only wants the cabin in summer, with its fragrance of pine needles and its little sap pockets on the tree trunks. This is the forest at its most efficient and enjoyable. In the face of all this change, there is something scary about the stalwart consistency of the forest, its assertive colour, its unwavering survival. Every moment of Rick's peacefulness is tempered by the reassuring thought that he will soon enough be back in the commotion of the city.

‡

At night, a slight twitch of Rick's bulk makes Sal blink into consciousness and fill with the instinctual urgency of investigating a whimper or call or thump that could be a human body landing on pine floorboards. But the dread evaporates with the slumber and is replaced with sadness. Perhaps remembering things is overrated. Sal sits awake for a moment, taking in the sleep-heavy desk and low, wide chest of drawers, with its surface covered with cologne bottles, mosquito repellent, sunscreen, powders, and tubes of flavoured lubricating lotion ("Happy summer lube," Rick had said, then tossed them in the shopping cart). The Emily Carr reproduction on the wall seems muted and alone, the totem poles easily mistaken for chocolate bars poking out of green wrappers. The scene is absolute and unchanging, even Rick's beefy extremities seem carved of marble, skin eerily blue in the moonlight. The scene reminds him of a book he adored as a child, *Goodnight Moon,* and the version of it he had made for Nonna one particularly rainy summer, with crayon illustrations and yarn to hold the pages together. All the original objects in the book were replaced with items from the cabin and "goodnight" was replaced with the name of the lake: *Go home Nonna, go home bees. Go home forest full of trees.* The book is probably still here, he thinks. The furniture in this cabin has not been moved in decades; what else has collected behind each piece? He pictures dust settled in layers, like the rings of a tree. Tomorrow, he decides, he will vacuum them all away, bleach the lime crust out of the shower stall, flip the mattresses. He and Rick could even renovate: replace and insulate the roof, get the pictures framed, buy some new furniture. The silence is so heavy, he wants to do it now. Instead, to break the flatness, to declare his animation, Sal loudly slaps a hand on the side of his neck, reviving the pain left there when Rick sunk in his punishing teeth during sex.

"She's dead," Rick says, voice lengthened by slumber. "Go back to sleep."

‡

During their second week at the cabin, Sal is in Nonna's room tapping a knuckle on the wall. He's followed the pipes in here from under the kitchen sink and is now trying to estimate the distance water must flow from the pump to the cabin — perhaps a furnace can fit in here. Through the window, he can see Rick's hard body splayed on the dock, golden from a week of swimming in the sun. Sal holds his pad up to the wall and writes down a few numbers. The room is stuffy and there is not even a hint of his grandmother's incontinence and decay; it smells of pine, now, and flowers.

Sal remembers Nonna best in this very room, leaning back helplessly on the bed. It was still early in Nonna's last summer and they had just arrived at the cabin, the cones of lilac still in bloom, brushing against the window screen. Nonna had been having muscle problems and fatigue through the spring. She had lost, too quickly it seemed, her ability to work with her fingers: chopping garlic, writing in cursive, sewing. In the kitchen, she had taken to ordering Sal around, telling him how to make things that required a lot of handwork, like lasagne and meatballs. And so it was Sal who brought together the little jars of insulin and rubbed them between his flattened palms, producing the familiar clicking sound he had heard twice a day for his whole life. She looked on with a wry smile formed from deflated skin. Her eyes examined him, magnified to enormous, concerned brown circles behind her thick glasses.

"You learn well, Sally."

"From the best," he said and peeled off the packaging from the back of a syringe. "Cross one over, then." Nonna folded one of her legs over the other. Sal filled the syringe and pushed the side of her dress up to her hip with his fingers. The skin there was pasty and blotched with small blue veins. She sighed and closed her eyes, the quiver of every wrinkle blown up by the lenses into a tremor. He poked through the skin and she did not react. He could see the plump plastic edge of her colostomy bag poking out from under the fabric of her dress. The plastic seemed cleaner, fuller, younger than her skin. She had not attached it properly and there was some brown leakage at the top of her thigh.

He pulled the needle out under a small alcohol towelette and threw the syringe away, but continued the swing of his arm to land atop her bag of plastic undergarments. With his free hand, he pulled the zipper open, producing a loud noise. Nonna responded by lifting her thigh slightly. Sal had been expecting this moment of necessity for years. He took hold of her leg and pushed the dress farther, up past the hip. The muscle in her leg was gummy and weak, it felt like tough caulking under the pressure of Sal's fingers. How temporary all this grisly biology seems, he thought, her stench intensifying, competing with the lilacs. The bags attached to her side with a wide elastic garter that was causing long pink sores in the fissures of her squeezed flesh.

The crack of the adhesive, like the quick pull of a plaster, seemed to shock both of them. Nonna started laughing first — a high giggle Sal had never heard before.

"When you were little, Sally, I used to do this with goggles."

"Why?" Sal said, surprising himself at how natural he sounded. He did not feel nervous or repelled, as he had expected; he found himself riding on instinct, steadfast, chatting even, like they were at dinner.

"Because when I changed you, you used to soak me. A little water gun, you were." She shook with laughter, the gummy thigh vibrating. Sal pictured her, like an aviatrix, three decades younger, bowed over him with a cloth diaper, anticipating an onslaught. "And now I would love to get you back." Sal chuckled, shaking his head back and forth, slowly pressing the adhesive strip of the replacement bag to her belt, and their laughter grew faster and louder, so loud that Rick heard it from the dockside.

‡

"Let's winterize," Sal says.

The sun is pouring over the remnants of breakfast in one fat beam through the bedroom door. The men are both leaning back in their chairs, coffee mugs in hand. They are well into their second week at the cabin now and Rick has noticed Sal taking measurements, staring up at the beams, sketching on serviettes after dinner while Rick smoked. In fact, Sal has spent very little time down on the dock — he's been scrubbing things and driving old pieces of furniture to the dump and taking pictures of leaky patches of ceiling.

"Let's not," Rick says, "and say we did."

"It'll be fun," Sal says as his eyes flit up to the ceiling, then at the dirty dishes, then out the picture window.

Rick feels Sal's anxiety like a fever reasserting itself. "Fun? Won't it be a lot of work?"

"Sure it will," Sal says. He's standing now, scraping the remaining food onto one plate and piling the dishes. "We'd have to fill the walls with insulation and get a furnace unit up here from the city. There's no basement, but we can put it in there. With heat, we can come up here for Christmas." He flicks his head towards Nonna's little room, with just a naked mattress corner peaking out from the door frame. "We'll need a better ladder — one of those big, butch numbers."

"You mean *you* will."

"No, I mean we," Sal says, carrying items to the sink. "It's our cabin now."

"It's funny, I still see it as hers."

"Well, I think Nonna would approve."

"If you want to do it, then go right ahead."

There is a clattering of dishes as Sal slides them onto the counter. The sound chases off Rick's thoughts of a few boyfriend-free weekends in the city while Sal is up here unfurling insulation. Rick looks over the table at him. Sal is shaking a little and his movements are quickening, uncertain, making Rick feel as though he should leap up and touch him, calm him down. But he doesn't — he doesn't want to provide Sal with any confirmation. The thought of having to come here during Toronto's busiest fashion season is absurd. And it is scary to think of Christmas, up here with just Sal, no distractions. The snow would preclude any swimming or walks or quick dinner trips to Crooked Bay. The attraction of this place is that it is fleeting, that there is only a small, sunny window of time when it can be enjoyed. Cementing the cabin to every month and day means it would always be there, hovering on the outskirts of Sal's thoughts, a cage where avoidance was impossible, where durability was built into the landscape.

"But I want to do it together," Sal comes in from the kitchen and places a hand on Rick's knee. "It really is ours, now."

"If it's anyone's, it's yours."

"And I want to give half of it to you."

"OK then," Rick says, squinting at the picture window. "You want to buy half a cabin? Cheap, cheap."

"Is that sarcasm?" Sal says, his voice cracking — sad and angry all at once.

Rick doesn't answer; he has never let Sal get this far in his hysteria before and he feels that if he doesn't stop it soon, the damage will be permanent.

"We're here every summer together. And in the city, we live apart. I'd like a place that's just ours."

"Oh yeah," Rick says, smiling, trying to steer the conversation away from the heavy tone of togetherness. "You'd like that wouldn't you, bitch?"

"You think this is a joke," Sal says. "Well, it's not. It's not funny."

Rick feels his smile melt away. He stands and walks over to the glass so he doesn't have to see Sal's face. "I'm just a guest here."

"Four years? You're no guest!" Sal calls out to him. "Four years and it doesn't make sense to winterize?"

"That's right."

Rick hears Sal approaching, so he takes a step back, shaking his head at the floor. "I'm sorry," Rick says and then pushes through the rear door, which slams back on its spring.

‡

The water is cold and invigorating. Rick swims hard, cupping his hands and driving them into the lake water, then lifting them out again, creating an expanding archipelago of water off his fingers, the globs becoming incandescent in the sun. He always swims with his eyelids shut hard into wrinkled patches. He cannot see the vastness opening up above him, but he can feel it, the strength of the wind and its nuance of fragrance change the further out he swims. Below, he can sense the watery distance between his pumping feet and the bottom of the lake: deep, black, cold, mysterious, and alive with unfathomable creatures.

He pauses and opens his eyes, thick legs spinning like a kitchen mixer. Half of his body is warm and yellow in the sun, and the other half is out of focus through the filter of the lake. He scans the trees along the shore opposite the cabin: a layer of pine needles, settled, like a freshly fallen layer of green snow. He has the urge to keep going, to finally reach the other side. But today, the water is black and uninviting, spreading out all around him in volumes so enormous and flat and encompassing that the docks and boathouses and buoys — and Rick too — seem incidental, present only because the lake permits it. His dominance is slipping, everything is slipping. Throwing himself into this place on a permanent — or even a seasonal — basis seems pointless and sad, like giving himself up to be dwarfed by the power all around him.

In the cabin, he feels the same way, only for different reasons; crowded in by the musty couches and the wall of aging *National Geographic*s and pine beams wiped clean of spider webs. And Sal, of course, who is wedged somewhere in that far-off greenery: *you're no guest*. Rick thinks of the huge project that was Nonna, the way Sal had shouldered the work like a duty handed to him by God. It was hard not to love a man who could do that. Where does that effort go now? Into the cabin? The relationship? Rick feels like he did that first summer; he wants to abort the trip, swim away. He looks at the opposite shore, where Go Home Lake Road curves back toward the city. The lake and trees have caged them here together — circumstance has taken away his visitor status.

But it wasn't my choice, Rick thinks. I never agreed to be any-thing more.

He dog-paddles back to the dock, wishing he could have been more clever with Sal. He wanted to say: "Do you know why they call it Go Home Lake?" But this was Nonna's joke and using it against Sal would have been malicious. Rick has heard it three different times as they pulled away, heading back towards Toronto. "Because if it was up to the lake, you'd just go home!" He laughs, hauling himself out of the water. Rick remembers Nonna on the sun-baked dock, it's planks still radiating the day's heat, at seven o'clock in the final evening of last year's stay. They could hear Sal nailing shingles to the roof — and the August wind was full of moisture, anticipating rain. The sun passed behind a cloud and then reappeared suddenly to bathe them in orange evening light.

"Fashion. Some people have no use for it," Nonna said, closing her eyes and absorbing the breeze and sun. A tree frog's alert began low and weak and then strengthened into a sustained piercing buzz. "But not me."

"No?"

"No. Eighty-one years old, I still take pride in how I look."

"You're a fine dresser." Rick always complimented her on her dress choices and Nonna would giggle.

"I know," she said. "And that means something, Amore." She opened her eyes and lifted herself into a more proper, upright position. "You are a good person. You know fashion. You and all the *frosholini* see. Except Sally."

Rick held up a cigarette and raised his eyebrows, asking for permission. She waved a hand and chuckled, turning away a little in mock embarrassment. "You don't need my okay. Smoke, smoke." Rick lit the cigarette. "You see this dress? I bought it special for this summer. So light, the material. Feel." He pinched a lump of it between his fingers. It was a three-quarter-length cotton muumuu patterned with over-sized paisleys, all smoky green and brown, rimmed with gold thread. The dress widened at the bottom, giving shape to her body. "It's perfect for the cabin."

"It's summerific."

"Oh, you *frosholino*," she said.

"Tell me, what does that mean, exactly?"

"Fruity," she said and lifted her little chin at him. "Like you." Rick laughed low, in shots of breath and smoke. The summer air quickly dispersed the cloud, pulling it out over the lake.

"There is nothing like a cigarette after dinner on a hot evening on this dock, with good company."

"Amore, I know! For years, I smoked. Will you give me a try?" Nonna said and looked at him, irises made enormous by her glasses. Glancing back toward the hammering, Rick leaned in and presented the cigarette. She leaned forward as well, and Rick could smell her, faintly, shit and talcum. "I know you mean it, Amore. About the good company. You don't mess around."

"I do mean it, yes," he said.

"Not like Sally," she said, as though she had not even heard him. "Like with fashion. Sally thinks you tell me nice things about my clothes to make me feel better. But you mean it. I can tell."

"Of course I do."

"Sally, he can rely on you."

"Of course." And they exchanged small smiles of satisfaction, eyes thin, lips thin, turned up at the corners. When they heard Sal approaching, Rick snatched the cigarette from Nonna's little fingers.

"Are you smoking in front of my grandmother?" Sal asked, his brow beaded with sweat.

"Yeah. Sorry, I'll stop."

"No, don't stop," Nonna interjected, turning toward Sal. "It's keeping the blackflies away." In the crazy way sound travels over water, their sudden burst of laughter went out to the other side of the lake, and then back to the dock. Even when he and Sal had climbed up to the cabin to finish packing, Rick could hear her laughing.

‡

On their second Sunday at the lake, Sal wakes up next to an empty divot in the sheets. In the air he senses moisture from the rain and the smell of coffee. As he pulls on his shirt, he can feel a tickle of pain at the base of his neck. Rick grabbed the skin there last night as Sal was stretched on his back with his arms tied to the bedposts. In the mirror, Sal can see bruises and little crescents of blood from where fingernails had broken the skin. Over the past few nights, Sal thinks, Rick seems to have lost his caution and crossed the thin line of mutual boundaries that made their sex so exciting. The whole week has been strange, in fact, full of small chores and quiet reading on the dockside: Sal staring into *Swann's Way*, Rick swimming far out into the lake, busy with his vow to reach the other side before leaving. Sal would often look up to check on him, a flurry of arms in the calm, flat water.

When he emerges from the bedroom, he finds Rick sitting at the pine table with a white mug. The light through the clouds is colourless, but Rick still looks tanned.

"I have some bad news," Rick says. His voice sounds cautious, distracted. "Do you remember my neighbour, Mr. Shoreditch?"

"The retired butcher? Of course," Sal says. He has shared the elevator with Mr. Shoreditch and his beagle a few times. He's a friendly old man, although the boys often joke about how he is oblivious to the sort of sex happening a few feet from where he sleeps.

"He passed away last night," Rick said. "Aneurysm."

"Oh, how awful."

"Yeah. His daughter just called my cell. I guess he had my number somewhere. She sounded pretty broken up." He turns away from Sal and squints at the window, even though there's no sun.

"Are you going to send flowers?"

"No. I think I should head back," Rick says casually, as though he'll just have to walk down the street. "You won't believe this, but he picked me to be one of his pallbearers."

Sal gives a disappointed moan. "Does that mean we have to go back?"

"There's no point in getting you all wrapped up in it. I'll just catch a bus this afternoon."

A vibration starts in Sal's jaw — the tiny, nervous chatter of his teeth. It is the signal that something has slipped out of his control. He feels a sudden need to get Rick's attention, to place himself at the centre of the Shoreditch tragedy. "You don't really have to go back, do you? I mean, how well did you know him?"

"Don't get like that," Rick says. He stands and walks over to Sal, placing a hand on the bruised neck. His fingers are warm from the mug. "I don't have a choice. I'm really sorry."

Sal suggests they drive back to Toronto together. "That way I can pick up supplies for the renovations."

"You really don't have to do that."

"It's the least I can do," Sal says brightly. "You know, it's sad — this is the second year in a row where we've had to leave because of a death."

Rick doesn't respond.

An hour later, right when they are ready to leave, the rain stops. When Rick goes outside for a last cigarette, he watches through the windows as Sal makes sure the water valve is twisted off, that all the garbage is in bags, that the windows are closed and locked. Now Sal is carrying bags of clothes to the front door.

Rick puts out his cigarette on the stone pathway and keeps walking towards the lake, arms on his hips. He volunteered to pull in the dock so that he could say goodbye to the view. He leaves his shoes at the path's end, socks balled up and stuffed into their mouths, and walks to the end of the dock. The wood is wet and soft against his feet and creaks slightly, making small rubbing noises as the frame scrapes against the sloping rock. After a firm, tough rain, summer takes a while to rev back up to its glory. For the moment, the skies are white, the lake is corrugated with little waves, and the air is breezy: wiped clean, chilled, and smelling of wood. This is the hour of quiet and careful resurgence of the sun. Distantly, the high beams of a car heading down Go Home Lake Road flash between the trees, like a code. The rain was hard, Rick thinks, but this place is stubborn. He takes in the view, filing it away in his mind, knowing that memory plays tricks. The images of Go Home Lake he'll carry with him will change long before the reality does.

the clearing

Patrick Callahan looks at himself in the chrome elevator doors of St. Joseph's Health Centre. He has changed over the eleven months that his father has been away. His face has filled out at the jaw and his chest has expanded slightly, just enough to be in proportion with his legs. The white dress shirt he has been issued for high school cannot be comfortably buttoned at the neck. He watches his reflection untuck it and he decides he looks better, the wrinkled edge of the material dipping down to mid-thigh, stark against the grey flannel of his pants. His hair has grown, too, the tips landing a centimetre above his left eyebrow. He flips the brown strands to the right side of his head. It is an action he practises whenever he has butterflies in his stomach, just before seeing his boyfriend. It makes him more attractive, he thinks, more seductive. As if it says: you think I look good now? Well, check *this* out.

At the third floor, he steps out into the intensive care unit and heads down the hall towards a waiting room fringed with sturdy chairs upholstered in black tweed. His mother is sitting against the wall, facing the nurses' station, a magazine opened but ignored on her lap. She's had her hair done, swept up into a curly grey hurricane. The fingers of her left hand are tapping against her thumb, as though she is counting them. She is wearing Patrick's least favourite top: a light-yellow blouse with embroidered flowers pouring out of the shoulder seams.

"Well, thank *God*," Mrs. Callahan says as he approaches. "I was getting worried."

"Why? Why worried?"

"Well, they've moved your grandfather down here. I didn't know if you'd be able to find us."

"And yet here I am." He sits down next to her and begins tapping his middle finger against his knee. The hospital has gone out of its way to make this space as inoffensive as possible. The buttermilk-coloured walls mute the fluorescent lights, that stripe the ceiling like music staves. There is a single print on the wall to Patrick's left: a view of Maple Street, Fiona's main thoroughfare, as it was at the turn of the century. There are horse-drawn wagons and gas lamps and shops with their names above the doors: Apothecary, Chéhab Funerals, General Food and Feed. The green hill of Exhibition Park rises behind it all, a half-mile in the distance.

"How was school?" Patrick's mother asks. "Where's your tie?"

"Fine and in my pocket."

"Don't get it all wrinkled."

"Promise," Patrick says. "Great hair."

"Oh, you like it?" Mrs. Callahan smiles, her lips disappearing into her teeth. "It's something new. Your father will love it. Won't he love it?"

"Well, let's ask him. Oh wait — he's not here?" Patrick looks around dramatically, with feigned desperation. "What a surprise. Did he leave you again?"

"Oh, be quiet." She gives her head a few little shakes, eyes rolled way up. "He's at work and you know it."

"I was at school and I still had to come." Patrick taps at his watch face — it's only three o'clock.

"He'll be by to pick us up," she says. Her cheer makes Patrick wince and swallow. He can feel the bob of his Adam's apple. He has news, but he will not be able to reveal it if he is looking right at her big, hopeful face. He distracts himself by peering into the nurses' station for his boyfriend, Dylan. He starts breathing through his mouth — little sighs, as though he is trying to force the news out like a burp. The staff behind the counter look with prolonged glances at Patrick and his mother. Fiona is a small town, and everyone here knows that, nearly year ago, Mr. Callahan left town at the same time as Patrick's violin teacher. Like Mrs. Callahan, they all assumed the pair had left to be together — the hussy musician and the dirty GM manager. Good riddance.

But last month, Patrick's father returned, roses in hand, begging his wife to take him back. A midlife crisis, that's what Mr. Callahan claimed. A phase. He had been in Toronto, he told Patrick, but didn't elaborate. He seemed contrite now that he was back in Fiona, brought more roses for the table and thanked his wife at mealtime — *look at this feast!* — then became pink-faced. Your mother and I, we're going to take another crack at it. Patrick believed him: Patrick who needed his mother to calm down, who thought that he could dodge scrutiny if his family had a semblance of normality. And their home seemed to be moving in that direction, until one night last week when Patrick was with Dylan at the Clearing — a notorious place on the eastern slope of Exhibition Park where men cruise for sex after sundown. In a wildly explosive millisecond, Patrick thought he saw his father stride past in the dark. He heard Mr. Callahan's pace quicken down the forest path towards the town's only gay bar. Patrick broke away from Dylan and stood on the edge of the Clearing to watch the small passage lit by the bar's security lights. His father's body passed swiftly and Patrick could not help himself. "I see you!" he screamed, feeling the ropes of tendons pull tight around his throat. "I see you, I see you, I see you!"

"I have my car," Patrick says to his mother. "I'll drive you home when he doesn't show up."

"Why must you harp on your father?" Her eyebrows, painted on thin as matchsticks, leap towards her hairline. "He's trying so hard."

"I have other things to worry about. Father will just have to take a number."

Behind the counter of the nurses' station, Dylan finally appears — short, with a thick neck and salt-and-pepper goatee — to receive orders from a nurse in blue scrubs. He's nodding at her, his eyes flick over at Patrick, a millimetre's worth of motion.

"Look at me, Patrick. Look at me sitting here —"

"In that blouse, I'd really rather not."

"*Look* at me, waiting here for a few precious last moments with my own father. You don't want to have the same thing happen to you, do you?"

"Grandpa was *around*."

"But you still don't seem to care one iota. You haven't even *asked* me how he's doing," says Mrs. Callahan, poking at a Kleenex shoved into her sleeve.

"You're just going to tell me anyway."

"Well, he's dying. It's official. I whispered it to him not two hours ago. Can you imagine having to tell your father that his life is to be snuffed out? Just like that?" She snaps her fingers. "He could go at any minute."

"They give him oceans of morphine," Patrick says. "I doubt he cares much one way or the other."

"Which makes it all the harder on me. *I* had to tell him."

"Is that why you look so awful?" Patrick says. He repositions himself away from her so he can peer more effectively into the nurses' station. Dylan is still there, preparing a cart of towels and trays and small plastic pill cups. The firm relief of the candy-striper's muscles is clear under his pink uniform. His head is wide, almost spherical, frosted with shaved hairs that outline a widow's peak.

"Do I? Do I not look sad?"

"Oh, you look *sad* alright," Patrick replies, his eyes fixed on Dylan.

"Is that sarcasm? Would it hurt you to feel just a little sad about this? I mean, believe it or not, your grandpa in there loves you. He *loves* you."

"Yeah, I know," Patrick says.

Mrs. Callahan sighs and pulls her shiny silver coat onto her lap from the chair next to her. "I brought a coat today. You'd think they'd make sure a waiting room was warm, not like this icebox. Is this comforting? I have a father dying in there and I've got to feel cold tears on my cheeks."

"Don't worry, Mom. Everyone can still see them."

"And this *colour*. As if sickness wasn't sad enough, they went and painted this place *beige*, of all things." She reaches up and pats her hair, ensuring its set. When the candy striper looks up from his work, Patrick begins to imitate Mrs. Callahan, daintily moving a flat hand against the side of his head. Dylan smiles. Patrick looks him up and down, then winks.

"You stop it."

"Stop what?"

"You know exactly what," she says.

"No, tell me. Vocalise, Mother. Ar*ti*culate."

"You understand perfectly well, I'm not going to create a song and dance."

"No, create a song and dance. You have a gay son. You can't tell me to stop doing something that you don't even ac*know*ledge."

"Why must you insist on giving me a stroke? It's a good thing we're already in a hospital. They can lay me down right there next to your grandfather and we can die together."

"I thought you wanted him to die in peace."

"Oh *you*." She turns away from him, bowing her head a little. Patrick looks at the streak of hairs frozen upward, away from her fleshy white neck. Patrick's muscles clench. He can feel his testimony gathering in his gut — he even imagines the look on her face: scrunching up in confusion for a second, then slowly draining of colour as her lower lip quivers and her eyelids sink into fierce little slits. He has practiced his own reaction, too: smooth and expressionless, eyes glowing with victory. Although scared of what else may follow this moment of triumph, Patrick holds dear the notion that his disclosure could obliterate his mother's pretty conception of their family — of the world, really — like a bug crunched under the wheel of a train.

"Stop crying," he says.

"I'm not crying," she says, turning back to him. "I just wanted to see if you were worried enough to ask."

Patrick stares at her with a face he hopes is impassive. She looks as though she's trying to keep a smile down.

"Well, I'm not," Patrick says.

"You *are*. You won't admit it. Obstinate, just like your father. But that's it. You *worry*."

It is true — sometimes, in spite of himself, he does worry. The day his father left, Patrick came home from the Clearing to find the house silent, except for his mother's muffled crying behind the bathroom door. Patrick knew she prefers crying on the front porch — loudly, to make sure the neighbours feel bad for her. This time, the stillness of the house forced worry on him; things were not what they were supposed to be. Patrick could only hear her clearly by sneaking his ear close to the door, hand flat next to his head. He imagined how she looked in there: puffy eyes, no makeup. Her lower lip jiggling like a square of Jell-O on a spoon.

"You are clearly delusional. Do you want me to get the nurse?"

"Yes, so I can complain about this waiting room. It is so much more dramatic than the one upstairs, don't you think?"

"Well, this is the icu," Patrick says. "They don't fool around down here."

"I should get the fbc to look into it."

Patrick is sick of the fbc — the Fiona Beautification Committee. This was the project Mrs. Callahan threw herself into when her husband left. She started by having the General Motors water tower ripped from the skyline and then moved on to the downtown. She wanted to bring Fiona back to a "simpler, more beautiful time." Over the past year, the sidewalks have been widened and given decorative stripes of pink interlocking brick. Stately iron lamps, with gabled tops and ornamental curlicues, have replaced the impersonal out-stretched arms of the old street lights. Neon signs were banned. Fiona may look better to people passing through, but the improvements just remind Patrick that his mother is a fool.

Every nurse at that station must feel the same way when they see such changes, Patrick thinks, looking past the counter to find the candy striper. By now, they all must have heard that she's idiotically let Mr. Callahan back into the family; Fionans excel at gossip. When Dylan finally reappears, pulling his cart out of the first room in the hallway, he raises his eyebrows at Patrick: *Have you told her yet?* Patrick shakes his head. Dylan scowls; his disappointment blows against Patrick like a current of air.

"It's too cold in here," Mrs. Callahan says. "And there should be a window. St. Joe's has some of the loveliest views in the whole town."

"Not today it doesn't," Patrick says. "It was still raining when I came in."

"It wasn't."

"It was."

"What a shame." Mrs. Callahan crosses her legs and smoothes out some of the hairs of her coat. "Do you know what I was just reading here, in this magazine, about the rain?"

"Now, how the fuck would —"

"That *word*."

"— how the *frig* would I know something like that? Can I read minds?"

"According to the man in this article, if a butterfly flaps its wings in Japan, in New York there will be rain instead of sun." Patrick leans to his right and looks down the hall, but Dylan is angry. He seems determined not to look back. "And that even the smallest little thing can set off the rain."

"Well, I doubt he was only talking about the weather. He was probably talking about the grand scheme of things."

"But this article, *this* one, is about the weather," she says, waving her rolled-up copy of *Science*. "And don't you find it reassuring, all this butterfly business? I mean, the butterfly didn't even *know* what it was doing. There was no real responsibility involved. Isn't that nice? To know that things are unpredictable?"

"No. It is scary as hell. For all *I* know, I am walking around causing all kinds of thunderstorms every bloody time I make a move," Patrick says. Dylan has nearly disappeared down the hall: a dark stick against the far window.

"I think it's *fas*cinating. I mean just imagine."

"I'd really rather not."

"You can trace things all the way back to a butterfly, but you could never — what's the word? trace forward? — trace *for*ward to the rainstorm." She jabs at the air with the magazine, as if indicating imaginary points in time.

"Humans are not butterflies, Mom," Patrick said. "The butterfly is just an ex*am*ple."

"There's no need to get huffy."

"I'm not getting huffy, I'm mindblown," he says. "Only you could bring talking about the weather to this staggering level of boredom."

Her face is blank. "Oh, you treat me so awfully."

"I don't."

"You *do*." Mrs. Callahan is running the nail of her index finger against the cuticle of her thumb.

"Can we just go in and see him already? Watching a man die has got to be easier than *this*."

"No, no. There's something we need to talk about."

"Oh God."

"Don't roll your eyes, this is serious." Mrs. Callahan lets out a long sigh and stares out towards the nurses' station. "It's about your father."

Patrick clenches his fists. "The invisible man? What about him?"

"We are not telling your grandfather that he has come back."

"We're not?"

"No. He disapproves." Her baby finger has found the cuticle now. "I've been honest with your grandfather all my life, but just this once I'm not going to be. For his own sake. It'll kill him for sure."

"Oh, the life of a martyr."

She looks right at Patrick now and lets the magazine go slack in her hand. "I just can't win with you," she says.

"You can't win at anything. Period." Her face remains still, expectant, as though refusing to hear him. I can ruin you, Patrick thinks. "Fine. I won't say anything."

"And you're coming home with me for dinner."

"I'm going out." He stares down the vacant hallway. Dylan's really angry — Patrick can feel it in his absence.

"Fine," she says. "Just fine. You do whatever you want. I'll drive myself home. A*lone*."

"Wait, wait. You have *your* car here?" Patrick says, turning to her. "I thought your reliable husband was coming by to pick you up. If you really thought he'd be here, you would *never* have brought that car."

"If you could only hear yourself," she says.

"If *you* could only hear *your*self. You won't even admit that I'm gay."

"That again?" she says. "You're seventeen years old, you don't know what you are. You think *e*verything is so clear. Well, Patrick Robert Callahan, nothing is *e*ver clear. I should tape this and play it all back to you someday when you have a better sense of what's important."

"Im*por*tant?" Patrick says, just under shouting. "You have no clue what's really important."

"And you do, I suppose."

"I could tell you a few things."

She shakes her head slowly and twists towards Patrick, placing both hands on the armrest of his chair. She looks like she will go for his jugular. "Things are never perfect, Patrick.

But we have to *try* to make them as perfect as possible."

"Is that why you took him back? That *li*ar?"

"You watch your mouth." She grabs Patrick's wrist. He looks at her. Her eyes are wet, vapid, round as quarters. "I need your father. I've forgiven him."

"There's something you need to know," Patrick says. He can't swallow. Her hand is sticky now and she shows no sign of having heard him. Her jaw is slack and her eyes confused

"Patrick, did I make a mistake?" Her voice is new — thin and dry as paper. She wilts, placing both arms on her lap. A chill takes the place of her hand on Patrick's wrist. He turns away, head heavy, desperate for a glimpse of Dylan. But he is not there. The nurses' station and the numbered doors all seem foreign, unknowable, as if Patrick has been dropped into a mysterious place and has been told to find his way back. But back where? He doesn't know and is frozen by a deep panic.

"Let's go in," he says.

"Did I make a mistake?" she says. She looks at him, face loose and open, full of tiny wrinkles. She has aged decades.

"Come on. Let's do this." Patrick stands.

"Give me a minute," his mother says. She heaves herself out of the chair. The act looks painful. She folds the new coat over her arm and pats down the fibres. Patrick lets her pass to lead him to the correct door. As they approach, Patrick turns down the hall, hoping to catch sight of Dylan. Mrs. Callahan places her hand on the door and sighs heavily.

"Will you be good?" she says, then pushes open the door and breezes through, not waiting for an answer.

‡

Over the last double-rumble of train tracks, Patrick finds himself outside the realm of the FBC. The street's name changes here, from Maple Street to Maple Street Extension (although it is all Highway 21) — it is wider, more utilitarian. There are large spaces between the gas stations and fast food outlets and lumber stores. Long, curvy streets lined with newer homes, even bungalows, intersect with the highway. This is where Fiona's GM workers and city employees live. Patrick's mother dislikes passing through this subdivision and always points out to her son that every car on these streets was bought on discount. Pontiacs, Oldsmobiles, Chevrolets. She calls it The Necessary District.

Patrick turns his Toyota into the parking lot of a bar named Scandals. A sad, soaked rainbow flag droops over the entrance. He is not old enough to go into the bar, so he walks around to the back. Patrick associates the smell of the dumpster with anticipation: old beer, fermenting on its rusty bottom, mixed with the biting odour of discarded liquor bottles. The smell follows him over a patch of grass brightly lit by security lamps, and dissipates as the path creeps up the side of the slope. On the other side of the hill, there are new nature paths being carved out of the forest by the Fiona Beautification Committee. The view from there is more compelling: it shows how the nearby rivers slide into one another and creep further out towards either Lake Huron or Georgian Bay. From this unsanctioned path, the path to the Clearing, adventurers catch glimpses of Fiona itself, with its bleak agricultural fringe and cluster of suburbs.

The rain stopped during the three hours that he and his mother sat next to the sleeping body of his grandfather, and now the bats are out, striping the royal-blue sky. The air is still moist, holding in it the mossy smell of the forest. The slow rise of the hill is easy on Patrick, although the ground is muddy. As a child, his father used to bring him here. Back then, there was a deeper ditch at the edge of the slope that snaked around to a playground, parking lot, and a decaying yellow bathroom: chipped paint, sandy walls, and rusty doors so warped they were impossible to lock. His father would park there and let his son choose a category for their hunt: "Flying ones," Patrick would say and then they would separate to trap flies or moths or butterflies in Mason jars. "Lots of legs" was another favourite. "Antennae."

The fun was stopped by the town council. Part of the beautification of Fiona involved the destruction of the old train sheds, water towers, and public washrooms. When this side of the highway was zoned for new homes and businesses, the area was closed off to bug-seekers and park-goers while the developments were underway.

Where the gradient levels off, the path widens by several feet and the space forms a rough circle, bordered on one side by a curving line of maples and on the other by a ledge that drops off towards the town. Patrick walks the circumference of the Clearing, looking into the gaps between the trees for the regulars. There is still too much light to attract other men — Patrick can still make out the details of the tree bark and individual sheep freckling the long, empty land — although he has seen other guys here as early as sundown, lingering, waiting for anonymity.

But Patrick is here to see Dylan, who usually meets him here at eight-thirty, after his shift at the hospital. The majority of their relationship has taken place at the Clearing — a refuge from Patrick's mother and other judgmental eyes. They met here for the first time three months ago. Dylan claimed to have been struck by Patrick's skinny, youthful form when he saw him around St. Joe's. When Patrick arrived at the Clearing one night, Dylan's arm reached out for him through the blackness and held its prize close. Patrick felt secure with this over-powering arm around his chest and could feel Dylan pushing off other men who tried to join their fun. On the night Patrick saw his father, the same brawny arm rubbed Patrick's back for an hour as Dylan listened to him cry. Patrick loves him with a fierce respect. Dylan is one of the few gay men in Fiona that is out of the closet; he works on the GM assembly line and volunteers at St. Joe's; he can laugh at childish jokes, but still maintains adult sturdiness, consistency, and protectiveness.

Patrick leans against a maple tree. He likes it here before the sun goes down. There is no pretension, just an excitement in strong counterpoint to the calm of dark. And the view, of course, stretching away from him now: points of light dissipating from the bright cluster of Victorian street lamps along Maple Street; the little cars passing through town; and even his own little house, right off Maple Street on Edward Avenue, with his mother's gold sedan in the driveway. St. Joe's is an overlit monstrosity of additions and parking lots. The tapering GM smokestack, poking up like a raised finger, is topped with a single cautionary red light that blinks on and off. Beyond Fiona on all sides is the quilt of Ontario farmland, green squares of various shades, held together by criss-crossing seams of trees and fences. From this awkward vantage point, night swallows the land from the sides as the sun disappears into the horizon — a bright orange ball set in blazing lines of cloud that break up the light.

He hears crunching behind him: the grit of the park's rocky soil against new summer leaves and the hard soles of shoes. Patrick can see the pink of a shirt moving between the trees.

"You didn't tell her," Dylan says, voice raised to cover the distance. Patrick watches him approach, stepping over roots, dodging trees. Dylan is still in his candy-striper uniform.

"Did you check on my grandfather before you left?" Patrick says.

"Why didn't you tell her?"

Three feet of earth separate them when Dylan stops and crosses his arms. Patrick lifts his back from the tree.

"You first," Patrick says.

"ok, he was still breathing when I left," Dylan says. "Now you."

"I couldn't," Patrick says. "She can't handle it. You saw her"

"I saw her treating my boy like *shit*. I saw my boy being a coward," Dylan says. "For Christ's sake, I thought we decided."

Patrick turns away. The sky is navy now, looming over Fiona. The moon is a bright pebble. "I'm not even going to discuss it if you're going to be like that."

"ok, ok," Dylan says. "I'm sorry."

Someone deeper in the woods shushes them. Dylan walks over to Patrick so they can speak softly and places both muscled hands on Patrick's hips. Patrick has a flash of an earlier anonymous encounter in the Clearing: hearing a man come towards him in the dark, able to determine little but the basic geometry of the stranger's body. Sometimes, when the moon is bright, Patrick can make out the placement of a stranger's eyes, mouth, chin, and think *Do I really want to go through with this?* But here are Dylan's familiar features coming at him in the twilight: thin dry lips; a small, hard nose, pointing up; calm brown eyes; goatee; a wide, creased brow under the rim of a faded Expos hat. Patrick had come for just this, to see Dylan before the night steals his face away.

"Look at you, Funny Girl," Dylan says.

"I'd really rather not," Patrick says. "Getting up here was so muddy. I'm a mess."

"You're a damn cute mess."

"My shirt's all gross and look at my pant cuffs." Patrick holds up his leg so Dylan can see the ring of dirt on his pant cuffs.

"Your mother won't like that."

"How you manage to do this to every pair of pants, I'll never know," Patrick says, imitating her. "What have *I* done to deserve a son with cuffs as dirty as *this*?"

Dylan laughs and a second angry shush comes from beyond the circumference of trees.

"We're breaking the rules," Dylan says. "Too much noise."

"This place is so depressing," Patrick says.

"You used to love it up here. You used to get so excited."

"Well, I've changed my mind. The desperation, the anonymity. All these men up here for a quick blow job, living a lie." Dylan's expression changes, his features fall. "Not you. I make an exception for you. You're here to see me. It's just that everyone in Fiona only cares about keeping up appearances. Look at my mother. All she cares about is making something pretty out of this shitty little town. And all the while her husband is nothing but a liar."

"That's why you have to tell her about your father, Funny Girl," Dylan says, warm mouth just behind Patrick's ear. The voice is smooth and deep; Patrick can feel the vibrations on his neck and back. "Otherwise, you're as bad as her."

"That's low," Patrick says.

"But true."

"What if she already knows?" Patrick tries to look defiantly at Dylan, but can't find his eyes in the dark.

"All the same — you should let her know that *you* know. That the whole town knows."

"The whole town doesn't know," Patrick says. "The whole town speculates."

"OK, forget about the town," Dylan says, and takes his hands off Patrick's waist. "What about me? If she knew, things would be a lot easier for you and me."

"Don't be so sure," Patrick says. "That means telling her that I was up here. She'll throw me out."

"If she does, I'll just take you away," Dylan says. "Simple as that."

"That again?"

"Yeah."

"And leave all this?" Patrick gestures all around them: the Clearing, the claustrophobia of the encroaching trees, the shimmering lights of the town. "Where would we possibly go?"

"Toronto, Ottawa," Dylan says. "I don't know. A city."

"And leave your job? Those spark plugs aren't going to assemble themselves."

"I think GM will survive without Little Dylan."

"Little Dylan?" Patrick turns to him, smiling. "That's so cute. Who calls you that? Your mom?"

"The boys at work. Our supervisor is a fat guy who's named Dylan, too. Big Dylan and Little Dylan."

"Little Dylan," Patrick says. "Funny Girl and Little Dylan."

"That's right. Us; alone together."

Patrick opens his eyes very wide and sucks in half his lips. He thinks about a table set for two in a far-off apartment with unpainted walls and aggressive noise from the streets. Dylan sits at one end and Patrick is standing in a corner, listening to the tinny, betrayed voice of his mother through a phone line. "I just don't want to leave her all alone. If my father was there, things would be different."

"You're father *is* there, remember?"

"Not really. He's not *real*ly there. In fact, he's probably here somewhere," Partick says, tipping his head towards the forest. "Besides, I'm not even done high school."

"There are schools everywhere, Funny Girl. That's not the issue," Dylan says in a firm tone.

"Oh, and what is the issue?"

"That we all have choices to make. I've made mine." Dylan puts his arms loosely around Patrick's waist and pulls their bodies together. Patrick's loose bottom lip disappears between Dylan's teeth and then is slowly released; Patrick can feel each fibre as the enamel scrapes over the tissue. "When fate deals you a hand as cute as Patrick Callahan, you don't just fold."

"I hate fate," Patrick says. Their faces are still close, but the features are sketchy in the dark. "Do you know about this butterfly business? That if a butterfly beats its wings in Japan, New York will get rain instead of sun?"

"You mean the Chaos Theory? I don't like it," Dylan says. "I like to think that everything happens for reason. A pre-*des*tined reason."

"Really?" Patrick looks at him, tries to find his eyes. "That must make the world pretty clear. I wish I could think that way. I used to, I guess. When I was a kid."

"You're still a kid."

"I certainly don't feel like one," Patrick says. They stand for a moment in each other's arms. There is a cold breeze against their extremities.

"Look, there's something I need to tell you," Dylan says. His voice changes suddenly into a deep whisper. "Call it fate or chaos or what have you."

"Oh no," Patrick turns away from him now to face the town, his back against Dylan's chest.

"I saw him again."

"A*gain*?"

"Yesterday," Dylan says. "While I was waiting for you." Patrick's eyes sink down to the town far below them, to the spot where one lonely gold car sits in the driveway of his house.

"Why didn't you tell me yesterday?"

"There was no point," Dylan says, quickly. "We'd already decided that she should know."

"A likely story," Patrick says. In the weeks after they met, Patrick was sure that he saw Dylan's Chevy Cavalier drive past his school near dismissal time and go by the house on Edward Avenue in the evenings. Patrick thought it sweet, this campaign of protection, but Dylan denied it so vehemently that Patrick let the subject drop — and a stiffness clamped onto Patrick's neck. It was the usual feeling that accompanies uncertainty.

"You chickened out. I *had* to tell you," Dylan says and pushes his thumbs into the fleshy space under Patrick's shoulder blades. Patrick holds onto the tension for moment, but then gives in, dropping his head and shoulders into a more relaxed position. "Your father's selfish little trips aren't going to end."

"Hurt me. Push harder in the middle."

Dylan presses until Patrick can feel the thumbs touch bone. "Like this?"

"Perfect," says Patrick, focussing on the town between half-closed eyes. "I hate him, you know."

"I know."

"That's what I mean when I say this place is depressing."

"So come away with me," Dylan says and starts kissing Patrick's neck under his white, starchy shirt collar and, momentarily, Patrick closes his eyes. The fingers of Dylan's left hand start making their way under the waistband of Patrick's flannel pants, the belt buckle pulled loose with the right hand. Patrick opens his eyes and reaches out to grip a tree. The town below looks like an exploded firework caught in freeze-frame against a black sky. The huge overhead lamps of St. Joe's light the cars that surround the main building.

A hint of movement breaks the stillness of the bright, black squares of the parking lot. A gold-coloured sedan is sliding over the pavement towards the hospital. Its shadow, tethered to the wheels, grows and shrinks as the car moves. Visiting hours are long over, so the driver has no trouble locating a space near the entrance.

"Look there," Patrick says. His clenched teeth vibrate with the words. "That looks like my mother's car."

Dylan peers down, too, over Patrick's shoulder. "Calm down. You're letting yourself get all bent out of shape."

"What if something's happened?"

"Let your father deal with it. She is not your responsibility." The driver's side door swings open, catching a flash of light in the window. Dylan wraps a thick warm arm over Patrick's chest. "Do you really want to make that mistake? Look what it's doing to you. I need you here." Dylan says.

Only the one door remains open. For a moment, Patrick hopes to see his father's long legs poke out — but when they don't, he starts to feel queasy, the butterflies at work in his stomach again. Dylan's arm is squashing his chest. Patrick imagines his mother sitting in the gold sedan, alone in the draft, makeup eyebrows already wiped off for bed. She's taking long stuttering gasps and touching a tissue to her nose. The arm crushes Patrick closer, but he feels pulled forward by an instinctive desperation. She's not rushing. She's weak. When Dylan says something else, Patrick can't make it out. He is already running toward her.

treasure

Two days ago, Carol watched from the kitchen as her husband walked in from work with his latest discovery. It was a metal detector, a long steel rod with a disc attached to the base and a set of wires snaking up to a box with two knobs. The device was labelled MajikWand. Lan laid the thing on the couch and, without a word to Carol, unplugged a pair of puffy green earphones from the stereo and attached them to the top of the wand.

"What are you doing with those?" Carol said. "Lance Goffritz, what are you up to?"

Deaf to his wife's question, Lan continued out to the front yard with the toy. She spied on him from the living room window, pie-eyed, clutching the curtain. After fifteen years of marriage, Carol was used to his discoveries, his eccentric insistence that they clutter up the house, but this time he was acting peculiar. He waved the wand over the ground for an hour, then climbed into his Astro van and disappeared down 7th Road. Carol picked up the phone to call her friend Joan in Toronto.

"Something's happened," Carol said. "Something with Lan."

"What is it this time?" Joan said.

"You'll laugh at me."

"No I won't," Joan was using her therapy voice, calm and reassuring. "There are cycles in every union, Car. For you, they're all marked by the same things. You get hysterical, you clean, you call me."

"Don't intro-to-psych me, Joan. Something's happened. It's in the back of my head and just will not quit."

"What happened?"

"I'm exhausted, Joan. I'm beat. I think I need a day. Come pick me up. We'll have lunch in the city and I'll give you the nitty-gritty."

Joan sighed and said, "Very well."

Two days later, on the morning of the lunch date, Carol opened the bedroom door and there was Lan, sitting in the vestibule, wiping the metal detector with a rag. He was smiling at it, eyes following the motion of his hands. He asked her to come with him to the beach to try it out. "Come on. We'll make a day of it," he said.

"No way, Jose. I'm going to the city later. Joan is on her way here to pick me up and I still have to vacuum out Cobble

Palace and run over to Triangle Discount for light bulbs. I'm not wasting the day with that thing."

"When all is said and done, Car, what's one spring morning at the beach with your husband?" He didn't not look up at her, and with this non-action Carol felt that the point when all is said and done may actually be approaching.

"I'm not going and that's that."

"Don't know what you're missing, Car," he said and looked up her. He had disappointed eyes over a prominent jawline, jug ears and omnipresent stubble like a field of pinpricks. He stood and placed a hand on the doorknob. "I'm running out to an assignment out on Bruce Row later, but I'll be back in plenty of time to pick you up in Owen Sound. Ten o'clock at the train station, as usual?"

"Fine."

‡

Joan is making her favourite drive: from Toronto to Cobble Beach along Highways 6 and 21. She adores the two hours of union between her body and the Audi, gliding from lane to lane, watching a driver's cigarette shatter against the road in front of her. She imagines possible dramas from her life or fills the car with off-kilter melodies of her own.

The sinister April of Toronto, with its bone-white sky and wafts of thawing dog shit, cracks open along Highway 6 to reveal a big blueness behind the Niagara Escarpment. In all the towns along the way (Port Elgin, Fiona, Inverness) there is a post office, a Stedman's, a Triangle Discount and streets named King, Queen, Maple, Oak, Elm, and Elizabeth. Between the towns are open fields of melting snow dotted with fences and silos and utility posts. Running next to her against the blue sky is the swoop-swoop of sagging phone wires, like the line of a melody. She rolls down the windows and sings into the wind:

She never was the stick-around kind
But kept all her boys in her head.
She never was the meatloaf kind
But, man, was she good in bed.

Three overlapping chevrons of geese appear in the southern sky. "That's my wedding," Joan says aloud; this is an old joke from the adolescence she shared with Carol in Toronto, when they ran through the house skeletons of the developing suburb of North York. If they ever came upon a drove of pigeons, they would shout: "That's my wedding!" in hopes that a similarly large flock of people would attend their future nuptials. But over the years of her friend's marriage to Lan, Joan has become disillusioned with the idea of matrimony. This whole trip, in fact, is to go and help Carol through her latest crisis. On the phone two days ago, Carol was typically elusive — refusing to reveal any details until they were face to face.

Ha! If that is what a marriage becomes, Joan is willing to settle for merely meddling in other people's unions. Joan is nearly forty and imagines any wedding at her age and with her luck in love as preposterous, more likely to be attended by a flock of geese than a gaggle of humans. She imagines them perched on padded chairs, drinking copiously from the punch bowl, and shitting all over the tablecloths.

Joan stops at a red light. It is the first in many kilometres, but hints at the town yet-to-come. Around the junction are tall, narrow poles of pine and muscular legs of maple. She lifts her body diagonally from her seat to catch a brief slice of her face in the rear-view mirror. She smiles, flares her nostrils, scrapes goo from the corner of an eye. Her beauty coup, Joan thinks, is concealing the immense girth of her head under flat, flowing streams of hair. She watches her reflection run a hand over it and, satisfied, proceeds through the intersection, tires rumbling over multitudes of fallen buds.

‡

Carol steps out of her house and turns left towards the lake, pulling a rattling shopping cart that holds a deep plastic bucket packed full of colourful cleaners, polishes, old pairs of Lan's underwear, and a massive key ring. Cobble Beach grows away from Lake Huron in a grid. A breeze blows crisp off the water and up the numbered roads. The beach still smells of winter, but as she moves closer to the town centre, the odours of spring take over: ripped-up earth and rotting cedar branches. Crows congregate in the shallow road puddles. Windows are opened to the warming sunlight. The cottages lining the southern streets of Cobble Beach are squat affairs, lifted off the sandy ground by concrete blocks. Serious buildings — with foundations and basements and invisible plumbing — have to be built in solid earth further from the beach. The summer homes appear sleepy, waiting for summer, tenants, life. Carol and Lan own six such cottages, each with its own name, and Carol executes their yearly cleaning with the same enjoyment she derives from scraping wax from her ear or vacuuming the minivan's glove compartment; it is a release of natural stuffiness.

Carol turns towards a cottage on 3rd Road, "Cobble Palace" according to the sign Lan posted out front, and pulls her cart over the yard's floor of pine needles. She finds the appropriate key on her ring and throws open the door. The kitchen and living room share the same low-ceilinged space, cluttered with ring-stained tables, unmatched chairs, and couches wrapped in worn velour. Every surface is covered in dust. She pounces: wiping, sweeping, coughing, spraying, polishing. She opens the main water valve and waits for the spurts of rust to disappear down the drain, then she fills the bucket and dunks the underwear. Each year, Carol is impressed by how these cottages are not merely temporary dwellings, but little homes. In a matter of weeks, Cobble Palace will be full of children racing through the rooms, sipping Kool-Aid on the deck, begging their mother to take them to the beach. This is the key difference between this place and her own bungalow, she thinks as she tosses a handful of dead flies out a window. Lan is the closest thing she has to a child.

When Carol moved in with him, she disliked the chaos of his home, which felt like a boy's secret fort. There was a stack of old board games in the living room, a pile of tin soldiers, a box full of old rotary-dial phones all tangled together. He still brings home all kinds of junk that he picks up during his assignments for the Bruce County Housing Office. His job is to visit the empty houses of the region — those that are silently rotting after a foreclosure, a death, or simple desertion — and dispose of the forsaken contents. In addition to the toys, Lan has also brought home items essential for living. They have an indiscriminate collection of cutlery, for example, and the furniture in their cottages spans every custom and style. As a newlywed, Carol came up with fanciful stories to explain all these items to her future children. She cherished the tales, even wrote a few of them down: why someone painted a picture of the local A&P; how a strange hunting expedition resulted in their bearskin rug; how their cottages got their names. But when Lan decided he no longer wanted kids, her stories lost their purpose. Now she just tells them to Lan.

Last summer, Carol exploded when she decided one of her creations had been violated. Lan rented the Honey Moongrove cabin to a gay couple with a pet snake. When he told her, she was stupefied by Lan's unwillingness to join her in one, unified panic.

"Aren't you the least bit concerned about what they are going to *do* to each other in a bed that *you* paid for?"

"The cheque was good, Car. When all is said and done, they could bugger the snake if they wanted."

"Rent them a different cottage. They can't stay at Moongrove."

"Why not?"

"If you can't see why not, then you don't deserve to know." And she stormed from the patio to the kitchen, sliding the door shut with a bang. Carol only calmed down once Lan asked her to tell her a story about a BB gun he'd found, with a boy's name scratched inexpertly into the barrel. He came running into the bungalow, holding the thing out to her, beaming, flashing Carol the face she loves: a slight, excited parting of his lips, eyes bright, and eyebrows raised.

The first time she saw him was when she was an intern with the Bruce County Social Services Office. When he arrived for his appointment, he walked up to her desk and his face lit right up, like that of a child swung into the air. He was polite with her, seemed happy just to sit in the waiting room. She snuck a peek at his file: *Lance Goffritz. New Hire. Standard exam. Born locally. Raised in foster care. Incessant discussion of other people's lives*, the doctor had written. On his way out, Lan grinned at her again and she couldn't help smiling back.

It is awful, Carol thinks as she sweeps the deck of Cobble Palace, that the things you love in someone can sneak up behind you and give you a jolt — even stab you in the back.

True, he invited her to the beach, but when she saw him beaming that face at the MajikWand, her forehead became pink with heat. And there was secrecy, too, with this metal detector. An afternoon drive to Barrie — over eighty kilometres — to pick up a special battery. Eighty kilometres had never gone unannounced. Eighty kilometres was panic.

Thank God Joan is coming. Carol has never known her friend to have a misguided reaction. When the two friends were lab partners in university, they were required to study brains. Real brains, in small cork-lined pans. Basic Human Neurology was compulsory for all students wanting to study psychiatry, as the girls did. Carol knew that she would have a brain slid in front of her when she registered for the class, but when faced with the reality of it she became queasy, like she was very drunk or very naked. She glanced at the pasty mound of tissue, it was heavy and ugly and seemed unnatural. She kept staring at it, eyes slit, leaning away from the desk. The brain didn't flinch. And Joan laughed at it. She *laughed*.

‡

On the outlying streets of Cobble Beach, where the road numbers break ten, there is a change in atmosphere. The yards are longer and the temperature feels higher. The houses at this end of town are solitary, unwaiting. On some lawns there are empty cars or huddles of stoves and doorless refrigerators on yellowed grass. Anchored into the ground, most of these dwellings once sheltered farmers and families but are now greying, crooked, and rotten. Lan and Carol used to speak about acquiring one of the less dilapidated structures and turning it into a bed and breakfast. After all, the area is not totally devoid of life. Some of the houses are still habitable and Lan waves through his window at one of the locals who is using the fresh day to shake a rug out on her veranda. Every year there is a day when forgotten spring opens like a box God found in his attic. Today is that day, and Lan feels released.

He turns the minivan onto a long gravel driveway leading to a quiet structure with eye-like windows poking out from its roof. The front stairs are gone and the door floats in the wall five feet from the ground, surreal and lost. With a clip-board and toolbox, he steps from the Astro van into a sea of long grass. The old, undersized farmhouse offers Lan scant acknowledgement of his presence: a windy wheezing and the clack-clack-clack of a lopsided pinwheel atop a post. Lan wades to the front wall, raises an enormous wrench above his head and knocks twice on the door, then leans forward to listen, as though this will improve the chances of someone answering. At each residence, Lan has the same thought as he knocks and listens. A few years back he was driving south on the 21 towards Southampton, when his CB radio coughed out his name. A friend at the Ontario Provincial Police had received a call from Carol saying that she was caught in their upstairs workshop. A female bear had pushed down the screen door and was poking through the kitchen. He squealed a U-turn and sped back through the night to their wooden square of a home. He remembers pounding heavily on his own door and listening. He heard no bear and no wife. When he finally turned the knob and entered, he did so gently, on tiptoe and with sweaty palms, feeling the weight of the possibilities balled in his chest. But at the top of the stairs, Carol was just sitting in a chair pulled up to his train set. She had placed tea lights in small saucers around the tiny homes and streets of the model town, making it glow orange as if at a sunset. On plates at opposite ends of the town were wide, steaming piles of corncobs, collard greens and chicken legs cooked in cinnamon and sugar. "Well, sit down then," his wife said through thin lips, "I'm not very well going to eat by myself."

At the house on Bruce Row there is no response to his knock and, smiling to himself, he walks around to the back door. With the wrench around the knob and a few hard strikes with the underside of his fist, the door cracks open. Lan steps into the musty kitchen, where old cupboards are gaping open, filled with dust. A mildewed breakfast table. Stedman's flyers. The floorboards are gritty with dirt and broken glass. He crunches through to the dining room, throwing open the doors of a corner cabinet. Inside, there is a rusted pasta mill and red-lettered bags of Redpath sugar, thatched with black lines and tears where insects have invaded. It had been a bad time for bugs because of the constant dampness. The heavy rain was last May, so the residents must have abandoned the house before then. The ceiling is bloated and there are brown stains streaming down the walls above the wainscotting. May, thinks Lan. Definitely after March, since there are screens in the windows.

Lan pulls a pen from behind an ear and wedges the clipboard above his hipbone. He is required only to list the items of "significant value," but Lan likes to list everything. Each piece of furniture, each poster, knick-knack, and bottle of expired penicillin may be important, may need to be researched later. What if there was a murder? What then? He scribbles for five minutes in the dining room cataloguing the rest of the house.

With every assessment, Lan is struck both by how predictable yet somehow unique each residence is in its discarded lives, its abandoned permutations of fate. The MajikWand could change a life, he thinks as he carefully climbs stairs that are lousy with rot, and it was just left for the taking in a shack near Oliphant. These souvenirs of life, they are Bruce County's heirlooms. Lan was raised in the local foster home and he feels like a product of his region, the prince of this rural kingdom. To him it makes sense these orphaned treasures are bequeathed to his care.

As far as his assignments go, the Bruce Row house is relatively barren. In one room he finds a huge novelty salt-shaker, a thesaurus bloated with dampness, and a dusty edition of Trivial Pursuit. The master bedroom has Polaroids taped to the wall, the images stolen by the humidity, and a pewter ring on the ground, nearly invisible against the floorboards. Small decorative hearts circle the outside. When he opens the linen closet, Lan finds dry leaves and mud pasted into a nest among shards of smashed Christmas tree bulbs. He flicks on a miniature flashlight and shines it over the shelf. In the nest are five baby squirrels, long dead, rotted into hard raisins.

‡

"His *what*?" Joan says, reaching over the table to flick some salt grains from the cloth. It has been spring in Toronto for nearly three weeks, a muted, humid city spring. The ladies are sitting at Café Peter Pan, in a window overlooking Queen Street West. Carol, facing east, focuses on the corridors of sky between the thin buildings of downtown.

"I don't know how to describe it without sounding dirty. It's a long stick with a disc at the end. A MajikWand — that's how it's labelled. He yanked it from a house in Oliphant." Carol outlines its shape with dry fingers.

"Like a metal detector?"

"Exactly."

Joan giggles, slowly shakes her head.

"You promised you wouldn't laugh."

"I'm sorry. Please go on."

"Well, he's consumed with it, Joan. Completely consumed. He's been down at the beach for the past three days straight. He's found almost five dollars in change."

"How do you feel about this wand of his?"

143

"Are you being dirty?"

"Totally. It's unavoidable here, I'm afraid," says Joan.

"Well, try not to be. I hate the thing. But what can I say? What could he be looking for out there? I watched him out in the yard that first day and thought to myself, 'Is this where I wanted to end up? Holding onto the curtains for dear life?'"

"What do *you* think he's looking for? Did you ask?"

Carol sighs. She loves Joan's insights, but it always takes so long to extract them.

"He says treasure. I say loose change and dead batteries. I don't *know*. I just know that I thoroughly disapprove."

"Well then, so do I."

"Oh, don't give me that." Carol takes a bite of focaccia. "You're a wand lover from way back." During their university years, Carol often went to the campus disco to stand among the boys watching Joan dance and smoke cigarettes. At one in the morning, Joan and some random guy would always walk Carol back to her dormitory. Carol did not understand how her friend could go home with strangers, although she always listened faithfully to the story afterward. Carol's imagination was much wilder than her libido. The image that scared her the most was a boy — the face wasn't important — on a streetcar heading home, his head against the window, sniffing his fingers and grinning like the Grinch who stole Christmas.

"Well, I can't deny that." Joan darts her eyes around the restaurant and whispers: "I had to let another one go last night."

"Another one?"

"A lawyer. Really tall, great apartment. But I had to dump him." Carol raises her eyebrows in response. "Well, he wouldn't stop calling me — even at the hospital. He had me paged. Twice."

"What do you do to these poor men?"

"I don't know. They just happen to me, the way tornadoes always find trailer parks."

"What are we going to do with our man problems?"

"Let's get drunk."

"No way, Jose." Carol's picture of Joan drunk comes from the reception after Carol's and Lan's wedding, when a drunken Joan stumbled on her matron-of-honour dress, leaned against the podium, raised her glass and said: "Lance Goffritz, you're one helluva sonnova bitch."

"Why not? What do you have to do today? Clean some cottages? Brood?"

"You have to work later. I thought we were going shopping for your new living room set."

"Tonight is all paperwork. No brains. And tipsy is the only way to pick out a good ottoman." Joan grabs a passing waiter and asks for a litre of the house red. She winks at Carol, but gets no response. "We're not done with Lan's rod, are we?"

"Stop being crude. You know I'm sensitive about all *that*."

"Still no joy there?" Joan's eyes dart to her lap.

"Can't you take me seriously for just one second?"

"Not really, no. The metal detector is an easy problem to

solve. Would it kill you to go to the beach with him? So what if he didn't ask you right away?" Joan is looking at her directly, unmoving. "Carol, you always have to find something wrong with Lan, but it's still the same old problem. You're jealous when he gives more attention to his things than he gives to you. It's a cycle. You remember last year with the gay couple and the snake?"

"That cottage was not for them. He should have *asked* me first."

"See? You can be petty sometimes. I tell you this every time you have a crisis, but you keep searching for new trauma. You should have given up being an analyst when you gave up being an analyst. Leave that to me." Joan leans forward in her chair and takes a decisive bite of her sandwich. Carol is silent. Her career as a therapist ended when she married Lan and moved to Cobble Beach permanently. But her feelings of inferiority to Joan began much earlier — on the day Carol switched her university major from psychiatry to psychology, seventeen years ago. Since then she has continuously tried to prove that she still has worthwhile observations of the world.

"Are you sure you aren't talking about yourself here?" Carol asks, herself leaning forward, as though conspiring. "You're jealous. You could never find satisfaction in your relationships."

"True enough, but stop projecting. Don't betray your B.A. How does this wand business make you feel? Not as a wife, but as a human being with wants and desires?" The wine arrives and Joan pours half of it into two glasses.

"I didn't get married for *that*. I know what you're suggesting." Carol is blushing. "But not everything is about *that*. This is about some stupid toy. He's pushing me aside for this thing. You should just see him smile at it, it's revolting. He's so bizarre."

"But you love bizarre. You love to figure things out."

"Don't be daft. It's a silly little trinket — if he insists on worshipping it, then I deserve to be angry. And don't tell me I bring all this on myself." Carol leans back and noisily gulps some wine. "And I feel a little bloated, to tell you the truth. You know, as a human being."

‡

In 1968, Sarah Calmwaters's name was inescapable in Bruce County. The three-month-old Ojibwa girl had disappeared from Cobble Falls Provincial Park and there was a massive effort by county authorities to find her. Posters, public service announcements, newspaper articles. Years passed without a trace. Her name became a local colloquialism: "My damn keys gone calmwaters on me," people used to say. By the time Lan opened the bottom drawer of an abandoned dresser in Inverness, most people in the area had forgotten all about the girl. But here was proof, before Lan's eyes: the warped head, like an egg upturned, bones like balsa wood pencils against the dark mahogany drawer-bottom. Each part of the skeleton was so small that the joints and sockets and ribs appeared to have been carved under a microscope. Lan stared. He instantly knew what the tiny, fragile pile once was. For an hour he remained immobile, then he returned to the minivan to report the discovery via radio to the provincial police.

It was Carol's idea for Lan to discuss the drawer incident with Joan. He had stopped asking Carol for sex, stopped responding when she asked about having children. As his wife and a qualified psychologist, Carol had initially believed that she could help him through this experience. But when she asked her questions, Lan just stared into her face and pulled his lips together, as if attempting to smile. One night, seven months after Lan found the bones, she called him to the phone, thrust the receiver at him, and then rushed out of the house, slamming the door behind her. She went to the beach alone and found a bench on which she could writhe for an hour, worrying.

Lan and Joan spoke every Thursday. Every Friday, Carol called her friend in Toronto to ask if she was making progress. Sensing that Carol's snooping was holding Lan back, Joan told her that the treatment was over. It wasn't — every time Carol flew off the handle, he secretly called Joan. It was part of the cycle. And so, after dropping Carol off at the train station, Joan returns home and unearths a thick blue folder labelled "Lan" from a peach-tinted file cabinet. She begins to flip through the contents: pages from notepads, photocopies from textbooks and a couple of *Bruce Country Reader* newspaper clippings Carol had sent during the Calmwaters incident. She reads over the last entry, from Carol's preceding explosion of hostility: "July 23, 2000. Talkative, positive. C. exploded, cannot take joke. Hot hot snake sex. Found 100-yr-old playing cards."

She pulls a pen from her ear and writes the date on a blank sheet of paper. When Lan picks up the phone he whispers, "She gone?"

"Yes, she's on her way home."

"She okay?"

"I think you'd better tell me about this MajikWand."

"Found it down Oliphant way, on a farm. City people. Foreclosed after a year. The metal's fine after I wiped it down. Very light aluminium. Easy on the wrist."

"With puffy green earphones?"

"She tell you that?" He chuckles. "They're puffy, yeah. Stuffed. Muffles the rest of the noise. I don't care if she thinks I look silly."

"I don't think that's the issue." Joan blows air into the phone. "Have you found anything special with this thing yet? Any treasure?"

"Coins. A kid's watch, too."

"Rusted?"

"Beyond repair. The inscription is dated twelve years ago. And now it's lost, I have it." Joan is scribbling. "It's not important stuff. It's just *in*teresting."

"Twelve years is a long time. The kid is probably all grown up now," Joan says. He is silent. It is the kind of silence Joan has grown to understand; it is now that she can break into that core of irrationality Lan has smothered in his practicality. She imagines Lan taking off his hat with the mesh backing and running a palm up his neck and head.

"Probably."

"Did Carol like the watch?" Joan drums her fingers on her pad, making the sound of a small horse galloping.

"She wouldn't even look at it. Junk, she said."

"Why do you think she reacted like that? It's not *her* watch, is it?"

"No, ma'am." She now pictures Lan standing with the phone, looking out the kitchen window into impenetrable rural darkness. The night still belongs to winter out there. His breath makes a circle of fog on the glass. "The inscription said Missy, not Carol."

"Did it make you upset to find this?"

"A little." Lan is speaking quickly now. "There was no story. It was just a watch. Usually Carol fills in the story for me. But she refused this time. It's not like with the cottages. She came up with a name for all of them."

"Tell me about them."

"Take Honey Moongrove. The trees all around it have thick, shiny leaves that catch the moonlight. Carol says they were planted, see. Planted by a woman named Honey, way way back, on Honey's honeymoon."

"Hence the name."

"Hence indeed. Carol likes to rent it to newlyweds only. And we find them, too, usually," Lan says. "But with the wand, no story."

"She has a fantastic imagination, but she can be quite brusque. How long have you and Carol got under your belt now?"

"Fifteen years." Fifteen years and Carol is still able to mount her thoughts like a horse and gallop away from him. Lan imagines his wife's face, that stern, symmetrical composition of colourless features — she hides there, behind that placid surface. He has to search her eyes for flickers of thought or emotion. "She has issues, but she's a good wife."

"She doesn't have issues, Lan." Joan sighs. "She has subscriptions."

Lan laughs, but then excuses himself. "What am I going to do with her?"

"Do you remember last time? What did you do make her come around?"

"I brought her one of my little treasures," Lan says. "But I already tried that this time. Didn't work."

"Try it again," Joan says. "But make the thing special for her. I talked to her, it will work."

"You're the boss." Lan checks the kitchen clock. "Listen, I gotta make it all the way to Owen Sound to get Carol. You let us know if you ever find the need for old Honey Moongrove. I'll clear some space on the calendar."

"Don't count on it, but thanks."

"Bye, then. You're one hell of a son of a bitch."

After Joan hangs up, she imagines Lan and Carol climbing into the Astro van and hurtling towards their ramshackle home. They are not talking. Carol is staring out at the vague nighttime shapes on the landscape. Lan is desperate to know what she is thinking. Joan closes her folder, shaking her head playfully as though shaking off thoughts of the couple. She looks at her empty living room with a self-admonishing rumble of disapproval, glad that her new furniture will arrive the next day. The condominium Joan purchased in Yorkville has bleached-wood floors and wide-slat Venetian blinds, operated with a dowel. The sunken room is airy, with white curtains, a peach couch set and black-fur throw pillows she bought to match her cats (a little secret she had told only Carol). The cats themselves — Pax and Thor — are bored creatures that love Joan in the reliant way hostages love their captors. She named them after her two favourite co-workers, Paxil and Thorazine. She imagines the bright loveseat and couch, metal chairs, and oval coffee table piled against the dismal grey of the back alley, waiting for the dustman or garbage vultures. These items have long been vessels of her life and hospitality, and the image of their abandonment unnerves her. She decides to call the Salvation Army instead. "You may be ugly," she says, hugging one of the pillows to her chest, "but someone will love you."

‡

At sundown the following evening, Huron is a lake of gold. Carol sits on a bench far from the waterline, wearing a tasselled shawl and cradling a copy of *Mysteries of Our Times*. She is sipping tepid coffee out of a plastic Thermos lid — coffee brought on Lan's insistence. They have been making a day of it.

"A day of *what?*" Carol said earlier in the vestibule.

"A day of treasure," Lan insisted. "We'll search together." He was fitting a new battery into the wand.

"I don't know why I'm doing this. This toy is a profoundly individual activity," she said as she put her boots on. But she does know why. Joan insisted.

The flat beach spans out before them and Lan is walking slowly on the compact sand, weaving between the metal garbage barrels. There is calmness to the whole scene; even Lake Huron expanding behind him offers no comment. The sun has dipped below the horizon and the sky is beginning to bruise. Lan waves at her periodically — a wide, friendly, full-armed gesture — the wand at his hip. When he hears a noise on the headset, he bends down ear-first, as if the buried object is actually calling him, as if he could maybe hear it better this way. Soon he becomes just a small fleck of familiarity.

"Car, come on down! Bring the spade." Lan's arms are both in the air.

Carol tosses the remainder of her coffee into the sand and tightens the lid onto the Thermos. As she walks towards Lan, she sees the boldness of the excitement on his face. "Here," she says, holding the little shovel in front of her body, the shawl flapping flaglike under her arm.

"Listen," he says and fits the earphones onto her head. She is immediately cut off from every sound and sees Lan mouthing at her, moving the disc over a small area of sand. A squeal grows in the earphones, like an animal in pain.

"What is it?" She does not realize that she's yelling. Lan laughs and bends down, marking the place in the sand with his finger. He hands the wand to Carol and begins digging. Carol slips the earphones off her head. "Well? What is it?"

"How should I know? I just found it," he says into the sand. Carol cannot help herself from peering over her husband's shoulder. "See, I told you this would be fun." They hear scraping and a small glint of metal appears under the spade. Carol is kneeling now beside him and there is warmth from the closeness of their bodies. She reaches in and clears grains of sand off the object, wedging her fingers around its edges. She pulls it free and holds it up to him in the dying light. It is an old, thick pewter ring. On its outside, there are small depressions clogged with sand, each in the shape of a heart. "It's for you," Lan says, teeth showing.

"Look at you. You're like a child," Carol says and turns back to the ring. She cannot look at that expression of joy for too long or else she will scream or collapse or laugh. Instead, she rolls the object between the pads of her fingers.

"Well, well," she says. "You know why this wand is magic, don't you?"

"No, ma'am," says Lan. "No, ma'am, I haven't the foggiest."

limb from limb

My mother was telling the story: "They were children, the two of them. Impossible to separate, always playing together in the Mortons' basement or at the park down past the Tim Hortons. The Morton boy was younger — that *Paley* Morton. He must've been four because Joey here was nearly six. Anyway, one day I am having a service at noon and it's quarter to and what do I have? A son on my veranda dressed in a huge bridal gown."

"Big enough for five brides," I interjected and accepted a bowl of carrots from my brother, Anthony. "That Mrs. Morton is whole lot of wife."

"You're not kidding. So, anyway, I say, 'Get the heck out of that thing before you put me out of business' — because anyone could see this, my boy on the front porch in a wedding dress."

"Not the best advertisement for a funeral home," Dad said.

"Not in the slightest. But he says he won't take it off. He says, 'All the plans have been made.' So I asked him, 'What plans are those?' 'The wedding plans,' he tells me, 'I'm marrying Paley Morton!'"

Everyone around the table gave Mother a little chuckle. The food was properly distributed now and we paused before eating to hear the end of the story, as other families would for a prayer. My father and my younger brother, John, beamed encouragingly, even though they'd heard this story countless times. Anthony stared into his penne.

"I argue with him for a good ten minutes, but he's as stubborn as I am, that one. So I have to bring out the big guns. I say, 'Fine, you marry anyone you like, but get off the porch with that getup or else you'll put me right out of business.' And he says, 'But, Mom, where will all the dead people go?'"

We all recognized this as the punchline and gave Mother the laughter she'd earned.

Of course, it crossed my mind to tell them right then. The circumstances were appropriate, all things considered, to reveal that I was gay — but it seemed too ceremonial a moment for a family like mine; after dealing with funerals all day, we preferred subtle rituals: stories, dinners, long conversations in the kitchen. I observed such small facts about us now that I was a visitor, not an everyday participant. We were sitting around hot, deep bowls of vegetables and a steaming oblong platter of pasta. This was my first meal since I had arrived in my hometown — Fiona, Ontario — from Montreal that afternoon, and despite Mother's enthusiastic mood, I felt like a guest: half spectator, half exhibit.

"I never tire of telling that one," Mother said, shaking her head for emphasis.

"Don't I know it," I said.

"Well, you can't blame me, Joey, I was hurt," said Mother from the head of the table. "I always thought you'd get married in my wedding dress."

‡

"I know why you're here," Anthony said. We had volunteered to go to the store on Maple Street for Mother to buy ice cream for the pie. We were both wearing T-shirts rolled at the sleeves and the evening sun shone down on us over the west-end rooftops. He walked at a wickedly fast pace, smoking an Export Gold with little tugs from his lips. "You're going to tell them."

"What gave me away?"

"You don't just come back for no reason at all. Why the hell else would you come home in August? It's like a Tennessee Williams play around here." This was true; when I moved away from Fiona after high school, I was overjoyed that I would not have to live through another August in Southern Ontario. Trapped between all those lakes, the

159

region sweated its way through long, humid Junes and Julys. But August was the stickiest. Even on our walk, at seven in the evening, the heat seemed not to linger, but to swarm our bodies, crawl under our clothes. Fiona residents reacted to this kind of summer just as they reacted to the chill-you-to-the-bone winters: with disbelief, as though they had stumbled upon the extreme seasons by accident, as though there had never been such weather.

"Maybe you're right," I said, pulling up my shirt to dab my forehead. "What difference does it make to you, really?"

"I just want to be prepared for the fallout."

"Isn't our family prepared for anything?"

"Not quite anything. Crying masses are fine. Dead bodies, no problem." He squinted his left eye, contorting his mouth. "Gay children are not our speciality."

"You haven't said anything to her?"

"Good God, no." Damn. The only reason I had told Anthony at all was on the off-chance that he would pass the information on to Mother. "I'm not letting you off the hook. You know, I don't think she'll be mad, necessarily."

"I wonder if she'll react at all."

"You never know. Just tell her."

"You just love a drama," I said. "You're just like Dad." We were at the store now and I smoked the rest of the cigarette while Anthony went in for the ice cream. The doors on Maple Street were propped open for the possibility of a breeze and air conditioners moaned, dripping their sweat onto the pavement. Most of the shops had been given makeovers since I left. Whimsical items sat in the windows while new signs, designed to look old fashioned, smiled down from pediments. Off of Maple Street, Victorian and Edwardian homes sat on avenues named Victoria and Edward. Like the houses around it, Chéhab and Sons Funeral Home was pristine and full of understated nobility, only paces from Maple Street down Elizabeth Avenue. Its exterior was hugged by a wide veranda where mourners could smoke if the weather permitted. My parents and two brothers still resided there, occupying the two floors above the visitation suites and expansive basement.

And I was the violator of all this backwater charm. There were gay people in Fiona, but none that had revealed what they were to my family — and if they had, I certainly had not been informed. As far as I knew, gay Fionans still lurked near the site of the public washrooms at the edge of Exhibition Park, or sat in parked cars near playgrounds, with candy in their pockets. But the town alone did not make me apprehensive. Secrets were something my family shared, and I was not playing by the rules. We were undertakers, and this gave us a type of we're-all-in-this-together ethic, like a war squadron or the Donner party. When I was five and Anthony was seven, our mother walked us down the front lawn and pointed at the brass letters above the sloped eaves. This, she said, made our house different from all the other ones in town. "Because our house has a secret." She then led us through a heavy wooden door off the basement lounge into a steely grey room with slanted floors and chrome everywhere warping my likeness. The room had a cold bite and reeked of latex and formaldehyde. "There is a border between death and life," she said, "and we patrol it." This struck me even then as a rehearsed speech, but a good speech. The same sentences were to crop up throughout our childhood. "We are as essential to the town as the grocery store or the GM plant or the school. Don't ask anyone to admit it, no sir, but we make it easier for people to let go."

Let go — two invaluable little words. We had all used them, picked them up from my grandfather's generation of our funeral family. They were the product of much refine-ment; the best way to say everything to a grieving parent, son, wife, husband, sister. They allowed the listener to understand something about death so quickly: leave it all behind now, this life is over, you are alive, you are free.

"It's true, I love drama," Anthony said breezing out of the store with a carton of ice cream in a brown plastic bag. "And there is no shortage of it when you come to town. You swoop in and get treated like you've been at war. You're not here for the day-to-day action."

We started walking. "OK, then, if you know them so well, what route should I take?"

Anthony gave a few sniggers out of his nose. "Don't try to implicate me in all this. I'm just a straight, innocent bystander. When you're around, we are all on a heightened state of alert."

It was my turn to snort. We climbed the side stairwell of the Home and pushed through onto the second floor, the sudden, relieving cold of the air conditioning enveloping us. Mother was still sitting with Dad at the table, drinking coffee, a sugar pie — my favourite — staring up at them.

"So, did you boys enjoy dinner?" Mother said.

"Of course," I said. "Dad has outdone himself. A home-cooked meal goes a long, long way for me these days. I'm stuffed."

"Me too," said Anthony, "I just *love* fatted calf."

‡

The discovery — not the one I had planned — happened the following evening. Mother asked me to come along for the service of Sammy Fricker, a man of seventy-eight who had been found earlier in the week face down on the counter of his shoe repair store. The only people at Sacred Heart Cemetery were the shoemaker's friends, gathered in a small cluster around the coffin. The heat bore down on us in our tight collars and ties and black dresses. Beads of sweat chased one another down my ribcage. As everyone watched the solemn motion of the box being lowered on elastic straps into the grave, Belinda Fricker, mad with gurgling, collapsed in grief onto the soft grass of the graveyard. "God, what a show

that woman is," Mother whispered to me as we stood dutifully outside the circle of mourners, a distance so respectable
and silent I considered slouching over to Mother and whispering, "I'm gay," knowing her reaction would be tempered by
the situation.

As Sammy's wife tried to stand, she wobbled slightly and
fell into the hole with the coffin. A number of arms shot
down to help the widow and the sound of shocked muttering
broke the silence of the graveyard. Mother and I guided
people aside with light touches to make our way through the
crowd (it is strange how light a distraught person becomes,
how they can be moved with a brush of fingers, like tapping
a balloon). Belinda was looking up with a bloody, puffed-up
lip and eyelids raw with crying. The casket seal had failed and
there was Sammy hanging out of his box, face flat with death,
arms frozen at his sides like a tin soldier. Under his right leg,
poking out like a weed, was a crinkly bag tied at the top with
wire and a tag that said BIOHAZARD.

‡

The local press had a field day. A police investigation turned
up dozens of amputated body parts, all sealed in BIOHAZARD
bags — all in the plots of Fionans buried by my mother. A
picture on the front of the *Fiona Spectator* made Sacred Heart
graveyard look like a minefield, huge piles of dirt and sod,
hastily dug up, framed by oaks. The constables on the scene

had severe expressions, hoping that a cat somewhere needed to be coaxed out of a tree. They were Fiona policemen, so unused to awfulness. Even I, a funeral director's son, was better prepared for this particular brand of horror. "Mistress of Death Buries Limbs with Townsfolk" said the *London Free Press*. But it was the *Toronto Sun*, suffering through a slow news day, that really went for the jugular. There was a huge picture of my mother, looking sweaty and smug, with a caption that read "Frankenstein's Dream Date." Two days into the scandal, I had to stop reading the news. It depressed me that every article waited until the last paragraph to mention why Mother — and Granddad before her — had hid limbs in the first place. These were the fingers and arms and feet of people that followed the Catholic or Jewish rules of respect for the body. No incineration, just burial. Just respect. Just dignity.

But my family's concept of dignity may have been slightly different from the one that predominated in Fiona. What kept funeral services solemn was based on what the mourners didn't know, on hiding messes behind heavy doors. No one wants to be aware of what happens to their loved ones after they die: the slicing and bloodletting, the injection of latex into the veins, plastic clips in the eye sockets, and facial bulges made of putty. And even though I was part of the family and I knew that presentablity was all tricks, I chose to ignore that awareness when I was in Montreal. I needed my own secrets; not everything was a dinner-table story.

"Morning," I said, dragging myself into the kitchen in my boxer shorts, a few days after the limbs had been discovered. Anthony and John were already seated at the large oak oval table, looking like something the tide barfed up, staring past their coffee mugs, dumb and puffy-eyed. Dad felt this way, too, but his manner of showing emotion was overcompensation.

"Hey, sport," he said, stirring sugar into a huge pitcher. "Lemonade?"

"Dad's chipper this morning," Anthony stated, barely moving his lips.

"Well, he does love a crisis." My eyes were searching the room for coffee. "But tangy beverages?"

"Just doing what I can."

"By making lemonade?" I said.

"It's for the reporters," John said. Of course it was. My father worked as an administrator at the local labour union, mainly dealing with the GM autoworkers, but he knew all the reporters in town from support rallies and press calls. I opened the door for Dad as he approached with the sweaty pitcher and a long sleeve of plastic beer cups under his arm.

"Anything juicy on the answering machine?" Anthony asked.

"Same as last night," I said. The answering machine at the Home had been jammed since the day of the Fricker funeral. "Disgraceful!" said one tinny but emphatic voice. "Far be it from me to judge," said another, "but what were you thinking?"

Most of the messages were just isolated moments of shock: the vibrating cries of old widows, long silences, shudders of disgust. Granddad called, too; his deep, reassuring voice telling Mother that there was no doubt about it, the two of them were in this together. Mother's liaison at St. Joseph's Health Centre, the Catholic hospital, had also left a message of support. Their morgue had been supplying our business with the defunct limbs of patients for nearly three generations.

I pinned the messages on the corkboard, poured myself some coffee, and joined my brothers at the table. Squeaks and pipe-rumbling hinted at motion upstairs in the master bedroom. My brothers and I were conspicuously quiet in anticipation of Mother's entrance; emotion hung thickly around us, around the enormous oak pantrydoors and over the floor tiles. It was not embarrassment or disgrace, really. It was the overwhelming worry of what-comes-next, of this-is-the-end-of-life-as-we-know-it. When she finally appeared, drifting into the kitchen and heading directly for the coffee maker, my mother seemed unruffled: fully dressed and made-up. She stood tall and straight, programmed with elegance. She had recently lost a bit of weight, I noticed then, and had taken to wearing longer skirts and fitted blouses that were plain, white or grey, and light on her shoulders. She had always done small things in defiance of her occupation, but strangely all the parts of her fit together in a balanced chord.

"Hello, boys," she said, reaching between John and me for the milk jug. I was feeling queasy; the coffee was beginning its insidious lap against the lining of my empty stomach. Anthony pushed out his lips and squinted in exaggerated confusion. I responded by opening my eyes as wide as possible, lifting my eyebrows, sending my ears and hairline back. John just shifted his pupils between us, agreeing with both expressions, confirming that this was uncharted territory; where we expected a damaged woman, there was just our unflappable mother.

"Has this family forgotten how to talk?" Mother asked, wiping coffee from her fingers with a tea towel. "I'll call hell and see if they're expecting flurries."

"Great suit," I said. "Is it new?"

"Yes, Joey. Thanks for noticing," Mother said. "After all, it is unfair for mourners to have to face an ugly funeral director." This was her typical argument to justify the purchase of a new brooch or skirt or, in today's instance, a flat, dark-brown suit with sharp lapels and graceful tapering at the waist. "Did you make those phone calls, Johnny?"

"Yeah," John said, "cancelled everything."

"Had they all heard?"

"Pretty much. I had to explain it to Mrs. O'Grady."

"Bless," Mother said. "She's quite the hermit. I'll give Mister O'Grady a once over before the service."

The heavy silence took over the room again and I watched Mother for an indication of what we should do, but she was just wiping lipstick from the rim of her mug with her thumb. Then I heard the door open from the parking lot and the mad scamper of my father climbing the stairs towards the kitchen — one of the journalists bellowing after him. I didn't hear the question, but my father, from the landing, was perfectly audible: "You know me, Frank. In the name of God, you *know me*."

‡

There was another home that was central to my family's life as well as the lives of many other Fionans. St. Joseph's Home for Chronic Care was attached to the main hospital, located on the eastern fringe of town, surrounded by semi-detached homes and lots still awaiting development. It was a sprawling institution with inoffensive teal walls and linoleum-tiled floors. I made a pilgrimage to St. Joe's on every visit to see my grandfather, the previous director of Chéhab and Sons. In light of the circumstances, my mother had insisted that I make my way to see him, more as a spy than grandson.

I found him in the gurgling aquarium room, sitting alone on a loveseat surrounded by towering windows and cloudy fish tanks. It was the only room at St. Joe's that was not air-conditioned and the oppressive sunshine bore down on everything.

"How can you sit here in this heat?" I asked.

"I got shouted out of the TV room. Bloody fools. The lot of them," Granddad said. His oak cane leaned between his legs. "Surprised these fish ain't boiling in their tanks." He shifted uncomfortably. My grandfather possessed a large nobility, full of camaraderie and concern. I remember how, when I was young, Granddad wandered the wide corridors of the Home, checking on small details, twisting together the ends of his massive white beard. During services or visitations, he would sit in the leathery basement lounge with his pipe and quietly talk with the mourners, offering them rye and scotch in clinking tumblers. Now he sat here, adding a touch of dignity to this horrid place, shifting next to his IV drip, still lightly squeezing an unlit pipe between his knuckle and thumb. "You're good to come," he continued. "It is nice to know that I haven't been buried out here all alone."

"Well, of course I came, Granddad," I said, sounding too earnest. "Especially in light of everything."

"Newspaper men have been down on the hospital lawn since daybreak. It must be a zoo at the Home."

"Yeah. This morning was a little crazy." I told him about the reporter chasing Dad up the staircase.

"Scavengers," he said and then leaned forward a little on his cane. "Tell me, my good boy, is your mother falling apart?"

"Not really." His little brown eyes were fixed on me. They poked out of his white facial hair like incidental features, the eyes of a snowman. Before this visit, it had seemed to me that Granddad had always been old, having plateaued in age around sixty — but now he actually seemed to have pushed past the stage of jolly old man. His skin was purple under the insanity of his beard, with his nose like a knot in the trunk of a tree. "Have you not spoken to her?"

"Oh, oh yes," he said deeply, "for nearly an hour, but I worry about her and her endless supply of bravery. I want to make sure that it is not keeping her from letting go." A mental flag went up, hearing that phrase in reference to my mother. I had always heard those words in certain way — let go, abandon. Now is the time to begin your forgetting. At that moment, though, the words sounded different. They were like a puncture; they sounded like this: release.

‡

Walking out of St. Joe's, I felt a shuffling in my gut, an anxiety so demanding yet unspecific that it frightened me. When the reporters saw me approaching Dad's car, they moved in my direction. I ignored them and turned left out of the car park, towards the newer, aluminium-sided subdivision.

"Joey Callino, as I live and breathe," Paley said, shirtless in the heat, his arms up behind his head as he put his hair into a ponytail. Paley stepped out of the door jamb and extended an arm into the foyer of his parents' house. "If you can call this living, that is." The Mortons were a different kind of Catholic from my family — they were Tacky Catholic, Weird Catholic, Ceramic-Pope-Head Catholic. Light bulbs in their house were more or less exposed, casting an unfriendly glare on pictures of the Last Supper and the candles decorated with pictures of Christ. The low ceiling and peeling linoleum of the entrance gave the house a shabby feel, and there were cobwebs trapped between the points of stucco on the ceiling.

Paley's mother was sitting in front of the TV, its sound over-powered by the loud rumble of a fan that she had pointed toward her full-fleshed form. For Fiona, this was a newer home, a split-level with two-and-a-half floors, including the basement. When reading about such houses in the Real Estate section in the *Fiona Spectator*, Mother always put such emphasis on the "and a half" part, the local real estate equivalent to the mark of Cain.

"Hi, Mrs. Morton," I called out to her.

"Is that Joey Callino? Welcome home." She didn't approach but waved wildly from the TV room. "Is it hot enough for you, Joey? These dog days of summer, what can you do?"

"Remain immobile?" I said.

"Good idea, I think I might just do that, Joey." And then, almost as an afterthought, "I'm so sorry to hear about your mother. You tell her I said so, too."

"I will, Mrs. Morton."

"I saw her on TV just now. A brave front she's putting up for us Catholics. I'm pulling for her. She's making a statement in less than an hour, bless her heart. God is smiling on your family. It may not seem like it right now, but don't you worry."

I was rushing to follow Paley, who had already descended the stairs to his basement lair. "I won't, Mrs. Morton," I called over my shoulder.

The heat lifted slightly as I made my way down the steps and I smelled that familiar mix of bong water and incense. Paley had eliminated a lot of furniture since we were teenagers and now the room looked bare: a futon couch, a crooked buffet cabinet and a wide, low glass coffee table with a substantial chunk chipped off one corner. On the floor he had put an orange rug that bunched up against a pile of bricks that supported a series of planks for shelves. There was a television on mute flickering in the corner, sitting on bare concrete.

"Ah, memories," I said and Paley smiled. In high school, I would often fall asleep on that couch, stoned, dreaming — and so my mother hated him. He had remained in Fiona after we graduated together from Our Lady of Victory Collegiate, making a little money by delivering pot on his bike. Every time he ran into my mother on the street he would tell her he was running errands for his mom. "Doesn't fool me for a New York minute," my mother always said. "Twit that he is."

She was right, of course, but Paley and his dirty basement would always have a pointed significance for me. It was here, under the sounds of Mrs. Morton moving about upstairs, that I kissed my first boy and gave my first blow jobs. Back then, I told myself and Paley that I was "just practicing" for future encounters with girls. Of course, he turned out straight, but for me, fucking Paley had been a religious experience — and, like most religious experiences, it was an event that could only resonate with certain people. For me it had been revolutionary, for him it had been like flipping his parents the bird.

He lit a bong made from a plastic pop bottle and then passed it to me.

"How's la belle province?"

"A riot," I said after holding in the smoke for a while. "There's a referendum in a couple of months." He was breaking up little leafy knobs of pot into small piles on the glass tabletop, looking at them with little, assessing eyes. "People are screaming in the streets. All the money's gone. I'm out of work. Everyone's out of work." The pot started on my brain immediately. "It's one big, fat sunshiney day." I held the mutilated bottle out to him.

"It's all yours. Welcome home."

"Thanks," I said. "Looks like God is smiling on me after all."

"What a load of crap," he said. "This Quebec separation thing, I mean. If I were there, I'd show them a thing or two about cutting a country in half." Fiona was composed almost entirely of immigrants, and the whole population sparkled with political opinion. The town possessed an unflinching devotion to Canada and a worshipful trust of the Liberal Party.

"Things are complicated. What can you do?"

"You getting laid?" He was under the table now, looking up at his little divisions through the glass. I looked at his head moving in and out of the smudges, out-of-focus pieces of a mosaic. Paley had lost a good deal of the fat in his face, and now looked slightly like Michael Jackson, as though he was made of sugar and had been left out in the rain.

"Periodically," I said.

"You still a big homo?"

"Periodically."

He laughed and let his head drop to the carpet. "You mean you are when you're gone, but not back in Fiona? Oh man, you take the boy out of Buttfuck, Ontario, et cetera, et cetera."

I was sure that there was a joke in there somewhere, but couldn't find it. Getting stoned with Paley again, I shifted to my old intoxicated enthusiasms. He was grinning into the table bottom, but I searched his face and body for other signs of his thoughts — signals of attraction. I didn't even want him; he was unshowered and reeked of patchouli. His green eyes were dry, like opal spheres, and he looked as though he were about to unravel.

"I do a lot of business out at Scandals or Secrets, whatever it's called," Paley said.

"Whatever what's called?"

"That gay bar on the Maple Street Extension."

"There's a gay bar here now?"

"Sure. Great money and everyone gives me the eye. Good for the ego." He rose onto his elbows, torso grilled with ribs, about forty-five degrees from the floor. His eyes were lower than mine so he had to push them against the upside of their sockets, like a dog watching someone eat. "Being gay must be good for your ego."

"Spoken like a true straight man," I said. We continued looking at each other — but I was the only one concentrating. He was expressionless, not focussing on anything; single strands of blonde hair put little spikes of shadow on his cheeks. I kept my eyes on him. If I stopped focussing, the pot would send my mind off like a reel of fishing line caught under a boat's hull.

"I'm glad you came by," Paley said finally. "I'm glad I'm still part of your life — you being Mr. University and everything." But I was instantly distracted, having caught sight of Mother on the TV screen.

"Turn around," I said.

There she was, smiling in her brown suit, her name splashed across the bottom of the screen, the Home standing regally behind her. A small crowd of locals had gathered. As her son, I was one of the only people obliged to see her as multi-faceted. I never had to forget her whimsical side, but the rest of the Fionans did, at some point, put aside their version of her shopping at the market or running through town with a yellow Walkman hooked to her belt and viewed her simply as the person who is paid to organize their grief. This latter version was what they were interested in now, gawking and looking concerned for the cameras.

Paley hit the mute button on the remote: "— privacy is a key factor in this business and our challenge is to conform to everyone's different concept of it," Mother was saying. She looked clean, honest, and infallible, her face neutral except for eyebrows that crinkled periodically in genuine concern. "I have done nothing wrong but try to respect the wishes of everyone involved. This is the privacy of my business, privacy in the public service. There is a border between death and life, and we patrol it. We are as essential to Fiona as the grocery store or the GM plant or the school. It is hard to admit, but we make it easier for people to let go." I closed my eyes, colours turning themselves on and off like fireflies against my eyelids. I could barely hear her any more, as the reporters' questions bounced off the Teflon of her resolve; my ears simply shut down, and I felt a familiar twist in my stomach. As I stood, the sensation rose and my arms felt scalded and powerless. I stepped over Paley's legs and through the doorless alcove to the bathroom, my gut lurching ahead of me as my knees collided with the floor, flanking the toilet. Lunch returned in a short gush, the bile filling my mouth with bitterness and shards of chicken. I slid further down to the floor, conforming to it like hot wax, my head sweaty and heavy as lead, eyes dry and cast out toward the field of little cold octagon tiles spread out before me.

‡

When I woke up the following afternoon, I wasn't sure I'd be able to heave myself from the bed. The previous night had passed into dawn before I was able to find sleep. I had stayed with Paley until nearly four, driving him on his deliveries, enjoying the small cove of air conditioning provided by the car. There had been a disturbing comfort and discomfort in me when I'd returned to the Home — the confinement of my old single bed and the chemical freshness of the sheets reminded me of the hours of sleeplessness during my adolescence: quiet nights of masturbation punctuated by the restful creaks and rumbles of the house. My mind had even raced with the same fantasies: Paley, hockey change rooms, Shannon Hoon, Alister from *You Can't Do That on Television*.

I stood in the hall, listening for signs of life. Nothing. I was scheduled to leave the following morning, and so I set off to find someone to have a final Fiona lunch with me. When there was no one at the Home, the smells of the place seemed stronger. The bathroom offered wafts of fresh-cut paper products and Wizard Orange Grove air freshner. John's room reeked of hockey equipment; Anthony's, incense. And my folks' suite — two-rooms that housed all of Dad's papers as well as their bed — consistently smelled of down feathers and Chanel No. 5. I wandered in there quietly, curious of whatever changes may have happened in my absence. Everything seemed the same, all well-tucked and fluffy; any potential messes were hidden away in drawers or closets. The shelf of books on the wall opposite the bed was so densely packed that as a child I believed that there was no drywall behind it at all, that the edges of the pages pushed up against the ceiling and kept the roof in place. I searched the volumes as I had so many times before, recognising certain titles from their enticing spines and fonts and colours: *The Alchemist, Shogun, Lives of Girls and Women. The Joy of Sex*, sitting high above the rest, was the dirty title Anthony and I used to giggle at. About midrange on the wall was a slim volume I had never dared to take down — *Stuck in the Middle: The*

Tribulations and Joy of a Middle Child, as though there were multiple tribulations and only one joy. The spine was black and cracked with white veins; the title was printed vertically in red letters, as if they were about to bleed like the words on a horror movie poster.

I reached out with my middle finger and slid the book from its place, but did not want to open it, did not want to delve into whatever secrets my parents may have snatched from what looked like an owner's manual, but for a human being, for me. I flipped to the index and looked up "gay," "homosexual," and "sexuality." None were there. In the text itself there were graphs and charts and big type, with sections highlighted. By whom, I did not know.

I shut the book. The house hummed from the air conditioners, somehow underlining the absence of life. The Home was mysterious, though. It seemed to swallow noises. I put the volume back and descended the staircase that grandly delivers people from the upstairs to the main foyer. I walked gracefully, with my palm flat on the wide railing, alone beside the pearl-coloured wallpaper that seemed to lean off the walls under its opulent weight. The suites were empty, too; just the claw-footed furniture and framed map watched me pass. It was a map of Fiona as it was in 1917, fractured, like a mirror hit swiftly with a hammer, into slices by merging and criss-crossing train tracks. I stared at it then as I did through my whole upbringing, the parts I knew well rose to the surface, all the venues of my former life. The Home, just south of the hammer's impact point; Exhibition Park occupying its hill; the old grist mill-turned-history museum. The Mortons' house was barely in the town lines, in an area empty in 1917 — just a blank, yellowing patch on the eastern side of the Canadian Pacific artery.

I heard shuffling in the basement and realized that someone must be home after all. I thumped quickly down the stairs and found my father in the cold room off the lounge. He was kneeling next to a white plastic bag drawn tightly at the top with wire. Its tag read: BIOHAZARD.

"Look at this," Dad said. His eyes were meaty from crying. "Wouldn't they know any better?" The bag was densely white, so opaque that only the knobby curve of concealed fingers hinted at its contents. I had been around the stiffness and decay of cadavers my whole life — but in this instance, something seemed to be tickling my gut. These appendages, rendered so completely useless by nature and science, were possibly the agents of the Home's undoing. I recognised the bags now — having seen them here and there when I still lived in the house. I had always thought they were some part of the funeral landscape, some part of that clinical dignity humanity imposes on death. And now they sickened me, struck me as pathetic, but still unbearably human, worthy of some respect, however forced.

"What are we going to do with it?" I asked.

"Well, we are *not* going to tell your mother."

"Can you bring it back?"

"It's not a sweater, Joey. It's not like going to The Bay after Christmas." My father did not look at me, he merely stared at the bag, teeth pushed together into the dramatic underbite he makes when he is worried or concentrating. Protector of my mother was one of Dad's more charming roles. It evoked the same passion he had for his job: banging out picket signs in a worker's backyard; driving people to their first day on a new job; screaming out chants on a bullhorn in the dead of winter, his fingers white and cracked and tight around its shaped handle. But this situation was new for him and for me. Sitting before us was something unthinkable, but not because it was chilling or macabre the way the papers had reported it, but something treasonous that turned around and scooped all the town's trust out of my family.

"Wouldn't the hospital have known better?" he repeated.

As it happened, it had known better. Our liaison at St. Joe's had called already and offered an alternative arrangement. Mother thanked her, but insisted that the limbs continue being sent to the Home. The bagged arm had already been received by my mother that morning and Dad merely discovered it after the fact. This struck me as odd, but I dismissed that thought immediately. Of course Mother had accepted the limb; she had commitments to both sides of the issue and was trained to deny her reflexes of repulsion. She made death palatable by severing herself from passion; by making bodies seem lifelike without making them seem alive, much like a drag queen wants to be like a woman but still have that hint of manliness to make sure the reality of things isn't lost. Too much rouge, too dramatic a visage: morticians, too, have to understand how to use hyperbole.

‡

Dinner was the main event of the day, the unit by which family togetherness was measured. When I was home from Montreal, my activities were calculated in dinners. "Home five days and only at the table for three dinners," my father would say in the dining room, a jovial photo of my grandfather looking down on us like a participant. I was running my flattened palms against the fabric tubes of the placemat, pushing little vertical tunnels to its tasselled edges. It went without saying that I was to turn up at this meal, my final one before heading back to Montreal. But when I arrived, there were only two place settings. My brothers and father were nowhere to be found.

"They're at mass," Mother explained, entering with the plates. "They'll say goodbye tomorrow morning."

"Won't they get hounded the whole time?" I said. "By reporters, I mean? They really should be here."

"Remember, I'm no chef," she said, ignoring me.

"I'm sure it will be brilliant." She made a fuss of pulling her chair out from the head of the table and then leaned forward on her elbows, into the steam rising from the pasta. Her eyes held that well-practised gaze, half sympathy, half I-mean-business. I felt like a toy that had been wound too far. This was my natural reaction to that look — the feeling of being anxious and quiet, at the principal's office or after spending all my allowance on candy. In my mind, I pictured tomorrow's escape on the train. There is a moment just east of Toronto where the train breaks away from civilization, from the fences and gullies and telephone poles. Suddenly there is nothing but a field of grass on one side and an expanse of water — Lake Ontario — on the other. This is the moment when I can finally relax in my seat. My shoulders come down and I let the train outrun my guilt.

"I'm glad we could do this, just you and I." I snapped back to the dining room, to my mother. She was smiling in that small way that leaves her face uncreased. "I love when you're home. Everything feels so much better."

"I know, me too."

"Don't lie to me. These moments are torture for you."

"Mother," I said, separating the syllables. In family moments, one-word arguments often pass for logic — but I was too nervous and continued. "Just because I'm happy out there doesn't mean I'm not happy here."

"Oh, I know. I wanted to get out, too, at your age."

"It's hard to believe that you were ever my age."

She rolled her eyes. "Believe it or not, I was a bit younger. I was twenty-two. Your grandfather wouldn't hear of it. We were sitting out on the front porch, well I was standing, he was sitting. And I said, 'Father, this is bullshit. I think I'm going to move away after school.'"

"I know you didn't swear to Granddad."

"ok, so I said, 'Father, after school I think I'm going to move away.' He looked up from his book and, without flinching, said, 'Don't be bloody foolish.' That was that. I went inside and sat in my room and cried for an hour. I didn't know the duct trick then." The duct trick was a technique we all used when we were working in the service of the Home to keep us from crying. You simply imagine that your tear ducts are sucking back their discharge; that you were, in fact, not crying at all. We were there to provide dignity, my mother always said, not tears.

"Rough," I said, gazing at a triangular shadow in the corner.

"Not really, Joey," she said leaning back away from the food. "He wasn't forbidding me from going. He just knew that I would be better off here." She sighed loudly and dropped her shoulders into dull corners of cotton. "And that is why I let you go — you are better off in Montreal."

"I appreciate it."

"So tell me, then — am I a bad mother?"

"What?" I nearly shouted, but I didn't know why; alarming statements were typical of her, it was a brilliant way to get information from us. "Christ, why would you say something like that?"

"Because here I have a son who can't even tell me he's gay," she said and whisked her hand in front of her, as though indicating the food. I stared into her mess of fettuccine, flecks of pesto looking like stubble against a white basin. I stiffened, although inside I was a jiggling mass. I recognized it as a calculated moment, but still felt obliterated and dug-up, exposed for the first time since my arrival on Friday. It was out in the open now. There was no point in denying it.

"How could I have told you with all these limbs going on?"

"That's no excuse, Joey. All this is nothing, it's a misunder-standing. All this is just a fly in the ointment."

"Hardly," I said. "It's all anyone can talk about."

"*Anyone* has a reason to be ruffled. *Anyone* doesn't under-stand what we do here. And they shouldn't have to. But I am your mother. I deserve to understand you."

"How could I possibly have said it?"

"You just say it. You open your mouth and out it comes." She was miming this, pulling invisible words from her mouth with her hand.

"I'm sorry," I said, and I was. Her face was like that of a plaster bust: permanent, unflinching, full of subversive under-standing. A sick grief had already settled below my chest, and it was getting restless, getting ready to jump grandly out of my mouth in the form of an explanation: I needed the perfect moment, needed to know that everything would be OK.

"I'm just so disap*point*ed," she said.

"I'm sorry for being a disappointment."

"Not disappointed in *you*," she said. And it seemed as though she wanted to continue, so we sat suspended in ten-sion, staring at one another, like we were playing a game of anticipation. All I could see was the barely perceptible tremor

185

of her bottom lip. Mother lowered her head and the tips of her hair fell forward into the pasta. She was trying to hide that she was crying. But I knew. I could hear her sniffling and swallowing; she looked foolish, like she should be a patron here, collapsed over a casket, bawling. I was surprised to find the pain below my chest dissolve into a warm, beautiful satisfaction.

Holding back my smile, I pulled her hair from her dinner and tucked it behind her ear.

alphabet city

I have this picture in my head: a tortured writer, alone at his messy desk, overflowing ashtray and typewriter set before him. He types a sentence, a word, a letter, and then whips the paper from the machine with a flourish, crumples it up and tosses the wad towards an overflowing wastebasket, around which are other crumpled papers: failed ideas lying scatter-shot across his floor.

This is not me. I cannot even get that far. First of all, I do not smoke and I do not have a typewriter. I work longhand on a sheaf of blank papers I plucked from the HP DeskJet 812C before hurling it at the wall. I stare at their emptiness or look up for inspiration through my only window: narrow, dusty, dotted with fingerprints. Today the skies are white with clouds — blank sheets framed by the brown mouldings that

I painted recently in a flurry of writerly procrastination. The walls, too. The baseboards. Everything. Yellow on the walls, with brown trim. Memories of Mahogany, the paint chip said, chosen because it matches my sheets. I should dream up such colour names for a living: Mocha Crème Nostalgia, Strawberry Alarmclock, Grey Matter, Tar Sands Midnight. The whitest shade would be the colour of the blank page: Writer's Nightmare or Hues of Block. I know this shade all too well, I'm afraid. Sometimes, for a distraction, I'll bang the papers against the desktop or gobble pieces cut from an oversized Lindt chocolate bar. I eat them right off the knife's edge. *Dangerous*, my mother always said when I did this as a child with cheese or fruit. *You'll slice your tongue to ribbons.*

But she is far away now and I can do what I like. She FedExed me the chocolate, so this hazardous way of consuming it feels somewhat rebellious. *Happy Hallowe'en, Marky!* said the card in her fat-lettered, drawn-out scrawl. I think she intended the chocolate as a peace offering. *Pick a place and we will pay to send you there*, she said, two months ago. The law has made my father rich and she could afford to banish me from Montreal. I was a risk to her pristine reputation as the hostess of posh gatherings, the maker of little narrow sandwiches, the brunch date of the mayor's wife. Of course, I picked New York: the most expensive place, but also the best place to be a writer. Her thinly veiled motive was to sever my ties to the greatest love of my life: Shank. Good, poor, old, loyal Shank who has been front and centre in my life for so long: my lover, my touchstone, my inexplicable passion, my Margaret Trudeau. He is tall as a spire and red-headed, overcome with freckles and moles. They find their way everywhere, from his forehead to the lumpy finish of his tailbone. Shank and I have been together for a year, and have been friends since high school, but have not seen each other in two months. Not since September, when he helped me move down to Manhattan and we spent a week in full romantic glory, hustling about from sight to sight. As an architect's assistant, he was amazed by the cluster of buildings in Midtown. We went on a strange walking tour, where he trailed behind me and I pointed to random skyscrapers and he told me when they were built, who designed them, and how they fit into architectural history.

But this is my story, not Shank's or my mother's or Midtown's.

Writers are always talking about their process. Here's mine: I cannot start working until one o'clock in the afternoon, after the sun has stopped beating down on my writing chair, after it has hurtled over Avenue D and begun its slow descent towards the Hudson. I used to work in the morning — I call it working, not writing — but after painting the walls, I had rearranged all the furniture in an attempt to make the writing desk my focus. I thought that perhaps my surroundings could influence my lax discipline. The desk is a wide, beautiful thing that I bought when I moved to Alphabet City. Built of heavy, solid cherry, it seems more permanent than anything else, certainly more permanent than the apartment itself. The plaster of the kitchen ceiling was flaking away in September, on moving day, falling slowly onto the floor and my shoulders. *I thought I moved away from the snow*, I joked with Shank, who may have laughed in some perfunctory way behind the box he was carrying.

All I heard him say was, *This is so typical. Who would move in here but you?*

I told you. This is Alphabet City. Perfect for a writer. This district had struck me as metaphorically inspired as I sat with a map of Manhattan folded out onto Shank's kitchen table in Montreal. Alphabet City. A grid of letters, ready to be populated with characters. This was where a writer should live. Practical, reasonable Shank did not buy my esoteric arguments. No destiny for him. No fate. He just looked up at the dodgy ceiling.

That's water damage, he said. *You're in for a messy time.* I, however, was too taken with the excitement of moving to worry about damage of any variety. I only started caring two weeks ago when the plaster started falling off in chunks. Bibi, the landlord, has begun repairing the building's pipes, but has yet to reach my little yellow studio. I have been making the best of it, turning the dysfunctional ceiling into a little game: part of the trial by fire that New York is supposed to be for a wee Canadian boy like me. Every time a piece falls, I allow myself to call Shank. I have even stopped saying hello. I just say, *You were right*. Shank likes hearing this, I am sure. Everybody does. *The righter you are, the more phone calls you get.*

Once upon a time, one o'clock was my self-assigned quo-tidian writing time. I could finally get down to work; with the sun having passed by overhead, its light could not invade my working space, could not boil the sweat right out of me. In the shade, I filled my chair and lifted my hands above the keyboard. I sat in the breeze from the opened window and searched for a sense of serenity, that place that allowed me to plunk down my fingers and mercilessly violate the computer screen with a deluge of words.

Or I used to.

Two months ago, I did. Yes, that week Shank was here I pumped it out at an admirable clip. The next-door neighbour even agreed with me. Shank and I often encountered Mrs. Sanchez in the stairwell. She nodded at us — quick little bobs of her long, long Giacometti head. *Sounds like you're getting lots done in there.*

Scads, I replied.

Then the repairs came. Two weeks ago, a schedule appeared next to the mailboxes in the lobby telling each tenant when their water would be turned off so that the plumbers could do their job. My floor got nailed with the midday shift. Four hours of daily waterlessness, from eleven to three. Showering at my usual time became an impossibility, so I sat filthy in my chair. One never realizes the significance of grooming until one is deprived of it. With my days off-kilter I was forgetting to shower. Something happened, however, that made me give up the bathing ritual at the same time as I became aware of my failure to practise it. I fell in love with neglect. My fingers have become particularly dirty, on their inside flanks. My hair lies flat against my skull, greasy and lank, and my scalp is riddled with lumpy white growths. With my uncut nails, I can reach under the hair and scratch them away, which can be painful. Not showering seems like a writerly thing to do, after all; part of my grand sacrifice for art. Sleep deprivation, too. When I read about the insomnia of Delmore Schwartz and Rudyard Kipling, I see how sleeplessness plays into their lives as artists. At night I keep the window open for a steady stream of noise and pinch myself as soon as I begin to drift. Today I woke up at noon. I have yet to master insomnia.

With the plumbing being repaired, it was time to get Procrustean. I started chopping up time into more easily digestible chunks, still not working in the nauseating morning sun, though — I'd be a horror of sweat. I tried working in the evenings, but the music and people on the streets ended that after one night. Since it is too hot an autumn to keep the single window closed, I could hear the ghetto-blasters — Latin music, happy stuff, would make me giddy — and the Spanish hollers from old ladies in their windows: laughing and chatting to passersby. Friends, family. I was jealous, in a strange way I had not expected. They made me feel estranged, from my country, from my boyfriend. *If you need something to get you going, why not write about your neighbours?* Shank said.

I informed him of his inability to understand me and my mind, a writer's mind. Secretly, however, I did try writing stories about them. I stared through my window and began a few faltering stories. I quickly concluded that I was right and Shank was wrong. My neighbours were ruthless, excitable people that I simply did not understand. The music, the language, the cackles. It all seemed otherworldly.

But my day. I never came to a solution, which is how I've ended up working unwashed in the late afternoons. The sun is not even an issue today, but I've still decided to stick to my schedule. The overcast sky is not inspiring, and I find myself suddenly curious about the time. I walk to the kitchen to check the clock on the stove, whose little digital message is angled just annoyingly enough towards the sink to be invisible from my desk. I walk back to my station to investigate the rectangle of sky. A single wisp of grey cloud, a cobweb's hint of change, is passing just north of the sash. A thumb-print, scrolling. I climb up onto the desk, knees rubbing hard against the desktop. This is my new habit — not just checking the clock, but craning my head out the window in a kneeling position to see what the skies have planned for me. I could not do this a month ago, as there was a computer monitor in the way. In a flurry of frustration, I rid my desk of that vulgar cube once and for all. The computer seemed revoltingly inorganic: I began to think of the words as pixels, not existent things, and began to rattle other thoughts around the roulette wheel of my mind — What is language? Is it expression or the failure of expression? — the sort of clap-trap writers invent to keep themselves from writing. I'll leave it up to Chomsky. To Jespersen. And that cursor! Flashing and flashing and flashing into perpetuity like the insistent cries of a bottled Sybil, begging not for me to write, but to kill it, to close the program, to play solitaire. To give up. I pushed the whole machine to the floor with one forceful heave of disappointment. I am a longhand man now, like Pepys and Austen.

There is nothing today but that single grey patch sliding its way across the whiteness, Hudsonbound, disappearing over the weathered pediment hung from the edge of my building's roof. This is the sort of thing for which Shank would berate me. I can practically hear his voice: *Get down off there, for the sweet love of God.* He insists that I am always finding excuses to avoid my work. We met in high school, waiting outside the vice-principal's office, having both been caught skipping class. That day he admired me for my excuses, praised the way I ejected myself from authority unscathed. Now, he would never let me get away with such weaseling. That is Shank, though. Mr. Balance. He always knows exactly when to cheer me on, when to treat me like a kid. He should be a parent, but he's an architect's draughtsman, working his way up, determined to put his mark on the world. We both are. We used to sit for hours together at his kitchen table, ignoring one another, each obsessively involved with our own passions.

Sometimes one would look up at the other to express some moment of joy. I would read him some page I had just put down, or he would flash me a picture of a marvel-worthy building. Love. Love because we were explaining things to ourselves, allowing our relationship to fuel our individual passions. And we remain experts in individual passions, even from such a distance. We have an open relationship, Shank and I. The decision came very easily — the two of us both attempting to broach the topic at the same time at a bar in the Old Port. We were sitting outside, I recall, a half-finished pitcher of Rickard's Red between us, Shank's fingers on my knee, playing with a stringy rip in my jeans. *I am going far, far away*, I said. *And it destroys me to think of you becoming lonely and celibate.* Shank started laughing. As it turns out, we had the same plan for the discussion: Get the other one drunk and throw it out there, then cower from the explosion.

Oh my God, Shank said. *I was going to ask you the exact same thing.*

Synchronicity. Just further evidence of how right we are for one another. We even have the same name. Mark. This is how we came to call each other by our last names: Ward for me, Shank for him, cut down from Cruickshank.

I do miss him and his forcefulness. He is good for me. He unclogs my brain. Perhaps another piece of the ceiling has fallen and I can call him. I contort myself into a sitting position on the desk, holding my legs as though chilly. Above the kitchen, I can see into the meat of the building through the wounded ceiling, all brown-rimmed from soaking and drying. There is no further destruction; just the insulation puffed out around the pipes, expanded out of its skin from the leak, auburn with age. The water has started its path of destruction down my newly painted wall, too, violating the yellow.

If I climb onto the counter, I can get my head almost entirely into the hole and see the damage, smell the dead mice. Rodenticide, too, Bibi has promised. He has not come though and I complain: to his answering machine, to Shank, to the lady next door who always replies with such kindly allegiance during our stairwell discussions. At night, however, I lie still in that empty bed, trying to keep myself awake, and she will start banging wildly on the wall. *Will you shut up in there?* At first, I thought she was crazy. I had shut up. The only noise I could hear was the traffic and the mice scurrying overhead. Lately, though, I've taken to responding. *I am shut up, Mrs. Sanchez*, I said last night. *Did they have the melons you wanted at the deli?* After a long, long pause I gave up on getting a response. But then it came: *No. The bastards.*

Another piece of ceiling hurtles stoveward, as though I willed it to fall with my stare. I watch it sail through the air and land between the elements with a little crash and puffs of plaster dust. My reaction is automatic now, Pavlovian, like I have no say whatsoever in the motion of my hand. I grab the cordless phone from its hook. *You're calling again?* Shank asks. *Let me guess, you're writing.*

Working, I say. *How's tricks?*

Hang on, he says. There is a lot of shuffling. He must have his hand over the phone, I feel like I have my ear up to a seashell. OK. *Back.*

I believe last time we were talking about you coming down to visit.

I can't, Ward, he says. *We've been through this.*

But I miss you. There is a long pause. I cannot hear his breathing, but I can hear him thinking. I know him that well. Poor Shank cannot believe that he misses me as much as he does and it sometimes hijacks his voice. *What was that noise?*

What noise? I didn't hear anything, he says.

It was really loud.

It was nothing.

Come to New York. I'll pay. You said you had news for me. Do not leave your lover languishing in anticipation. I hardly mind taking a week off my working.

I'll bet.

We can do another walking tour, I suggest. *Downtown this time.*

It was a beer bottle, he says, as though it had just occurred to him. *The noise.*

Oh. I am confused. Sometimes I simply do not understand poor Shank, sitting home alone on Hallowe'en, drinking. *What kind?*

Ward, do your writing. It's a Rickard's. I have to go.

Happy Hallowe'en.

Right.

Cheers.

Bye.

That boy is strange, but you have to love him. I feel sorry for him, actually, the way I feel sorry for poor Nick Carraway, all alone there at the end of *The Great Gatsby*: Left by his enigmatic partner, cut off by everything, adrift in some kind of disgusting ocean of the self, continually getting tossed back — beat back, if you will — against the shore that is me.

Yes, that is lonely Shank, but this is my story. This is the story of a wee Canadian boy who left everything behind so that he could write about it with a clear head, severed, as it were, from the Great White North and transplanted into the deep, fertile ground of Alphabet City. I've followed through on a Canadian artist's rite of passage — escape to somewhere else, to look back with an Osbornian eye at the place I left behind. Cohen did it. Mitchell, Richler, Young, Davies. And now me.

They — I — had to leave, at least for a while. Up north we would have ended up getting too enveloped in all that snow and weather and dire, dire provincialism to produce anything of merit. All I could see were the metaphorical trees — I could even see metaphorical insects burrowing into them — with absolutely no perspective on the forest itself. And what a forest. In the United States, that is how everyone sees Canada: one giant, sprawling, romantic wilderness populated with burly folk who pump out lumber and good beer and folk singers and little else. I'll show them. I'll write a great work. It will show my homeland as it is: a glut of characters huddled in a horizontal line along the 49th parallel, all deep and conflicted and interesting — a country of Salinger-level dysfunction and beauty and profundity.

The boys at the bar here ask all the same questions, always in the same order: *What's your name? What do you do? Where do you live?* Mark, writer, Alphabet City. *Are you writing the great American novel?* And I laugh at them. Americans are obsessed with that concept. *I am Canadian*, I say, *and there is no such thing as the great Canadian novel.* This is true, apart from being sparklingly clever. Mine is a country of stories, each embedded like diamonds in the ore of all that geography. And this story is mine. The tangled masses of my head are worthwhile; I know this, I am positive. I often flip back through my old stories and am reassured. I shined. The move to New York was not just my family's need to excommunicate me from its untarnished reputation, but an attempt to transform my talent into some mineable resource, to run all my passion through a Chekhovian regimen of work so that I can put more and more and more of my head onto the page, turn myself into the sentence factory I have to be. It takes a while to get into the right place to do it, though. Depression, it seems, is necessary. I sit at my desk and close my eyes and lie to myself: I am no good, I am without anything worthwhile to put on this page. I grip the pen and think of my anonymity, my Sartre-inspired hell, and can feel myself disappear further and further into the cavern of my skull; my fingers turn purple against the shaft of the pen. And, once I am in this Plath-like state of serene self-deprecation, I let myself go and out it splatters: adjectives gravitate towards nouns, and in the collision comes the shrapnel of periods and commas and semicolons, all finding their mark, making the story hum.

Writing is hell.

I suppose I owe something to my parents for making all this possible, whatever their motivations. Thank God for their money. My mother's most expensive habit is keeping up appearances. She does it for my father. He and my mother had a series of raging rows over the gay issue, on nights after he'd come home from *making connections with other attorneys* down at Winnie's, his favourite bar on Crescent Street. I could hear them through the laundry chute. Dad would dictate his orders to Mom in the same way he would dictate them to me or to a client: with utter conviction of his infallibility. Winnie's must serve quintessence by the keg. I can never get the whole story from Mom afterward. She likes to think of herself as the mother from a Paul Peel painting, or one of the more opulent Norman Rockwells. She pays through the nose to keep the image perfect, to keep the underbelly of her family well licked-over with paint. *Mark? Why, Mark is living in Manhattan now.* Oh, if her family only knew that I am a writer. Those brothers of hers — all five of them — would immediately draft injunctions and gag orders to keep my scribbling from ever being published. There would be money involved, too, enough to prevent the picture from being fouled. She must keep it all from them, those lawyers, those five sibling fools that circulate like a haughty Anglo aristocracy in Montreal's richest neighbourhood, perched up on the mountain, staring down at the rest of the city. What a life she must have had, that mother of mine, growing up in the shadow of those monstrous brothers. Father drinks with them, scotch in thick tumblers, pushes people around for them, leaks items to the *Gazette* and the CBC, stays on Crescent Street late on weeknights. What could she have been thinking, marrying such a man?

But wait, this is my story. Mother had her reasons, her excuses, for lunching with Mephistopheles and coming out on the wrong side of the bullshit, for paying her son to stay south of the 49th parallel, way out of view. And now what about me and my enthusiasms? My reasons? I need to keep my passions intact. My forceful need for beauty, creation, greatness.

A wind blows through the window, just strong enough to carry a few sheets of paper to the floor. I fling myself from desk's edge and bend to pick them up. I wonder if stronger wind carries a guarantee of rain. The rectangle of sky is darker now, after all, and the blanket of whiteness is now spotted with darker sections, like a paper towel lining the bottom of a basket of fries. New York has gone for weeks without rain. City officials are starting to worry. The skies have clouded over like this before and everyone gets excited, including me. But there is no payoff in precipitation. The next day the air is heavier with humidity, more unbearable. There is a reason New Yorkers live here instead of LA or Florida or Houston. Blazing sunshine beating down uninterrupted on a city becomes boring for them. They expect seasons, expect things to happen quickly, change quickly, and the weather is not exempt. It is one of Mom's favourite phone topics. Searching for something to say, she interviews me about the weather like some kind of meteorological spy. *It's threatening rain*, I told her last week, and not for the first time. But the threats are empty. We are deprived of the climactic, cathartic finish to our expectations. It is like this with so many things. Poor Shank must feel this way about me, left alone way up there. And writing, too, is like this. I sit and stare, but the page remains as dry of ink as the streets are of rain.

The papers are together now, between my palms, and I knock them against the surface of the desk, bang-bang, then lay them perfectly centred, in front of the chair. They glare at me. How long was I staring out the window? Has another piece of ceiling fallen? Somehow it seems as though I should sit back down and there would be something on these pages, penned by some mysterious hand, some opening sentence, or even a word, that could trigger my great work, puncture my subconscious and let the ideas pour out onto the page. This would be brilliant: some sort of celestial confirmation that I am on the right track, a small act of God that could forgive me my doubt, let me run wild with sentences the way I used to — not two months ago! — when Shank was here, sitting on the Murphy bed with the *Times*, and me at the desk, fingers dancing over the keys like Glenn Gould taking on Bach. Green eyes that unlock me, that is Shank, that is Mark Johann Cruickshank. With him next to me, the world becomes a Botticelli clam, pried open, beauty pouring out everywhere. One night in the Murphy bed he said: *Close your eyes and picture St-Louis Square. The fountain and the iron fence. It is two weeks ago, remember, we are lying on the grass together? You are afraid of staining your khakis. It's hot, but every now and then the breeze carries over the spray from the fountain. Everything smells slightly gross, because of the garbage behind the ice cream parlour on Laval Street. Those two Hungarian midgets are playing their harps. See it?*

Of course I see it. I see it perfectly.

This is how I want you to remember us.

ok, I said. *You are my madeleine moment.*

I went out and bought harp music on tape. I have no stereo, but I have a Walkman and I listen to the tape when I feel lonely, or after I wake up with someone else in my bed. Whoever it is always wakes us up to find me there, next to them, bright yellow Sony earphones over my head, turned away, because I can hardly let them see me crying.

Has another piece fallen? I wander over to the stove, phone in hand, and examine its enamel top. Possibly. One smaller chunk seems new, having landed close to the back-left burner.

The piece is chalky and slightly damp in my hands, triangular. I forgo one message of fate for another and dial. *Boo!* I say. *Did I scare you? It's Hallowe'en, after all.*

Yes, I know that. Let me guess, you're going as a writer.

Right. I have not showered in four days and my hair is a mess of grease. I am still wearing my boxers and that green T-shirt riddled with holes. I look as though I've been shot.

Who shot you?

I live in Alphabet City. I suppose it could have been anyone.

That's great.

What are you going as?

A sailor. He lets a lot of time go by here. *Ward, I can't really talk right now.*

But I can't work, I say. *And you always fill me with stories.*

There are stories everywhere, Shank says. *Look out your bloody window.*

Stop suggesting that. It does not help one bit, I reply. *There are buildings everywhere for you to stare at. Stories are not so obvious as that. You would not understand.* And he wouldn't. How could he?

If you're so goddamn misunderstood, he says, *then explain yourself. I know you better than anyone and I don't get you. You better do a better job of making me understand.*

You're drunk.

Maybe I am. What difference does it make to you?

We always used to get drunk together.

But we are apart and it's Hallowe'en. I have a life.

Don't change the topic.

Oh, sorry. That's your job. The sky is darker now, more uniform. The white spaces between the low, heavy clouds have closed up and the heavens look like a blackboard, coloured completely over with white chalk.

Sarcasm, I say, *is the last refuge of the fool.*

Whatever. There's someone at my door. I have to go.

Don't go.

But someone's here. I have to go let them in.

Call me back.

Goodbye, Ward. Write something.

There were happier times, when he did not feel so threatened, when his defence mechanisms were not squarely aimed at me. I try to picture St-Louis Square and the fountain and the smelly ice cream, the sun coming down. My head is on Shank's bony shoulder. He has given me his diary to sit on so that I will not mar my trousers. Poor Shank and his silly diary, with its sad sketches of buildings, each with a unique but wonky perspective. Diaries are for teenagers and girls. Then again, perhaps on some distant day he too will publish his series of journals. He may very well be the homo-Canadian Anaïs Nin. For that to happen, however, I must get down to the business of being his Henry Miller.

I will write a great thing.

I will write a great thing.

I will write a great thing.

Ah, but can I write a great thing? Can Mark Ward create a *Tropic of Cancer?* Is this how Miller did it: the pages just staring up at him: white, perfect, with their sharp little corners? His stomach shrinking, echoing the emptiness of the page? Did he have to look out the fucking window? I get back onto the desk, kneeling with a straight back this time, the front of my underwear creasing up against the window screen. The clouds are the colour of mercury; the wind seems to come from below, humid and warm. A city wind predicting rain. The street is desolate, colourless. People are moving slower now that the workday is done. A few kids are in costume. Two Latino fathers, probably mechanics or garbagemen or thieves, with thick wedges of hair on their upper lips, smile widely as they carry their little girls along Avenue D. Both children are dressed as princesses, glittery dresses all the more silvery against their dark skin. One of them is showing her father a little chocolate bar wrapped in a metallic envelope. The men are talking, laughing, the girls trying to get their attention. Hallowe'en at my house was never like this. It was a grand affair — tabletops weighted with food platters and wrapped in linen, decorative bats hanging off all the corridor candelabras, professionally carved pumpkins looking out from the dessert tables at Montreal's wealthiest revellers. In my Hallowe'en, those Avenue D fathers would be wearing aprons, mixing drinks. I would be holed up in my room eating the candy I had collected an hour earlier, before the guests started to arrive. I did not get the treats from the other Westmount homes, but from the patrons at Winnie's, where my father would deposit me onto the carpet with a pillowcase while he sat at the bar. *Just go to the tables and say 'Trick or treat,'* he advised me. *It's just as good as going to people's doors, only without the legwork.* And I would. The pillowcase would fill with pretzels and loose change — sometimes candy, from those men who had been there in previous years and knew this was the secret tradition my father and I shared, not to be revealed to Mom. I would get whole chocolate bars sometimes, from older men with loosened ties and vulgar, coughy laughs and overspaced teeth. *This here's Ward's boy*, they would say to their companions. The women typically leaned forward and kissed me. *Well, aren't you the cutest little thing.* And they were right, too. Whatever costume I was wearing had been in the making for weeks. Once I had an idea — the Little Prince, John the Baptist, Icarus — my mother would take me to the tailor, to the hairdresser, to Simpson's. I was impeccable. The year I went as a mummy, my father called me down from my room so he could show me off to every party guest, saying, *This is my son Mark. He's going as Margaret Thatcher this year.*

But that was then, and this is now, flung out of Westmount, out of Quebec, out of Canada all together, spending Hallowe'en alone in my little box. I suppose things have not changed terribly. I can still look down out my window and see everyone else trick-or-treating. Most of the kids in Alphabet

City are dressed as bums, though, or in one of those sorry excuses for a costume, a plastic apron with an outlandish superhero printed on it and a mask held on with a length of cheap elastic string. I wish I had my old costumes now. I would give them to my new neighbours or to Bibi for one of his grandchildren. When Shank and I looked at the apartment, Bibi told us the story of his life, as if trying to distract us from the building's flaws. He had emigrated from Armenia as a child, wrapped in a blanket and strapped to his mother's chest. She literally walked across Europe with a gang of what I assume were gypsies. Right through Nazi territory, right through the craziness of the war, to Portugal, where his mother had to pass herself off as a Spanish aristocrat to get on the boat to New York. He, the only surviving male from his family, now has eight kids and an army of grandchildren. He lives in Brooklyn. All that, just to come here and rent me a roach-infested hovel in the East Village. I do not even think he heard me and Shank quibble about the place, just kept laughing into his cellphone, speaking a language I could not understand, then looking up at us and saying, *Yes or no?*

Hang on, Shank snapped at him.

I like it, I told Shank. *It is the perfect place to languish in exile, like Stein or Nabokov.*

It's a dump.

That's the whole point, I said. *My mother would have a stroke if she ever saw this place.* Boxes are still stacked on the floor next to the computer, whose smashed components sit in a pile like bad art. There is a wall full of shelves that I dismantled in order to paint and have not bothered to reinstall. I have no books out in the open and do not understand all those writers who, in magazines, are photographed in their homes before a massive wall of volumes, as if to say: *Look what I've read. See how I conceal all these people's ideas in my writing?* Not for me, that. I do read, of course, quickly and comprehensively — Oscar Wildely, I would say — in my chair at my desk. When I finish a book, I hide the thing safely away in a box. When a boy comes over after a successful night at the bar, he always asks, *Did you just move in?* I say, *Maybe.* The less they know about me, the better. The true sign of unfaithfulness is to open up to someone else, and Shank deserves to have all my mental energy and output, even if he cannot have the physical me. When the great work is finally published, the dedication will read: for Shank, who let me share myself with the world.

But I must write it first.

I close the window. No more excuses. No stalling. I simply must get off the desktop and sit in that chair and attack the pages. But when I do, the frustration becomes physical; I tense every muscle available to keep it locked in my gut, but it escapes nonetheless, moves to my arms and to my fingers, which grip the pen so tightly I can feel the edges of my nails dig into my nerves. I surprise myself, even, suddenly clutching the pen like a knife and slashing it across the page in huge strokes, a scantily clad Dorian Gray going at his own likeness with a blade. And then I stop, feeling embarrassed, as if I have been caught. My heart is knocking at my ribcage, insistent and overworked, as I sit still and try to calm down. I know that another piece has yet to dislodge, but I dial Shank's number anyway, dipping into my overdraft with fate. I will not call when the next chunk falls.

There are noises in the background, music and laughing. *Hello?* I am focussed on the cold sky. The wind is carrying the mugginess into my studio now.

Are there people there?

I can't believe it's you again.

I'm sorry. Do you have people over? He sighs loudly. The sounds in the background diminish. *I'm so glad you're not alone.*

You know I have people over, you're not quite that dense, Ward. The doorbell rang while I was talking with you.

I'm not dense at all.

You have to stop this.

Stop what?

Calling.

Are you mad?

Of course I'm fucking mad.

Are you drunk? He sounds drunk, voice raised, using short, declarative, Hemingway sentences.

Of course I'm fucking drunk.

Do you want me to call you back?

No, don't, he says. *Don't ever call back.* My knee starts pumping like the needle of a sewing machine. The clouds move faster.

I beg your pardon?

You heard me.

Is that a threat? It certainly feels like one. It feels like urgency, like seeing the text end mid-way on the next page of a book: sad anticipation.

No, it's a request. This isn't left-field stuff, Ward. I've been thinking about things for a while. This is what I wanted to tell you when I came down.

I don't understand.

It's over. I can't keep doing this. Neither can you. Silence. Awful, mysterious telephone silence: no face to read, no place to look. *I hate these phone calls. Hate them. And you are not writing.*

Working.

Whatever you want to call it, you're not doing it. It's a bad, bad scene.

I don't understand. Conditions are not as bad as you make them out to be.

Well, they are, Ward. They are. When all I do is come up with excuses to stay with you, that's a bad scene. I'm turning into you. I can't save you. Excuses are a waste of time.

I don't understand. Outside, someone turns on Latin music and people clap, start dancing. They don't seem afraid of the dark clouds. My whole body feels held together by skin alone. The very idea of dancing makes me feel as though I'll fall apart. *I don't understand anything.*

the dead roommates

Luke stands in the doorway of the living room, still drowsy from sleep, wearing only a pair of shorts. He has been dreaming about driving at night, in the snow. He was not sure where he was going or coming from, but was certain that the car was gaining speed, the needle of the speedometer straining against the wrong side of its resting peg. The snowflakes, glaring white, leapt into view outside the windshield and were gone instantly. In the rear-view mirror he saw that his teeth were falling out and his gums were bleeding, black, rotting away. There was a screech and then he was in bed, light pouring in around the blinds, Billie Holiday singing "God Bless the Child" in another room.

His roommate Adrian is sitting on the couch across from him, motionless, white T-shirt camouflaged into the white couch. Outside, puffs of snow are still falling like feathers. Luke shivers. "Why are all the windows open?" he asks.

"Because I can't get the door to the roof open and this is the closest I could come to duplicating the atmosphere," Adrian replies, flicking his eyes momentarily at Luke's chest.

"Are you OK?"

"Yes. Just sad."

"Me too. Is the music helping?"

"Yes and no."

"Did you sleep?"

"Not really."

"I did. I just had the craziest dream."

Silence.

The funeral is tomorrow — a joint funeral for their other two roommates, Jason and Giovanna. This seems fast to Luke, considering the accident just happened yesterday. Not that he minds; the less time he has to spend with Adrian, the better. Luke cannot remember a single conversation with him since they moved into this apartment in September. Sure, there were little domestic exchanges, like the one yesterday when Adrian delivered the news about the deaths. They discussed schedules, booked train reservations (the funeral was being held in Toronto) — but there was rarely any depth to what they said. Even exchanging condolences seemed necessary, transactional. No, Luke thinks, we are more likely to communicate without speaking. It had not taken long after moving in for Luke to detect a touch of desire in Adrian's spooky glances. This is particularly true at moments like this, in the living room, or when they cross paths in the hall, Luke planning for the glance and purposely waiting until then to pull on a shirt or buckle his belt.

But there is something new in Adrian's stare this morning. This look, here, from the couch, it is not making Luke feel any more attractive. Now there is sadness. Those pathetic eyes and the bruise-coloured pouches that hold them — they hint at a deep grief that is foreign to Luke even while it is right here in his living room. He remains in the door frame for a moment to take in Adrian's image, and then walks back down the long, long hallway toward his room to get dressed.

‡

Adrian thinks: they're dead. Jason and Giovanna lost control of their car and were snuffed out, victims of the snowstorm, of the slippery roads, ten kilometres east of Kingston. The blizzard had, in its delicate danger, turned Adrian's life into a calamity. Of course, life has always been a calamity, but this was a push into deeper torture, without reference points or the friendly padding of sanity provided by Jason and Gio. Now there is just a sickening interior collapse, the sensation of his insides turning to liquid, gushing, flooding the parts of him that still work with chaos and grief. If only Jason had been taken, maybe then it would be bearable; Gio would be on this couch, a mourning partner, willing to slide an arm behind Adrian's neck and speak to him calmly. He does not blame Giovanna and Jason; they were too kind to have consciously abandoned him. But what a vulgar joke for fate to play on Adrian, to leave him here without consolation, to writhe and snivel with only comfortless, beautiful, half-naked Luke. Surely someone, somewhere was laughing about this.

Adrian looks up at the door frame. His roommate is gone now, making noises deeper in the apartment. The Din of Luke, this was Jason's term for how his roommate seemed to permeate the whole apartment, how everyone knew where he was because of some whistling or clattering of dishes or guitar chords. Adrian can still picture him here: his clay-coloured skin, the relief of his chest and stomach rolling down to his waist, the hairs on his thighs just starting to get thick and long before they disappear under black boxers. Then there's that cocky face of Luke's, that half-grin, those arrogant glances and inflected black eyebrows. And that self-conscious charm, fully loaded, even seconds after waking. Adrian had taken stock of these things when he first moved to Montreal five months ago. Gio, who had been friends with him since they were ten, was already attending university here and offered him one of the rooms in the sprawling apartment she shared with her classmate Jason, another Torontonian. The other available space went to an old friend of Jason's, the singer from his band — Luke.

"Just what this apartment needs," Adrian whispered to Gio as they watched Luke carry an amp from a moving van to the room at the end of the hall, "more fags."

"He's not gay," she replied. "I'll bet dollars to doughnuts."

By Christmas, she and Luke were sleeping together every night. Adrian heard her sneaking past his bedroom door. It changed the way the household worked. Adrian felt annoying and small, like a mosquito. He began interfering with Gio's and Luke's intimacy, although he did it subtly, from a distance: turning up the TV, talking on the phone in the hall so everyone could hear. He couldn't admit his jealousy, she would have laughed at him. It was better to let her think something was terribly wrong. In this apartment, the distances are natural: a living room with a bank of drafty windows that lets breezes down the whitewashed corridor, past four unmarked bedroom doors. At the very end of the hall, past Luke's room, past the bathroom, are thin, twisting stairs that lead to the laundry room and the courtyard. It is easy to avoid someone in such a place — Adrian and Gio were barely speaking to one another when she left Montreal for Toronto to celebrate Christmas with her family.

That was two weeks ago — Jason volunteered to go with her and split the price of gas. Luke, too, had gone away for Christmas (to Hawaii with his family) and Adrian spent the holidays alone in the apartment. For New Year's Eve — three days ago — he watched porn on the communal TV and went though his roommates' drawers. Gio had taken her diary with her to Toronto and Adrian only found one reference to his campaign of silence, in an email she had written to her mother: *I think Adrian hates me right now.* Good, he thought.

It was comforting to think that he was owed something, some twinge of guilt, some extra attention.

And now she's dead. The huge weight of all that silence — a silence he thought punitive — has landed squarely back on his shoulders. To make matters worse, her mother has asked Adrian to write Gio's eulogy — "You were her closest friend, dear, she would have wanted it this way" — and he does not know what to say. He has written the opening several times, but little else. He has the pad and pen here on the coffee table, but he cannot stop staring out the window at the quiet, malevolent snow.

‡

Luke pulls his guitar case to his knees, lifts the lid. The instrument has a slim plastic body with a high-gloss black finish. Its face is decorated with stickers, gifts from Giovanna. They blare out bands' names in stylized letters or offer clever sayings against orange and red backgrounds — *Life's a Bitch, Canada kicks ass!* She was most excited about a package of stickers showing figures in various sexual positions on loonie-sized neon circles. He begins peeling them off, running a thumbnail around the circumference of the first. This seems like an appropriately grief-stricken activity, he thinks. If he were to speak about Giovanna, he could use it in a eulogy. But he's not. He's been asked instead to say something about Jason, who was in the car with Giovanna when it struck an overpass support during the blizzard. Jason and Giovanna's parents thought the symmetry would be appropriate — to have the two surviving roommates speak about the two dead ones. "I didn't really know the musical side of him," Jason's father explained over the phone, "and I thought that you'd fare better. I spoke at his mother's funeral and I couldn't bear to do it again." In high school, Jason and Luke were always in some rock band or another, where Luke sang and Jason played the drums. They had some success in recent months, recording ska covers of "The Rainbow Connection," "Deeper and Deeper," and other unlikely songs.

In spite of all this, Luke feels as though he should have the choice of cadavers because he will write the better eulogy; he is a creative person — a rock star, a songwriter, a literature major — and Adrian wants to be an accountant. Besides, as a result of their fling, he has more material about Giovanna than Jason. He's written it all down because he hates his ideas going to waste. It would be a crime for it to go unheard by her loved ones. Besides, Luke's already finished his eulogy for Jason: seventeen pages, typed and stacked. On many of them, he has highlighted sentences that would make excellent lyrics. Luke lays the pages out before him on the black bedspread and sings a couple of the words. The covers are fun, but in Luke's mind they remain only novelties. Dead songs, reanimated. What he truly wants is to sing his own compositions, like this one, about Jason. Luke writes them here, alone in his room, the door open so that the sound of each attempted chord is sent down the hallway to the rest of the apartment. Collected, they make a repertoire nearly large enough for him to become a solo performer. Jason's death comes at a convenient time. It provides Luke with a reason to dissolve the band.

Is that callous? This is a time of tragedy, he thinks, whatever that means. But Luke has always seen himself as living in a bubble, keeping a necessary distance from people so he can write songs about them and not hurt them. Maybe a eulogy is different than a song. As he writes his memories of Jason, Luke feels like a fraud. Jason was so political — always out protesting, asserting some kind of wistful lefty dream that Luke never understood. And Adrian's display of sadness doesn't help — in fact, it underlines Luke's disconnectedness, makes him feel lacking, fluttering just outside the realm of emotion. He is fluttering outside death's crippling force, though, and surely that counts as survival. In a week, in a year, Luke will be the one who has moved forward; he'll be writing songs and performing and recording while Adrian will still be sitting, staring, sobbing. That cannot be what Jason and Giovanna wanted. Isn't that what everyone talks about after a death? What would the deceased want? Luke's not dead, after all. Jason would want him to go solo; Giovanna would want to see him succeed. Imagining their intentions like this, Luke's coldness is sensible — he should to do whatever it takes to be productive, hard, victorious.

‡

Adrian cannot stop thinking about the storm. It hit Montreal last night, foreshadowed by a wind blasting down the streets, taking over, searching the city for him. From the roof, Adrian watched the branches of the trees moving in the wind. The trunks creaked, back and forth, like an autistic child predicting something horrible but unable to express it. All evening, drifts built up at the curb, into driven curls, like spun sugar. Throughout the night, he got out of bed to check his window. The blizzard raged until morning, obliterating everything. Now, the snow has nearly stopped, the tail end of the storm that killed them.

Adrian looks at his pad with contempt. The corners of the sheets are peeling up in the breeze. His pen rolls onto the floor from the coffee table. How can he be expected to cobble together a tribute after such an injustice has been thrown at him? His thoughts are sluggish, trapped like a June bug in a car, bumping and slapping against the glass. He wants to smash things. But how can one lash out in these situations? Jason would have found a way — he always did. Adrian had gone to a protest with him once. They stood in front of the Sheridan Hotel, the November wind stinging their faces, holding signs condemning a meeting of the International Monetary Fund taking place inside. Jason screamed up at the windows, led chants and then started throwing snowballs made from the nasty exhaust-grey snow. They hit the hotel windows with satisfying thunks. Adrian pointed out that Jason was still achieving nothing, but his friend seemed not to hear. There must be a release for me, too, Adrian thinks; a resistance to forces larger than himself. But here is nothing, nothing but endless walls and empty corners and pages that need to be filled with sad celebration.

Mournful chords from beyond the living room arrive to compete with Billie Holliday. Adrian wishes he could be on the roof, looking down on the world, cut off from Luke and the apartment and the eulogy. The weather has conspired against him, though. The snow has fallen thick and heavy against the roof door, making it impossible to open. Luke's strumming becomes more intense. This indirect show is clearly for Adrian — there's no one else to hear it now. But even before the deaths, Adrian was sure the music was for him. Gio didn't need further seduction and Jason was too laid back to care.

And the show does not just entail music; it is a subtle current that includes everything Luke does in front of Adrian. The first time the four of them sat together in this living room, Adrian was reading a book in the armchair. Gio was on the phone. Jason and Luke were practising their songs on the couch near the window, sipping beer, arguing about the lyrics to "The Windmills of Your Mind." The back of the couch tugged on Luke's shirt, and there was a line of flesh visible above the waist of his jeans. Adrian flicked his eyes in Luke's direction. This little alluring bit of skin was so incidental and off guard and irresistible that he felt he should get an eyeful in case he should be denied it forever. Luke slouched further down the back of the couch, dragging up the hem of his T-shirt, then moved his beer bottle to the V of his crotch, holding it fistlike, with his whole hand, and Adrian knew that there was a purpose to it, knew somehow that it was directed at him. Adrian responded silently, rearranging himself to get a better view. Then, with total insouciance, Luke slid his fingers down the back of his jeans, as if he had an itch, and then left the hand there long after scratching. There were many moments like this — countless now — where tension inflated like a party balloon, where a prick of awareness would ruin everything. Even when they were performing some chore or doing schoolwork or watching TV, Adrian felt the game was on in the background, like the hum of the furnace. Adrian knew where Luke was, knew what he was up to, knew that there was an invitation to respond.

It has to stop now, Adrian thinks, the music still drifting in from Luke's room. With just the two them left, there is no more need for camouflage; it feels glaring, inappropriate, robbed of its sexiness. This is why he wants to be on the roof — it's the only place where the game is off, where the hum disappears. Adrian suspects there are other motives at play — that Luke doesn't want Adrian to concentrate on the eulogy, doesn't want Adrian's thoughts to contain anything but Luke himself. Adrian picks up the pad. He must not get distracted, he must keep writing. He reads, *There are few people in the world as unique as Giovanna. Now that she is gone from my life, I don't know what I am going to do with myself. I feel like there is*

223

a cavity now that can never be filled and, like a real cavity, it is causing so much pain, then throws his pad across the room.

‡

Luke cannot get on a roll. Every now and again, he stops playing and listens for signs of life elsewhere in the apartment. He wonders if Adrian is still in or if all this music is going unheard, swallowed up by indifferent rooms. Luke's finished his memorial to Jason and, now, as an exercise, he's decided to compose song-eulogies to all his roommates. Death has provided him with this strange moment, a time to remember Giovanna and Jason while observing Adrian's pitiful show of grief. Yet each strum sounds hollow and the words are not falling into place. They sound forced, clumsy.

Perhaps it is the absence of smoke. Luke has just quit. He adopted smokng years ago as a rock-star accessory, like black sleeveless T-shirts and studded belts. Last week, however, he'd begun feeling a tightness in his chest. Every cough reminded him of his own mortality. He left his remaining half-pack of cigarettes on Adrian's bed as a Christmas present and has not smoked since. Luke recognizes the emptiness in his fingers, mouth, throat, but takes great satisfaction in each day's delivery of frothy phlegm. His body is clearing itself out. He is using his guitar to occupy his hands and lollipops to satisfy his oral fixation. He has to; temptation is everywhere. Adrian has been smoking near him. Increasingly, it seems. Luke tries to see this as a challenge; he knows Adrian is doing it on purpose, to get noticed. Even before the accident, Luke would stumble upon Adrian sitting motionless on his bed, on the couch, on the toilet, pants all the way up, washroom door open, staring ahead with a cigarette unattended in a nearby ashtray, smoked by the room. Adrian's such a sad creature, and yet people actually care for him; they connect with him in a way beyond sex or happenstance. Both Jason and Giovanna could talk with Adrian for hours. How did he manage camaraderie with his mopey victim's regard for the world? It's baffling. People fall into two categories: those who want to serve and those who don't. Jason never wanted to serve — luckily, that never interfered with the band. Jason had bigger, impossible dreams of control. He wanted to stop poverty and exploitation, sling mud at the American consulate, set flags on fire. Adrian, on the other hand, is the definition of servile. He reminds Luke of a big dog, a husky, who waits patiently, sadly panting, until he's called over to pull a sled or fetch a stick. Adrian's attention makes Luke feel powerful and magnetic, but Luke also seeks it out for Adrian's sake — a game like theirs is just what Adrian needs to feel good about himself. Maybe Adrian needs to be offered more opportunities for this kind of happiness, Luke thinks. Maybe that's the connection.

Luke has filtered these thoughts into a song he is writing about Adrian he's calling "The Brink of Something Terrible."

He starts with a few slow plucks, each note ringing momentarily on its own before he plays them together, a full, sad minor chord.

‡

Adrian hates this song. It sounds facile, he thinks, as he picks the pad up from the floor. He hides it in his dresser before heading to the bathroom. He closes the door on Luke's music and latches it — he does it all quietly, so Luke can't hear, can't misinterpret any sound. This huge apartment used to be full of rich noise, he thinks as he peels off his white shirt — Jason hammering banners for his protests, Giovanna skipping down the hall, band practices, the modem squealing, a stir-fry sizzling in the wok. The flat is so empty now, so open to Luke. The grumble of the water heater and hiss of the shower cannot even drown out his guitar.

Adrian steps into the greyed porcelain tub and seals himself in with the plastic curtain. He makes the water hot so he can feel his blood charge faster — the pain is proof of life. The steam turns this little wet cloister into another world, a foggy-white place with safe, soapy odours and unquestioned privacy. But Luke invades even here, Adrian thinks as he steps out of the spray to lather his face and shave. Here are Luke's shampoos, conditioners, mousses, and depilatories cluttering the little wire caddy. They have relegated Adrian's gear to the tub corners. Gio's and Jason's things are gone, but hinted at: the residue of his pulpy oatmeal soap, the green circle left by her bottle of body wash. Where are these things now? In a police locker? Flung into a highway ditch, little specks in the snow ten kilometres east of Kingston? Tears cut paths through the shaving cream on Adrian's cheeks. There is more territory now, more room for Luke to expand. He can dominate the apartment, Adrian thinks, because he avoids sentiment with that slithery emotional manoeuvring that is at once repugnant and enviable. Luke has a knack for survival, a calmness that makes Adrian feel incapable of being human, of dealing with both life and death — the basic parameters of existence.

How quickly can Adrian get away from him after all this is over? Could they live there together, just the two of them? Before the accident, Adrian often fantasized about that exact scenario, about drunken nighttime slip-ups, mistaken doors, confusion of sex, of orifice. Now all this seems morbid and catastrophic. Luke's attractiveness is corrupted: that macho swagger now announces his insensitivity, his unwillingness to hand himself over to loss. Luke deserves to be dismantled, his strength unveiled to be exactly what it is — cold, selfish idiocy. Adrian smiles at the thought and puts a small cut in his chin. In the mirror, he can see a bulb of dark red blood build out of his skin. He tilts his head slightly and lets the water dilute it to scarlet, watches as it runs down his neck until it dissipates into nothingness.

‡

Luke hears his roommate in the shower. He gathers up his eulogies — the one for Jason and the one for Gio — and walks down the hallway, loudly, slamming his soles against the floorboards. In the living room, the breeze tickles his flesh into goosebumps. Adrian's pad and paper are no longer sitting on the coffee table, there is just the little nest Adrian's made for himself on the couch: balls of paper, tissues, cigarettes, mugs lined with cold tea. He leaves Jason's eulogy on the table and then walks over to Adrian's bedroom — it's the closest one, just next to the front door. It's locked. Luke is familiar enough with this door; he slides his student card between the door and the frame, pushing aside the barrel of the lock, and the door opens easily.

The single bed is unmade and there is an open copy of *Fifth Business* on the nightstand, next to a scattering of crumpled tissues. There is a potted tree dying on the floor near the window — a Christmas gift from Jason. The dresser in the corner is grey. Luke slides open the top drawer. Tongues of paint have leaked down the sides of its interior walls, pointing down to a regimen of videotapes, with thick, wild fonts announcing each film's title: *Swim Meat 3, Boys 'n' Toys, Guess Who's Cumming to Dinner?* Little pieces of pink, purple, fleshy body parts are muddled into a mosaic of skin so random and crazy that, for a moment, it seems animated. Luke opens a second drawer. Adrian's pad is there, sitting on top of unpaired white socks, jumbled together like oversized larvae.

On the top page, there are a few blocks of scribbled text, separated by spaces. They are all beginnings of eulogies. He reads one and then another. *Gio thought our apartment was pretty bleak, so one day she showed up with some paperboard and an X-Acto knife. I helped her cut out all these smiley face stencils and then we painted them on the wall in our living room. They are still there. Every six inches there is one with a different colour. When someone like that dies in a car crash, how am I supposed to care about anything else?*

This sucks, Luke says aloud. He leaves Adrian a crisp piece of loose-leaf paper. It says: *Knowing Giovanna was like reading a novel. Every page you turn there is a twist and nothing is what it seems to be in the beginning. And my opinion of her changed, like reactions to a novel's plot: love, intrigue, excitement, challenge. She made me think, but at the same time could turn around and let loose and be fun. Often I had no idea if she was conscious of it. I trusted her in this way, confident that when I was done with her I could leave and take her effect with me everywhere. I can hear myself quoting Giovanna years from now, then smiling.*

‡

Adrian comes out of the shower to find Luke's door closed. Today is the first official day of the winter semester and he hopes Luke has not gone to class — their train leaves for Toronto in three hours and Adrian is already imagining having to tromp around the snowy campus in search of his roommate. But where else could he be? Luke only closes his bedroom door when he leaves the apartment.

Adrian enters the living room to retrieve his cigarettes and notices that Luke has left his eulogy on the coffee table with a note: *Read this fucker and tell me what I should cut (if anything). L.*

Adrian counts the cigarettes. Luke has not taken one.

Smoking, he begins to read. *Death. The spectre of this looming figure influences us all in a different ways. For some, it is an impetus to complete as many goals as possible. For others, death is something to be avoided; it forces such people to seek safety. Jason lived his life in the former grouping. Jason was there with me as I started a band, played in front of even the smallest crowds. Now, of course, I play for a much bigger audience, but those initial days were hard for me and Jason was my right hand man. From today on, when I am up there on stage in front of all those people, I'm going to dedicate every show to him.* Luke probably believes this writing is brilliant, Adrian thinks. It isn't. He flips through the rest of the text and his eyes pick out the overwhelming number of 'I's on the page. He can't believe Luke's going to read this at a funeral, but starts to cry anyway, just thinking about Jason: he was so determined, so unflappable. He wrote letters to Members of Parliament, he put his dreadlocks in pigtails, and sang kids' songs at summer camps. He gave people trees as gifts. There is none of this in Luke's eulogy, no actual sense of Jason. Soon the tears keep Adrian from seeing the words. He is cold, wearing only jeans. His hair is wet and the windows are still open. The happy faces painted on the wainscotting are just blurs of colour. When he thinks about the eulogies and the people they represent, Adrian ends up letting go of reality and tumbling back into sad panic. He needs to devote himself to more practical matters, he decides, like hygiene and packing.

Adrian goes to the kitchen to fetch a drink. The walls here have never been painted. The white primer is all he sees: uneven, full of the brush strokes. On the stove is a bag of multicoloured lollipops spewing out onto the black enamel surface. Adrian is angry with Luke for quitting smoking. Luke should bow to the sadness. Break down, light up. Luke is flaunting the ease with which he has replaced one habit with another, more alluring one. The lollipops ride Luke's tongue from one edge of his mouth to the other, with enticing motion of the traveling stick between his lips.

The fridge is all cold, white light. The water pitcher sits empty on the shelf — Luke has forgotten to fill it. But Adrian does not drink Jason's organic orange juice because it is too expensive, and although he is dead and had money, he feels guilty. He drinks tap water instead and keeps the fridge door open, staring into it. Jason's and Gio's groceries are still on their assigned shelves. His tofu; his bundle of lush, green broccoli; her chunky multicoloured salsa; her McCain Deep & Delicious cake. Who is going to eat all this food? He briefly considers eating it himself or splitting it with Luke, but this seems vulgar and inappropriate. He throws it all away, ties the garbage bag closed and leaves it in the hallway. He then fills a bucket with warm, soapy water, gets down on his hands and knees and wipes the shelving clean. Is this what I will write in the eulogy? She ate well? he says to the suds. Is this what the funeral-goers want to hear? Her parents? Her sister's boyfriend? Her fourth grade teacher?

‡

Luke presses his ear to the door, ready to hear an exclamation, some sort of gratitude, some sort of acknowledgement. He opens the door and moves back to his bed, where he's laid out black T-shirts, jeans, underwear, all folded and pressed and wrapped in sticky paper bands from the laundrette. For the visitation and the funeral, he has two suits, both black, and two crisp dress shirts, both white. For a tie, he picks dark red silk and spreads it out on the white shirt. It will bring out the colour in his face. Before zipping all this into a garment bag, he examines how striking the tie looks splayed on the shirt. He wonders if anyone else will connect it to Gio's and Jason's blood on a snowy roadside.

He picks up his pen to write this idea down in his journal, scribbling faster as he continues; lyrics, after all, are everywhere. Luke loves to immortalize his thoughts. He knows that if he does not take note of these little observations, one day he will forget them all. He imagines some point in the future, after his death, when biographers will come across these very notes. He thinks appreciatively of how leaving that small chunk of writing to help his roommate is like his own lick of colour. The elements of the world — the storm, the ice, the speed of the car, the mistimed pull of Giovanna's hand against the wheel — have shown Luke that there are still things he can learn, that death should never be attractive, that he has a lot to give, a lot to leave for posterity, no detail is to be spared, the world is full of small revelatory moments of colour.

‡

Adrian is angry at Luke for going to the first day of classes — how could he, considering the circumstances? Part of him is relieved, though. Now he can pack and maybe even write without being distracted. He empties the pockets of his jeans onto the dresser — keys, cigarettes, lighter, a few pennies — then pulls the pants off, folds them and puts them into the suitcase he's opened on the bed. Wearing just his overwashed briefs, he keeps packing, carelessly lining the bag with sweaters and underwear. He folds his silvery-grey suit — the only one he owns — over his arm and slides it on top of the wool overcoat that is reserved for dressing up in the wintertime. He opens his drawer to collect some socks and sees that there is a fresh piece of paper on top of his writing pad. Adrian reads it — *I trusted her ... my opinion of her ... she made me think ... when I was done with her* — and feels suddenly under attack. He lowers himself onto the bed, the gush returning in his chest. Luke's been in here. Doesn't he know the game is over? He's violated things, opened the drawers, read the eulogy. Maybe even crawled onto the bed, between the sheets.

No. Adrian can't let himself get turned on like this, the way he does every time Luke breaks into his room and takes something or leaves something behind. Adrian always tells himself that he's appalled by this behaviour, but knows that it means something more: that Adrian's life is worth investigation, that he's provoked Luke's curiosity. But this time, Adrian can see the enormity of the scheme. The game has to be over; their friends are dead.

"Come down the hallway and comfort me!" he yells, knowing that his roommate's not here. He wants to stand up to Luke now, Jason and Gio deserve to have their memories defended and he is the only one that can do it. His sense of injustice crystallizes. "Stop your stupid act!" he yells.

Then, suddenly, Luke opens the door — his black shirt is unbuttoned and his face is flushed. Adrian feels a warm pump in his own body now, a determination.

"Oh," Adrian says, "I thought you were at class."

"What the fuck are you screaming about?" Luke says.

"I know what's going on," Adrian tells him. "You want me to read your eulogy for Gio. Well I'm not."

"I was trying to help," Luke says, unkindly.

"You want me to read this? Well, I won't do it," Adrian says and sweeps his foot along the floor in a spike of exhilaration, sending the piece of paper flying against the wall.

"Who do you think you are?" Luke says and takes Adrian's wrist in a vise of fingers, easily bending the arm behind Adrian's back. The tender skin is pulling like an Indian burn; Adrian can feel his blood beating through the squeezed veins. "I'll tell you. I'll tell you who you are. You're a complete failure."

"Fuck you," Adrian says. With his free hand, Luke grabs some hair and pulls Adrian's head back, pushing him against the dresser. Adrian can feel the lip of the open drawer digging into his calves and flesh pulled tight over his Adam's apple.

"Yeah? Yeah?" Luke's breath is hot against Adrian's neck. With blinding force, Luke flips him over and traps Adrian's free arm between the dresser and his torso. He holds Adrian's cheek against the surface of the dresser, pushing; the pennies there are cold, shoved into his lips, and taste like blood. He hears the tinkling of a belt buckle, and then Luke is bent over him, pulling down the flaccid white briefs, and fucking him. With the fistful of hair, he yanks Adrian's head against his thick, hairy neck. Adrian is completely split open, the edge of the dresser pushing into his abdomen, harmed, weak, a penny stuck to his cheek with sweat, only able to submit. "You're shit."

No. This has to stop, Adrian thinks, halting the fantasy, sitting on the edge of his bed, alone, his cock in his hands. There is whistling in the hallway. Luke is announcing his presence — has he been here the whole time? Has he heard Adrian's exclamations? Disappointment gathers in Adrian's mind: he wants Luke to have heard. Talking to him will go nowhere — they never talk, not seriously, they have no rules for that kind of exchange. He must get out of Luke's range. He has to find another way to lash out. But there's nothing here, nothing but the toxic mingling of desire and grief. He is a failure — a failure suddenly shot through with a wild urge to leave.

‡

Luke, still whistling, is pawing through the lollipops on the stove. He is taking out all the liquorice ones to bring with him to Toronto. They're black, perfect for a funeral. As he considers whether or not to take strawberry, too — red, to match his tie — he hears the slam of Adrian's bedroom door, followed by the slam of the main door. Where is he going? The train leaves in two hours.

He stuffs the candy into a pocket and walks into the living room to investigate. Jason's eulogy sits on the couch, turned to page six. He smiles — Adrian is still leaving clues. He carries it to his room to put it in his travel bags, and picks up his towel. Luke has to walk all the way down the corridor to the shower. He knows the sound every roommate's saunter made down that sixty-foot stretch of floorboards. The bouncy skip of Giovanna's sandals; the lethargic shuffle of Adrian's boots; Jason's confident heavy lurch.

The water pressure feels good against his skin. He feels the moisture in his lungs, loosening things up. He begins coughing. He smiles into the shower-mirror and, for a second, the shadow of his lip plays a trick on him and he thinks he is still in that absurd nightmare, mouth still rotting. He drops the smile and practices looking sombre, imitating Adrian. He imagines the grief-stricken faces of the mourners staring up at him. He can hear his voice pronouncing the eulogy. They are listening to every word, crying harder. Luke rolls the bar of soap in his right hand and steps back out of the spray, reaches down and grabs his cock, moves his lathered hand up and down in a wild soapy froth.

‡

Adrian slams his shoulder against the door to the roof. A small crack of light appears and cold air brushes his face. He repeats the action until the door has ploughed a wedge out of the snow. Adrian squeezes his boot through and steps down onto a cleared patch of gravel on the surface of the roof. He pushes further, shins braced for the cold, until he has created a trench to the far wall. The sky is white and big; from four stories up, he can see in all directions. On the north side is Mount Royal, white, striped with leafless trees. South, he sees down to Ste-Catherine Street, abuzz with New Year's sales. It is garish, he thinks, for people to be capable of normal transactions when friends can be mangled on highways, when Adrian can be abandoned with someone like Luke.

Adrian prefers life to be like this rooftop: uncomplicated and white, undisturbed. Luke has not taken over this place, not yet. From here, Adrian can pick his thoughts without any pressure to act on them. Everywhere else, the world happens to Adrian — he can never reach out, never influence what's around him. On the train, for example, he will spend four hours pretending to sleep, feeling Luke's warm proximity, heart beating strongly, listening to the drone of Luke's theories. His roommate will likely force him to reread Jason's eulogy, or worse, read it out loud. He imagines Luke's mouth, candy clicking against his teeth, stick dancing, Ontario fields going past in a long, white blur. Everyone on the train can hear him. When Adrian finally turns to show the other passengers his embarrassment, every person in the car gives him a look of taciturn but palpable sympathy.

The warm pity of strangers may serve him well in that moment, but there are other things to consider — the memory of Jason and Gio, consoling their families. This eulogy has justice staring Adrian in the face and he still hasn't been able to act on it, to pick up his pen and place his own indelible stamp on the world. He has to prevent Luke's distractions — and his own distractions, his own urge to float away in that updraft of miserable longing. Adrian will finish the eulogy on the train. He has no choice now.

‡

Luke steps out into the courtyard from the laundry room, right fist clutching a bag of garbage that was left in the hall. Most of his legs disappear into the whiteness. He walks into the centre of the courtyard, pushing shafts into the snow with each step. He is the first person to come through here since the storm ended. Disturbing the snow seems perverse and enjoyable. A few flurries continue to fall, but without any purpose. They are individual and solitary, signalling the storm's end. White confetti against a white sky. Luke sees the weather as a weapon wielded by some greater, admirable power. All around him the walls of the building rise up out of the drifts, perforated by snow-laden windows and vents. The sky is divided into little triangles by the telephone cables that hang over the courtyard, each one heavy with snow. Nothing is untouched by the storm. Luke scoops some snow up to his face. It is heavy and shimmering. He squeezes it in his fist: this is what did it. This is what killed them. And here I am, he thinks, alive, disturbing it, manipulating it, defeating it. He tosses the bag over the side of the dumpster.

A thump sounds not too far from his head. He turns to see a circle of snow on the side of the bin. He turns further, facing the whole courtyard. A second snowball comes hurtling towards him, but misses, disappearing into one of the drifts. Luke raises a hand to his brow. On the roof of the building he can make out a silhouette raising its arm and throwing. This one hits him in the shoulder and pain shoots through his arm. Another, on his chest. He feels like he's been shot. He loses his balance, throws a hand out against the dumpster's door for support, but misses and lands in a sitting position engulfed by a wet, penetrating cold. Another snowball speeds towards him, and he is able to grab at it with his hand — that produces a sharp pain in his palm. He opens his hand, there is piece of gravel sitting there, cold from its snowy casing. Distantly, he can hear the rare sound of Adrian's laugh.

ordinary time

one

On Saturdays when I was young — five and six and seven — Sinatra would greet my aunties as they arrived. Frank's confident voice blared from the dusty, scratchy phono "Only the Lonely" as I watched Maria and Lucia shamble up the driveway towards the side entrance of our house, their faces bright with teeth. They pulled on my ears, squeezed out my cheeks and lifted me from the ground with deflating hugs, their wintercold coats or summertoasted arms brushing my neck.

"He's getting big, this one," Lucia said, squeezing the meat of my arm, as if she intended to buy it. "They grow so fast. How do we keep up, huh?" This was during the time that I refused to speak — but she said it anyway, every week, and then flashed me a hopeful, vivid face. Of course, I wanted to respond. The urge was there, but the answer wasn't. *I don't know* — that was the best I could come up with, and it seemed stupid, unworthy of her, a non-answer. I just smiled.

Bless my Zia, the woman who raised me, who sensed the fear in my silence and walked over to us, singing along with Frank, lyrics as big as she was wide. Sometimes we let her finish the song, dipping at the knee and shuffling across the alcove, fleshy arms thrown out in a V. After the final lyric, the aunties clapped and laughed before descending into the kitchen to swarm the orangetop table: pulling out chopping boards, unpacking groceries, tying on aprons that smelled of forgotten meals. Zia always started the cooking, lifting a huge cauldron of water to the stove and dropping in pieces of puckerskinned chicken. The broth was made every Saturday since it was useful for a number of the week's meals. There were other foods that could be counted on, too. Lucia worked on the meatballs that her husband and sons adored, loaded with garlic, Parmesan cheese, and her homedried breadcrumbs. For Maria it was gnocchi, with the potatoes carefully peeled and riced, then rolled into snakes of dough to be cut. It seemed that there were twice as many hefty bodies around the table with large laughs and flurries of hands — white with flour, oily with butter, gloppy with meat.

My job was to fetch. I was just skinny enough to slide between the aunties' chairs and the waxywood cupboards.

"Cannelloni this week," Maria said.

"This cheese is for Lucia."

"Potatoes over there for now, you want to scrub them?"

"Bread crumbs over here, Bello."

"I need that ground beef from the basement."

And I would run to get it, down the stairs and into the cold room, as quickly as possible. I wanted to help, but I did all this mostly for the appreciative little show they performed when I returned with the right item.

"Look at that, took him all of five seconds," Zia said.

I beamed proudly.

"A meek little marvel, this one," Maria said. "Your wife'll be the luckiest lady in St-Michel."

The whole family lived in St-Michel back then, a glut of ungainly homes full of Italians, on the northern perimeter of Montreal. And these three women were all zias, techni-cally, but I only called one of them by this Italian word for "aunt". Childless herself, Zia and her husband — Zio ("uncle") — took me in when I was four, after my parents died in a car accident. Lucia and Maria were called the more Canadian "auntie." They all participated in raising me — raising, in this case, meant assigning yardwork and overfeeding me. Each weekday, I walked from my elementary school to a different auntie's house and passed the hours with my cousins: raking, shovelling, playing basketball, watching TV, throwing snow-balls, depending on the season, depending on the auntie.

Yet it was Saturdays that reigned supreme. I enjoyed watching how my aunties talked, how they bullied their ingredients into nourishment and flavour. More importantly, it was as though my longdead mother was there, too. As I rushed around, I would often catch a quick glimpse of Ma, whose picture was pushpinned to a corkboard near the stairs. It was black and white, and seemed to offer a different message every time I looked over. It showed my mother as a child, sitting on the edge of a bed, hand extended to pet a cat. Her hair was a thick mass of black, dramatically juxtaposed with her white dress and a white silk bow drowning in the strands. She had turned from the animal to look at the camera, smiling, surprised, eyes like black marbles, as if thrilled to be getting away with this action, as if she never expected the kitty to permit it. Her little hand was behind the cat's ears, barely making contact with its fur. I often imagined her touch, her touching me, just like this.

Soon, the kitchen smelled like coffee, even sounded like coffee as the percolator in the corner grumbled and puffed along with "Willow Weep for Me" or "A Wing and a Prayer." Zia poured it into three mugs and the conversation accelerated. The food always seemed secondary to the talk, as though the meals they prepared were excuses to pull everyone together — first to make the food, then to eat it. I felt like the elite cousin, privy to details deprived of my equals.

"I'm not claiming that he's helpless," Lucia said of her husband. She was scissoring parsley into a bowl of ground pork. "But Devo can't even be trusted to dress now. Tonight I'll have to lay out all his clothes for mass tomorrow. It's his turn to read the Prayers of the Faithful." I looked over at my mother. She had been part of the church reading group, too: a collection of parishioners who got up in front of the whole congregation to read prayers and passages from the Old Testament. I thought of all those faces, listening, looking up at her. She was brave. I'd be frightened behind the podium — paralyzed, my small voice not even making it past my teeth. In the picture, her excited grin seemed fearless and determined now, full of faith.

"Age!" Zia said. By now, she was skimming the fatty bubbles from the surface of the chicken stock and slapping them off the strainer into the sink. "Soon they'll be unable to dress at all. What's a wife to do?"

"Laugh," said Maria. "It's not worth the worry."

"Can you defrost that beef you brought up, Bello?" Zia said to me. I was the only one to have mastered the microwave.

"Ba. That machine," Lucia said whenever Zia handed me a frozen block of meat. "Don't rely on that gizmo. There's a process to everything. That's what makes things good."

I had something to say here, but spent too long turning words over in my mind, trying to formulate anything as indelible as my aunties' phrases. *But it's so fast* — that was too trite. *It speeds up the process* — no, they'd see I didn't understand the process at all. *It gets the job done* — better, rhythmic, but still small and forgettable.

"Not good," Zia said. "Better." Three words. Zia always made it seem easy, this business of communicating.

"Yes, it's like with the pies," Maria said. "Cecilia always softened her crusts in the machine."

"True! Remember the pies?" Lucia said to me. "Your mother was the lady with the best pies."

"Never too lazy to cut the butter right into the flour," Maria said.

"And fillings like candy. We didn't know what she did to them to make them so sweet, none of us."

"Taken so young, but what pies!"

Maybe God wanted to taste the pies, too — but instead I just smiled, accepting the compliments on behalf of my mother as though they'd been bequeathed to me. Were such revelations supposed to give me some knowledge of the lady that had grown me, pushed me out into the world? They succeeded only in making me aware of how little I knew of her, of how any intimacy had been stolen from me by some painful force well outside my comprehension. The aunties understood it, though; they were infallible. For me, my parents' deaths had been sudden and confusing. I was a flurry of questions for crying aunts in black, to answerless uncles with wine on their breaths, to Father Giando, even, who told me that God wanted my parents in heaven. It was not until the funeral, three days later, when these people all got up to speak, that I was finally offered clarity. Bold words about loss blasted out over the shiny coffins, vibrating the pews. *Their home was their castle and their son was their treasure.* These were definite words, spoken through blubbering grief. I felt for the first time that my mother and father were gone. It was impossible not to. *Today we must balance the tears of our sorrow with the tears of our joy.* I could not explain what all this actually meant, but that didn't matter, really, because the lines felt true. I could hear the scope of my family's desperation, their need to confer immortality upon my parents — and they succeeded, somehow, with these phrases that opened up onto oceans of sadness. *Sorrow from loss, but joy from knowing that they are in a deserving place.* How could I compete? *The divine message is our sweetest comfort.* At home in bed, on the first night of my silence, I replayed every word in my mind. I had nothing to say that could be as powerful as those tributes. Later, my family members decided that it was the deaths had silenced me — but that wasn't the case at all.

"Where or When" now, Frank getting a little blue.

Zia began pushing garlic skins and crumbs of buttery flour into a cupped hand and the orangetop table glinted with wetness. I felt a collapse of disappointment in my chest, knowing that the Saturday ritual was almost over.

"One more cup of coffee," Zia said. "There's only a drop left." They all shot their eyes to the clock, seeing how much time remained before the men came back from their card game. The broth was nearing its potency, its odour having overtaken the smell of coffee.

Zia took her chipped mustard-coloured saucer from the windowsill and placed it on the table before lighting a cigarette. She smoked two per day, when she was sure Zio wouldn't catch her in the act. It was understood that everyone could leave once the cigarette was done. They finished wrapping up their creations and sat in the now-spotless kitchen discussing their children — grades earned, chores botched, soccer games won. There was a noticeably calmer tone during this last chunk of conversation, but I was still pumping with the energy of the day and stood with my back to them, rinsing the cooking utensils, sliding them into the dishwasher.

"What's a mother to do?" Lucia said. "If my son wants to date a French girl, he'll have to live with my wrath."

"You met her?" Zia said.

"Yeah, she's got some English, that one. And she's as big as this table if she's an inch and a half."

As luck would have it, I was at Lucia's house the day this French girl came by. On the days that I went there after school, her teenaged son Franco liked to order me around. He used my silence to his advantage. I brought him forbidden snacks (he was on a diet), money from Lucia's purse, and bottles from Uncle Devo's beer fridge. On this particular day, Franco had sent me out of his room while he changed for his night out. I sat on the top step and waited for him, listening to the conversation Lucia was having with the Quebecoise in the foyer. Lucia was right. She was a big girl. I remember thinking that they looked alike, these two women: heavy set, with dark features, golden hoop earrings, and sensible flat-soled shoes. They were like before and after pictures of the same person: awkward youth/hardened mother.

"She's not one of them, is she? A troublemaker?" Maria asked.

"Well, I didn't ask her." Lucia said. "Politics is not what I'm going to bring up in the twenty seconds I had with her. She's a Catholic, though, if that's any indication. A good one. Every Sunday with her parents. Or so she claims."

"Bless her heart," Zia said. She always came to the defence of the troublemakers, the Separatists.

"Don't know if I trust her on that and I'm not taking my chances," Lucia said. "Can't always rely on them, you know. And I told her so. I said, 'My son doesn't take any malarkey.'"

But that's not at all how the conversation had gone. She'd been far more timid. What she'd actually said was, "Take care of my Franco. He's a delicate monster." I remembered it distinctly, because I had rolled that phrase around in my mind all night, thinking it utterly true — *delicate monster*.

"They're not all in the National Assembly," Zia said. "Some of them wouldn't lie."

"Most of those Frenchies wouldn't spit in your mouth if you were dying of thirst."

The sisters laughed, my mother chuckling along from her position on the corkboard. I froze there, in front of the gaping dishwasher. They were complicit in the lie — no one pointed it out, no one even asked her about it. I didn't want to either. I wanted to believe that the mistake was mine — that I had misheard, misinterpreted. But the prospect had already materialized; behind all those clever phrases there was potential trickery. My mind started to fall back into previous Saturdays, all more or less the same, when similar talk filled this room. It was so definite in tone, so clever. I must have swallowed other deceptions, maybe even held them dear.

"Franco should stick to what he knows," Maria said. "I'm sure he'll meet a nice Italian girl one day." She stood, making her statement dramatic and final. Zia's cigarette was out by this point. It was time to leave.

Goodbyes, like hellos, were maulings. I was hugged, pawed, told I was cute and growing miraculously. I let Lucia hug me, but made sure to stay stiff in her arms. As she pulled away, I searched her face for any indication that we shared her lie, that we were in it together. There was nothing, just a smile and wrinkles clogged with powder. I continued watching Lucia from the sink, waiting for her to come clean as they stood in the open door, food-heavy bags dangling from their fists, offering pleasant comments about the coffee, the conversation. When the door finally clicked shut, I watched my aunties' backs shrink down the driveway. Maybe she'd run back at the last minute, pop her head in, admit that she'd lied, and then hurry along to catch up with Maria. But she didn't.

"What a day!" Zia said, rushing back to the kitchen to rinse out the yellow saucer and slide it back onto the windowsill. There was always the threat that Zio would return early and scowl at the crushed, orange cigarette butt. She opened the window and allowed the smoke and coffee and broth smells to escape. I lingered in the kitchen, watching her pour the broth out of the pot into a large plastic tub — in winter, in the draft, immense cottony clouds of steam would roll off the liquid. She set this next to the backdoor overnight so it could cool and the remaining fat would congeal on its surface, like ice on a lake. In the colander there was a mountain of overboiled carrots, onions, celery, and chicken fallen from the bone. We sat together at the table, picking through this greyish mass for the best pieces of meat that would turn up later that week between slices of bread or held in quiches.

"You were terribly helpful today," Zia said. "I don't know how we'd get on without you."

I smiled half-heartedly.

"What's with the long face?"

I shrugged.

"You can't fool me, Bello. I can read you like the Bible."

I looked up at her fat munificent face and jet-black hair in short curls. My fingers were burning, wet with broth. I wanted an explanation. But now I was trapped. Zia's words — *read you like the Bible!* — were so measured, so careful, so natural. I was too embarrassed to voice the clunky, inadequate questions forming in my mind: *Are you allowed to lie? Did I miss something? Am I stupid? Doesn't God hate liars?*

"OK then. Can you finish this? It's the shower hour," she said and looked down at me. I must have appeared desperate and confused. "I'll just be gone for a minute, Bello."

I shook my head — I wanted answers.

"Here," she said, scooping soup out of the tub with a bowl. "Eat this, I'll be back down in a minute."

She dusted the broth with Parmesan cheese, turning it cloudy, then left the room. I sat there at the table, staring at my shadowy reflection in the fatty surface of the liquid. The sound of the shower filled the house. Frank had sung his last song for the day, and the record would not be flipped or replayed. That day's memorized phrases were bouncing around in my head — *there's a process to everything, take any malarkey, as big as this table if she's an inch and a half.* I looked over at Ma. She seemed satisfied now, the cat looking up at her, its face turned from boredom to reverence. Sometimes, if I could keep up the hush, a voice so soft — but unmistakably hers — rose in my mind: "What's the matter, Bello?" she said.

"Lucia — she lied," I thought.

"She was always a show-off, that one."

"But you can't lie," I whimpered in my mind, almost crying into the soup. "Zia always told me ..."

"Yes, it is a sin," Ma said. She looked happier now, angelic, full of divine understanding. "But that doesn't mean you can't be forgiven for it."

two

Between the two masses, parishioners would stand on the front lawn of St. Leo's Church. Those exiting from the ten o'clock ceremony were one Sunday closer to redemption and looked triumphant. The other half — my half — were just arriving for the noon mass. Zio, Zia and I always came early in order to go to confession. The two groups mingled, shook hands with the priests, remarked on friends' outfits, and exchanged nuggets of gossip. The lawn was punctuated by a huge stone sign announcing the name of the church. In the springtime, the magnolia trees smelled sweet and in the autumn, dead leaves blew up against everyone's legs. I stood close to the entrance of the church, watching the river of Catholics pour out, trying to get the attention of a heavy-set Italian boy who went to the ten o'clock mass — Carlito Fisteri. He was the only kid I liked whose family came to St. Leo's.

When he appeared, I grabbed him by the wrist so we could race ahead into the reception hall to get the jammy doughnuts before they were gone. We experimented with the beverages — amazed that they were free — by filling the Styrofoam cups halfway with coffee or tea and then daring each other to taste it based on combinations of additives: milk, cream, sugar, Sweet 'n Low. Each week, to Carlito's chagrin, I shortened his last name to Fister, and he got back at me by handing over some brownish paste made of coffee and shovelfuls of non-dairy creamer.

253

"It's a potion," Fister said. "I'd be real careful if I were you."

"What'll it do?"

"Magic," he said.

That was easy enough to believe. At church, it seemed like magic was built into the rafters — all the chanting and praying made God take notice of us. I saw St. Leo's as a portal to heaven, and all the priests like witches with spells, coaxing out powers beyond human understanding. I drank the sweet, grainy goo. I didn't feel any magic, but I pretended to by shaking violently and closing my eyes, before shoving a sugar cube in my mouth to stop my gag reflex.

Every Sunday, Fister wore the same black-collared top, black pants, black wingtips and white tie. With his oiled midnight hair, the tie looked like a stain, like the colour of his face had run down the over the strained buttons of his shirt. He found many ways for us to be horrible: crank calls from the phone in the reception office, climbing the magnolia trees in the garden, or stealing cucumbers from the Chinese lady that lived next to St. Leo's. Often we'd lock ourselves in the washroom, turn off the lights, then spin ten times, shouting "Bloody Mary!" When we stopped, we each claimed to see her in the mirror — but I never did.

"You're going to drive me to drink," Zio always said when he came to collect me and take me to confession. I was usually halfway up a magnolia tree or sliding around the ice in the parking lot. "In your Sunday clothes, I mean really," he said, fingers around my upper arm, even once I'd grown as tall as him. "I guess you'll have plenty to confess this week."

Back in the chapel, Zio and I waited in a pew with some people at prayer, crucifixes swaying at the ends of their rosaries. The organist was practicing, playing versions of "Ave Maria" or "How Great Thou Art" with melodies stretched out long and weighty, as if to force solemnity. Each time someone one went into the confessional — an oak cage for the priest, flanked by two spaces draped with velvet — Zio and I scooched down the pew, getting closer and closer, like an assembly line. In my mind, I always thought of this as the Forgiveness Factory.

While waiting, I entertained myself by reading the prayers in *Your Sunday Missal* or the lyrics out of the *Catholic Book of Worship*. This was my own prepenance ritual because it proved to me that God existed, that confession was worthwhile. The first verse of each hymn was divided into syllables with dashes, running along under the musical notes. God, it seemed, had the power to break up language into all its little parts, even have His own ancient and lovely vocabulary that would require such divisions: *ag-nus de-i, kyr-i-e e-le-i-son, Eu-cha-rist*. More proof: I understood these words, but not in a literal way. Spoken or sung, they were translated into emotional information, sanctimonious and cantatory.

In the Missals, I was obsessed with the liturgical calendars. God had gotten into these books, too — He had power over time, as well as language. The prayers were organized according to how God divided up the year — the Fifth Week of Pentecost, the Twenty-Third Sunday of Ordinary Time. What a tantalising coupling of words. Was this day ordinary? Or that day? What characterized extraordinary time? Extraordinary minutes? Seconds? Sundays at St. Leo's, like the Saturdays of foodmaking, were ordinary enough — they simply existed, unquestioned; they anchored the week. The day of my parents' deaths — that was extraordinary because God had momentarily intervened. The day I began to speak again was extraordinary, too. It had happened during mass. My Uncle Devo was behind the pulpit reading the list of group prayers. "For the meek," Devo said, as though making a toast, "that they may find kindness and discourse and the proper path to God." This is where the congregation was to reply, automatically, in a monotone: "Lord hear our prayer." I never understood why. It is such an enticing sentence — the pleading, the selflessness. That week, though, it seemed pulse-poundingly urgent that God receive this request. I was meek; I could still hear Auntie Maria's voice calling me a "meek little one." *Lord hear our prayer!* And I said it — my little voice drowned out in the group. No one heard me but God. Every time thereafter, at the Prayers of the Faithful, I'd be convinced that they worked, that the message was being transmitted, that divine powers were afoot.

The lady ahead of me stood and went into the lefthand confessional. We moved down the pew. I slid the book I was

reading back onto its shelf in preparation. I was next. The
people in there were taking a long time, it seemed. When the
organist stopped playing, the room was suddenly drained of
life, replaced by a sacred silence. I was taken by a heightened
sense of gravity, Fister forgotten, convinced that something of
huge consequence was waiting nearby. A girl of twelve, with
hair the colour of Mars, exited from the righthand confessional. She looked pale, dreadful. Zio looked down at me and
lifted his tufty eyebrows. I entered the booth quietly, closing
the velvet curtain all the way. If no light could leak in, then
no sins could leak out.

The space was the size of a shower stall. The milky-sweet
taste of the coffee was still in my mouth and the faint smell
of incense and varnish clung to the air. More waiting now,
in darkness, kneeling, listening to the mumbles of the lady
confessor in the opposite booth. She sounded tragic, beseech-
ing and the kneeler rumbled with Father Giando's unfazed
voice. I strained to make out some scintillating words —
adultery, cocaine, theft, murder — but couldn't make out anything through the closed casement.

Father Giando's face filled the window as the barrier slid
away. His head was jewelled with sweat and his nose was
tipped with a web of veins — the whole visage partitioned
into diamonds of flesh by the iron lattice through which I
was now expected to bear my soul. He coughed. Over the
centuries, priests have mastered that cough: a clearing of
the throat that says, "Go ahead, I acknowledge your existence,

tell me everything." I kneeled straighter, almost painfully, in a perfect L. At these moments, God was judging everything, posture included.

"Bless me, Father, for I have sinned. It has been one week since my last confession."

"Very well, my son. Proceed."

And now the sins — usually the same ones:

"I stole some cucumbers from Mrs. Chang's garden," I said. "She lives next to the church. And I took one of those cardboard tubes from the box in the washroom. It has a string on it. I know it's for ladies only." Once I began, I could not look at his face, thinking it may be judgemental, or worse, bored. Father Giando listened in silence, inhaling and exhaling through his mouth with a slight gargle of mucus. "I didn't listen to the readings during church last Sunday. And I spoke during the consecration."

"Is that all?"

"And I dirtied my Sunday clothes playing on the lawn."

"What about sins you committed when you weren't here at St. Leo's?"

It was very hard to swallow. Trying to verbalize sins was like trying to point out a specific star in a dark sky. I knew that I'd done things that felt wrong, but now could not explain exactly why they'd had that effect on me or why I'd done them in the first place. Being unable to articulate my transgressions seemed like the worst sin of all.

"When I was younger, I didn't speak," I said. "Everyone was upset with me because I didn't want to talk. Everyone except my mother."

"Son, you don't have to tell me that every week."

"I feel bad."

"Well, you have to talk. How else do you say please and thank you? How else do you express how you feel? What's in your heart?" Father Giando said. "And stealing, you know stealing is wrong, don't you, son? How do you feel when people steal from you? Your toys? Your games?"

"I feel bad."

"ok then. Five 'Our Fathers.' Ask the Lord for guidance," he mumbled. "And stay out of the women's washroom."

"Yes, Father."

"ok then. I absolve you of your sins, in the name of the Father and the Son and of the Holy Spirit."

When I re-emerged, Zio had already disappeared into the other confessional. People were starting to come into the chapel for noon mass and I wanted to keep my distance from their penitent bodies and sounds. I walked to the front-row pew, from where the ornaments of the altar appeared large and close. Jesus's face was handsome — pallid and peaceful — despite his wrecked body. I folded my hands into a mess of fingers, clutched tight and pale.

"Our Father, who art in Heaven," I began. This was the part of Sunday that appealed to me the most. Repeating the same lines over and over — that rhythm — made strange and wonderful things happen. Fister and I had said "Bloody Mary" ten times into the bathroom mirror to make a ghost appear, but that was the wrong kind of language. Prayer was sharper, stronger, tried-and-true — it lifted guilt from me the way pain evaporated after swallowing a pill.

"Our Father, who art in Heaven —"

Conjuring words: measured, magical, exciting, cut into a specific shape like the grooves of a key.

"Our Father, who art in Heaven —"

A tiny voice came up; not someone else in the chapel, not human at all. If I concentrated, whispered, surrounded the voice with silence, it would ring clearer. I was alone, the world dissolved. True solitude was the company of this voice.

"Our Father, who art in Heaven —"

I felt a shiver, a surge of divinity.

"Our Father, who art in Heaven —"

"You do not need forgiveness for your silence. The whole purpose of a ceremony is its silences," the voice said. It was just a hint of a sound, a vibration. "Rituals are just doors."

three

Fister and I walked downward through Parc St-Michel, the gravelled path carrying several other high school students with us through the trees. The woods on all sides were black, impenetrable, with branches raised against the citynight sky like the arms of drowning children. We could hear the rumbles and strums of our acquaintances playing their guitars and tam-tams. It felt tribal, following a drum that resonated in the gut, the reverberations striking deeply, pulling us all along. On such Friday nights, this didn't seem at all like a trip down to a party in the valley, but to the underworld.

We were drawn to Parc St-Michel by its sprawl — unpatrolable and wild, full of possibility and risk. We could create a setting there for our savage experiments in joy: a bonfire (now visible there between the trees), uncounted bottles of beer, pot, acid, pills — levity that we never dreamed could break through the barrier of the surrounding trees.

As we approached, music blew loudly against us and the darkness would disappear behind our backs as we stepped into a large clearing with a fire in its centre. Teenage bodies stood in clusters to joke and flirt and pass joints. Close to the fire was a ring of five or six benches made of half-logs bearing little messages carved into the seats with keys and penknives. This was where the musicians sat, the party's epicentre, slapping drums, whispering chords to one another, taking requests, the flash of the flames bouncing off their guitars. Dave Boccinni and Roberto Galleti were the central players, making up jokey lyrics for popular rock songs — "In Bloom" or "Rusty Cage." Kevin O'Malley was among them, the lone Irishman at my school, his cherry-red hair pouring over his head, curling up into dainty hooks at the temples.

He looked concerned, moving his head from left to right, determined to get the fingering right.

Fister and I made our rounds together, high-fiving the people we knew. The flamelight softened the focus, dulling stubble and pimples and scars into sleek patches of soft, touchable skin. Fister reminded me that he came to these parties for my benefit. His policy was to hate almost everyone — the jocks with boisterous laughs, the hippies, the girls in their hoodies unzipped to reveal deltas of cleavage. Depending on the season, he covered his wide masculine shoulders and sizable paunch with a huge T-shirt or a heavy ski jacket, convinced that people were making fun of him, calling him thunderthighs or lardass as they had in elementary school.

"Still tame yet," Fister said. "No one's even puking."

"People are just getting here," I said and pointed to the pathway, where others were still arriving.

"Well, if I'm going deal with these people," he said, eyeing his knapsack, "I oughta be fucked up."

Then he pulled out The Concoction. Fister had prepared it in his basement several hours before: wine, rye, crème de menthe, Kalhúa, Fin du Monde, Goldschläger, whatever else he could find, mixed together into a one-litre milk jug. Although it tasted different every week, The Concoction always got the same offended reaction from my throat and stomach, a half-retch, easily suppressed.

"Big guy!" Al Bouchard said, coming around the fire in his school hockey jersey. He clapped a hand onto Fister's shoulder. "What's in The Concoction this week?"

"Arsenic," Fister said, not looking up. "Want some?"

"Ya big bear, I'm trying to be friendly here."

"And I'm trying not to be."

"What kinda attitude is that?" Bouchard laughed, keeping things jovial. "We were wondering if you'd give us a hand getting some wood for the fire here. See, there's this oak back there just dying to be burned. A whole tree. We need a big strapping lad like yourself to get the bitch down." This was common enough — each week the hockey players would try to top themselves by igniting something memorable: Kevin O'Malley's guitar case, a six-pack of Wildcat swiped from one of the wimpier kids, a D-cup bra found in the trees rumoured to belong to Cindy Bronfman (the musicians played "I Am Woman" and we all sang along).

"Pass," Fister said.

"Some friend," Bouchard said and then took off to ask someone else.

When a space freed up on the benches, Fister and I sat down and I pulled out a tinfoil ball from my pocket. In it were my selections from the treasure trove of Zia's velvety Crown Royal bag, which she hid at the back of the bathroom vanity. Vicodin, Valium, codeine, Contac C, SleepEze D, Demerol, Anaprox — the pharmaceutical history of Zia's nerves. Against the shimmering foil, the pills looked innocuous and small. Unlike Fister, the perpetual driver, I could always push myself to take more, go past last week's high. Lessons in risk: that was adolescence. The dosages depended on my mood. Codeine meant numbness, except when combined with alcohol, which added up to shortlived giddiness and giggly shock at the loss of feeling in my fingers, feet, arms, face. Valium meant a steady peace — mix it with too much alcohol and I was a zombie. With a halftab of acid I was daring: no tree was too high to climb, no fire too high to jump, no face too angry to slap. Anaprox turned me to jelly; cocaine, when I could get it, turned me into an asshole — but cut it with enough 222s and I was a philosopher. On Demerol, I was poking the fire, entranced. Histamines made me dopey and cloudy, staring off at Kevin O'Malley's face: bloodless, flamelit, exquisite, and proud of the night's musical achievements.

Properly self-medicated, we walked around the periphery of the party. As the drugs began their assault, I felt like a falcon coasting, collecting observations. The firelight lit up something for everyone — a boy fondling the drawstring of a girl's hoodie; satellite groups now passing joints; some laughing and dancing, wild with intoxication; others, more timid, were making their first tentative steps closer to the musicians, listening, stoned, spellbound. The players them-selves were well into their repertoire of made-up lyrics, inviting others to sing along. The songs could change in mid-melody, morph into something new, and bring the partymood with them. But what seemed most important on these Friday nights was the realm of invisibility. The darkness of the surrounding forest was a sphere of mystery entered only by sexually adventurous souls and the music. Ending the night in the woods was the desired outcome for all. I watched with a drugblank mind, confounded by the woods' magnetic effect.

When the musicians' melodies became sloppy, everyone could sense that the party was winding down. To fight off the denoument, some of the revellers would concentrate on some pointless stupidity: a fire-jumping contest, smashing guitars. Or Bouchard and a line of jocks would come screaming from woods, the wounded oak held above their heads, and heave the tree into the bonfire. In no time, the bark ignited and fire climbed the trunk, quick as shivers up a spine, then expanded along the branches, vaporising the leaves, until the whole thing was ablaze and unreal.

Fister and I exchanged exasperated looks and, without speaking, began our walk up the pathway to his old rusty-rimmed Mazda.

"If you're going to puke," Fister said, "puke now."

I stopped moving and calibrated how I felt. Nauseous, yes, but under control. Just my mind was spinning. My body was numb, but had the uncanny feeling that it was in freefall. "I think I'm okay this week," I said.

"You sure?"

"Yeah," I said and started walking again. I had only ever thrown up one time and knew, even as my dinner and bile poured out onto the street through the Mazda's open door, that I'd never live it down.

"I think I might throw up myself," Fister said, unlocking the car doors. "Who do these people think they are?"

"Our friends?"

"Hardly," he said.

"Well, it won't last forever. Graduation's not far off." I found myself saying this a lot.

"Let's get out of this ugly suburb," he said and we shot out of the parking spot with a squeal. We barrelled out of St-Michel, taking quick corners, ignoring stop signs, passing what remained of The Concoction back and forth. This was our idea of danger. We could choose the music, the speed, the destination. It was brazen, pointless freedom.

We went down St-Denis and shouted at the university students who — just then, at three in the morning — were stumbling from the bars. They waved back. We drove down Ste-Catherine Street and theorized about who was in the limousines parked near the strip clubs, then pushed further east into the gay village to see if we could illicit compliments from the men walking down the streets. We crossed the Jacques Cartier Bridge to Longueuil, another suburb, a French one, where we slid past flashy roadside bars with their huge, crumbling parking lots. The street proposed a beauty of inversion. Unlike the path to the party, this was a tunnel of dark road surrounded by light. We were flanked by gorgeous vintage signs on long posts, ovals of little bulbs — yellow, blue, flashing, calling, insistent — making up stylized letters that spelled out the names of the passing establishments. Suburban

Montreal's Las Vegas strip: insane, outdated, electric.

As we weaved back to St-Michel through Montreal, Fister twisted the conversation towards sex.

"Why do all those hockey goons get to have it?"

"Random fucking in a forest?" I said. "Is that really what you want?"

"It's better than nothing," Fister said. Our clothes and the Mazda smelled of bonfire. "They think we're freaks. We're no better than they are."

"Of course we are." I tried to be hyperbolic about this sort of thing, pump him up, but had few references outside the simple truths we'd decided were universal — being odd is better than being vain, sex is overrated, those who enjoy themselves in high school spend the rest of their lives paying for it. The tiny assurances of adolescence.

"I don't know how to talk to girls," he said. "They won't touch me."

"Neither do I."

"But you're skinny and cute, and I'm fat and hairy." I rolled my eyes, but the compliment mingled with the drugs to make me feel warm, glowing, ideal. "I'm going to be jerking off for the rest of my life."

I thought of Fister's room, littered with Skinny Puppy CDs and smelling of semen. "We all are."

"But you know how to talk to girls. You've got all the right words."

"I don't want any of those gangly party bitches."

"That's why they like you," he said. "Because you act like you don't want them."

I had no response — it wasn't an act. Every week, I'd think that this common teenboy conflict would finally get to me, this belief that sex equalled justice, but it never did.

"My fingers are numb," I said eventually.

"I feel fine," he said. "But I need to get back. Do you want me to drop you at home?"

"No. I'll walk and sober up."

At Fister's parents' we coasted into the driveway in silence. I felt dizzy and nauseous from the car ride, getting near the end of my high. We hugged and I gave Fister a little boost so that he could climb into his bedroom window from the driveway. He poked his head out to me, giving me the thumbs up. We mouthed goodbyes.

Then, with drugs ebbing and dawn hinting at reality, I walked to my own house. St-Michel seemed new and beautiful: light frost on the cars, the long lawns with their ordered gardens, the cookiecutter houses with their blinds closed. My eyes went in and out of focus — the doubletrees and doublecars and quadruplefeet, if I concentrated on them, would bring the overlaid facsimiles into a single, proper vision under the eerie cyan morning sky. In these sharp, sober moments, I saw the world with staggering accuracy. Every colour was stronger, every texture more dramatic, exemplary, safer, realer. I was able, for a split second, to differentiate the sharp moments that belonged to the real world from the mysterious moments that belonged to the drugs. As the real moments grew longer, I could hear a divine whisper in the diminishing seconds of drugged understanding. "This concludes our broadcast day," it said. "Here's life in perfect focus." And I was left with the swish of my corduroyed thighs, one against the other. The walk home was the tragedy of ephemeral moments, I thought, and had the urge to write this down, to remember it tomorrow. "You can immortalize them," the voice said, just before it disappeared, "but they can't last forever."

four

Nina Simone was my prelude to a night of dancing. Since I lived closest to our favourite clubs, my friends and I met at the apartment I shared with Fister. They trooped in: hyperselves, all plucked and coiffed, dressed for dancing. Jimmy, with a few bottles of cheap wine from the dépanneur, usually arrived first, sometimes an hour early. Then Sean and JP showed up, sometimes an hour late, with Montreal kisses, a peck for each cheek.

"Look at *her*," one said to the other, as though I were a mannequin. "Scruffy artist boy goes on the town."

"I see we've finally figured out the razor then," the other added, running a hand down my freshly shaven face.

"Gotta be gay," I said and led them into the living room, where they exploded with more greetings, kisses, and compliments delivered as insults for Fister and Jimmy. Wine was poured and I staggered in with a column of dessert plates topped with a pie.

"Oh, strawberry rhubarb! Right to my thighs with you," JP said, eating his portion like a slice of pizza.

"Yeah, I hope Weight Watchers sent you a kickback this month," Sean said. "Did you make your own pastry?"

"Nothing but the best for my fags," I said, dribbling the last of the wine into my glass.

"I should have brought more," Jimmy said. "Sorry."

"Don't be silly," I said. "Let me see what I can rustle up."

Jimmy had put himself through university as a bartender, so I tried to set up a minibar for him on the coffee table, complete with shot glasses, shakers and a little cutting board for limes. He expertly turned my little collection of spirits into beautiful, fantastic cocktails: White Russians with their swirling collision of liquids, margaritas encrusted with salt, seedy strawberry daiquiris, pinkish wine spritzers. If it was someone's birthday, we toasted eternal youth. "How old are you this year?" someone would ask, and the birthdayboy would reply, "Dead, in gay years."

When Nina was through, I put on Madonna.

"Yay!" they shouted. With one boo — from Fister, the only straight man in the room.

"You boys shatter no stereotypes," he said as the tinkly opening of "Holiday" kicked in. Fister pretended to dislike my gay friends, but secretly enjoyed these weekly visits and their attendant attention, like the way JP ran a flat hand down his chest and said, "How drunk do you have to be to live up to that nickname of yours?" I was proud of how disarming the group could be, the way they could drain tension out of every situation. I was proud of them, and with apartment, too, its pell-mell beauty — the Salvation Army couches, the coffee table made from a slab of orange Formica, the warm yellow walls and the light bulbs softened by squares of map I'd clipped from an outdated atlas and thumbtacked to the ceiling. The place had a strange layout, with communal rooms upstairs and the bedrooms below, sealed off from the world, accessible only through a narrow staircase that was meant for servants before the building was converted to apartments.

"Let's go to The Underground," JP said. "Let the beauty search begin!"

"Looks like JP wants a little sugar in his bowl," Sean added.

We looked at the time. If it was past eleven, we all agreed to start walking towards the club — it would be absurd to arrive any earlier.

I asked Fister if he was sure he didn't want to come along.

"Positive," he said. "I'm having a quiet night at home."

"Shall I stay so we can snuggle?" JP asked, blinking flirtatiously.

"JP," I said, "no night with you could ever be quiet."

In line outside the club, we could feel the beat, winding everyone up like toy soldiers. Ahead of us in line, skulls bobbed and torsos swayed. Inside, after a quick round of drinks, our collective pushed itself onto the dance floor with eight elbows, clearing a little circle close to the centre. All four towers of speakers were pointed at us, the relentless thump of house music driving through every song. The lights flashed and swept with the beat, the melodies soared and landed with it, limbs flailed, reached, dipped, and folded with it. Even in the washroom, the circles of water in the toilet bowls rippled with the rhythm. They were called gay anthems, these loud booming songs. Looking around, I thought the name was appropriate: everyone was smiling and moving together, squeezed into a communal frenzy, arms thrown above their heads as the music climaxed. I never understood it, though — to me, the songs were a necessary evil, a lowest common denominator, a sort of musical maypole around which we were all expected to dance.

There were recognizable faces in the melee — the regulars, standing in predictable spots with the same friends. I exchanged a specific kind of glance with them, a hint of a nod. In this category was my cousin Franco, who passed by every now and again, or danced with the same heavy girl whose handbag sat on the floor between them as they jiggled and shimmied. For him, I had a special look, a conspiratorial look. We did not speak, we were too different — he was older than me, stocky and balding; according to Zia, he worked in engineering, was a Separatist sympathizer and still never brought girls to St-Michel to meet the relatives. But we shared a strong link, carried the dynamic weight of our family with us everywhere. And now we shared this, too, this beat, this lust, this city, and this look acknowledging that our lives were pinned together in two places.

Late in the night, JP always took off his shirt and tucked it into the waistband of his jeans. The rest of us theorized that he'd shoved an arsenal of drugs up his nose or down his throat during a trip to the bathroom. "It's time to get down to business." He had put in his time with us and now focussed his attention to the night's true mission. "Which one of these boys should have stayed home tonight?" he said with only partly ironic malevolence. He turned from the group and faced the other revellers in a declaration of intent.

Here I began the process of elimination. It was a tricky ritual since the faces in the fagswarm were lit only in flashes, and in those floating microseconds, I had to assess the orchestration of boys' faces, how the features played together: is the nose large enough to balance wide-set eyes? Ample enough lips as to not get lost in kissing? Eyes undilated? From every shift of eye and swing of hip, I could determine a stranger's degree of willingness. I dismissed everyone dancing on the stages and the risers as exhibitionists. The shirtless, too, were not considered. Too vain. My eyes stuck on specific boys, those with offhand, effortless beauty, wearing jeans and a T-shirt, whose eyes would look over for a moment, checking that I too had a sustained interest. A touch of macho, of self-conscious swagger, worked in their favour. It gave me the chance to give them what they wanted: an award for their affectations.

Charting my approach, I would orient my body towards my prey and begin to dance nonchalantly. If the boy didn't immediately begin moving away, I knew that I had him, that I could continue this gravitation directly into bed.

"Hey there," I said.

"Oh hi," and we discussed the following subjects in the following order: where we lived; what we did for a living ("A poet?" he said. "Wow."); the gay scene, how we're sick of this place; how I have a queensized bed; whether or not we would take a cab to my place. It was the kind of exchange that prevented the transfer of any real information, anything that could pierce the beauty advertised on the dancefloor.

A short taxi ride later, we walked into my living room and I asked him if he wanted a drink.

"Sure."

"Beer? Vodka? Just water?"

"Just water's fine," he said. "This is a nice place. Great maps."

"Thanks," I said. "I'm particularly proud of the bedroom."

"Really? Does it have as many windows?"

"You can count them if you'd like."

In the dark of my downstairs room, boys all looked the same: blond, brunette, redhead; black, white, red, yellow; francophone, anglophone, allophone. I relied on my finger-tips for directions, messages; waited for a shudder of pleasure as I ran my nails over a patch of vulnerable neckflesh, or a grunt of relief when I pushed my thumbs into his back, or a blowjob gag, or the thrust of big male hips when sliding myself between his thighs. The language of sex.

Afterward, he bolted. Like most boys, he had his own post-coital scurry plan: "Thanks. Maybe I'll see you around," and I locked the door behind him. I never cared if my one-night stands remained or disappeared. Their beauty, as far as I was concerned, had already been conquered.

I'd climb back into bed and stare up at the repeating patterns of the window's shape, each with a different intensity of shadow, splayed against the ceiling. Everything — the closet door, the desk, the split condom wrapper on the floor — would seem excessively still, cast in the blueish citynight glow. I closed my eyes, awake just enough to feel my muscles twitch, heralding sleep. There were no sounds, no motions, just slumber growing out of drunkenness, pulling me into oblivion like a receding tide, the day's memories left on the beach of consciousness: indelible images, beautiful sounds, collisions of words, JP's tapering naked back, the musical brakes of the subway bouncing off the station tiles. And it suddenly seemed essential that these fragments of imagination be immortalized before they finished as dreams and evaporated with waking. I couldn't stand to write them all down, the liquor had me pinned to the bed; the chore of verticality would overtake these thoughts, send them spinning out my mind. So I was determined to commit the

275

images to memory before my body had decided on wakeful-
ness or sleep, convinced that I'd never been so alone, never
be able to coordinate the words as perfectly as I could at this
tenuous moment when I was allowed access to a dimension
of honesty, adjacent to my own, on the flipside of beauty. The
flashes of sentences were spoken in a small voice, familiar
but unplaceable, that ran all the words together in a celestial
mumble.

"Beauty," the voice said, "Beauty is a red herring."

five

I start alone, here at my desk, eyes pointed at the semicircle
of little metal arms in the guts of the typewriter. There is
yesterday's period on the paper before me, a dried black
blotch that marks the rushed-to finish of an idea, an image, a
sentence. I've been asked to read my poetry at a bookstore
tonight — so I know that someone thinks this is all worthwhile. I read my last few lines. I reread, slower, each word on
its own, each sound measured. Then again, quickly, as though
by rote, as though reciting a prayer. But the inky dot stays
with the paperwhite abyss gaping below it. There must be a
trigger there, in the mess of yesterday's letters. Yesterday,
the abyss wanted violating. Yesterday, I was brilliant.

Just like yesterday and the day before, Fister is at
work. The apartment is full of compulsory silence, that huge

emptiness that encourages distractions. The furniture is lonely. The coffee is getting stale. Do we need butter? Perhaps the mail is here, shoved through the doorslot four hours early?

I've read yesterday's lines enough times now to have them stick in my memory and play back to me when I close my eyes in the silence, my own voice whispering in my head. I think of the next line. *There are truths hidden behind everything* — no. That's powerless, puny, obvious. *It's like a dream* — absolutely not. I close my eyes tighter, enough to feel skin bunching at their corners, but I find nothing worth writing down, I just see rows of faces waiting to be entertained, to be transported. I'm too aware this afternoon. Magic can only be made — and found, for that matter — on an ordinary day, and then only exploited at extraordinary moments, like it will be tonight from behind that podium. I'm stymied; the mechanics of what I do are laid bare. Yesterday it was easier to take a risk, to get lost, to get intoxicated with language, which is the only way good poetry is written — when you can believe your lies. Tonight, if my lies are handsome enough, people will want to believe them. Where I can, I try to attract people with beauty, guide them with the touch of the words, towards my little truths, those doors that open onto the divine.

Doors that open onto the divine — maybe. It has a beat, a rise and fall. I type it onto the page, the click and slam of the machine breaking the quietness for the first time all afternoon. It looks good there. I push the typewriter's chrome arm to start a new line, the roller moving slickly back to the left-hand margin, then continue staring at the page.

The boom of Fister's footsteps brings the rest of the room to attention: the messy desktop, the rickety IKEA armoire, the snapshots on my wall, the dreamcatcher in the window across the street. Fister calls out: "Woman, where's my dinner?" I stare at the day's lonely little sentence with an immediate fear that I will never be able to produce such a sentence again mingled with an untoppable satisfaction. Six words: a day's work.

I climb the small flight of stairs to the kitchen. Fister is there, his tie pulled loose, flipping through the mail. The rest of the apartment reeks of burnt coffee. Out the window, I can see the sun kissing the western edge of Mount Royal, giving everything a buttery glow.

"Christ, what time is it?"

"After four," Fister says, looking up. "You must have had a good day if you don't know what time it is."

"It was ok." I slide a casserole dish from the fridge. "I marinated chicken for dinner. Rosemary and lemon."

"You're such a homo." He descends to his room and calls out, "Are you nervous about tonight?"

"I haven't even thought about it." The poetry reading is at seven, but the bookstore is located nearby so it should be a quick walk. I sprinkle some saffron onto the chicken breasts and slide them onto a skillet. Fister returns in jeans and a black T-shirt, transformed from a PR representative.

He presses play on the CD player and Leonard Cohen comes on — "Famous Blue Raincoat." The chicken sizzles and pops. "So you're not even the slightest bit freaked out? All those people staring up at you?"

"Maybe a little. I'm more concerned that I'll get up there and realize I have nothing to say. There are two other readers, though. One of them has two books. Maybe they'll be good."

"Hacks," Fister says. He pours white wine into juice glasses. He holds one of them up to eye level and I do the same. "You're better than them and you know it."

There is jazz music playing in the bookstore when we arrive — an aural backdrop of swishy drums and a mandolin. I leave Fister with Jimmy and JP who are flipping through men's health magazines at the periodicals rack. The wine has done its work and the aisles of books pass like lampposts alongside a moving car. At the back, six sparsely occupied rows of folding chairs circle a podium. Two kinds of people come to these things — those who know the readers and those who actually have faith in books, love poetry, have walls of their apartments devoted to shelving it. I recognize some of the faithful: the academic couple, gay, both in tweed coats and black turtlenecks, and the androgynous girl with curly dark hair and breasts, as Zia would say, till Tuesday. She's also wearing a black turtleneck. And Sylvie, of course, the stout Quebecoise who owns the bookstore, head shaved, face impassive, waving at me from a corner. Under her black-tasselled shawl she looks like a gargoyle on a stone building.

Auntie Lucia and Zia are standing near an immense folding table covered in plastic wine glasses and a fan of cheese slices. Age has finally caught up with both of them. They look more wrinkled than at Christmas dinner, just three months ago. I had not thought that either would come all the way down from St-Michel, especially to a gay bookstore, just to listen to me read. But I was wrong. Zia said she "wouldn't miss it for the world dipped in gold." And since Uncle Devo passed away, Lucia has become enamoured with the city and makes Franco drive her to downtown events every chance she gets.

"Look at how big you've gotten!" Lucia says, grabbing my face. "How do we keep up, eh?" she asks Franco.

"I have no idea," he replies, giving me a look of annoyance.

"I'm so excited! Your mother would be so proud!" Zia says. "And to think, you never used to talk!"

"Well, I'll be talking tonight," I say. I pick up a cheese slice, warm and squishy from the heat.

"It's no good," Zia says. "We made you some cannoli and pitzels." She places a box onto the table and opens it up.

"You didn't have to do all this."

"It's only a couple dozen."

"You brought your own food?" says Sylvie. "Italian desserts! It's just like one of your poems!"

I introduce her to Zia and Lucia.

"We just love your nephew's work. He has such a clear voice. It's so *real*."

"His family's very proud," Zia says. "They all wanted to be here."

Sylvie takes my coat and places it on a front-row seat with a "Reserved" sign stickytaped to it. Flanking it are the other featured poets — a frumpy lesbian from Wales, with a disapproving frown, and a cute blonde man from Ottawa, younger than me, chatting with a gaggle of effeminate friends. They are from opposite ends of the spectrum, these two poets, but it is definitely the same spectrum — that of the bookish types who linger in places like this, who exchange diffident looks and quips about the loathsomeness of everyone they tolerate.

Sylvie turns off the jazz and waves everyone to attention. "I'm up first," whispers Ottawaboy with a charming nervousness. I smile back. He makes me feel, at twenty-seven years old, like a seasoned veteran. His hands shake as he walks up to the microphone. I shoot an evil look at JP and Jimmy, standing near a mountain of books, loudly plotting Ottawaboy's deflowering.

The poet introduces himself, offers a few disclaimers about his work, clears his throat, and then speaks of a broken heart, of a condo in Hull overlooking the river, of billowing curtains, of navels plugged with cum during the long afternoons of summer. His shaking ceases and he begins to float on his words. There is a delicateness to the way he speaks —

a confessional, inspired tone. He's the first reader, so the audience is still attentive and sharp. They clap in genuine appreciation when he is finished, giving me extra assurance as I walk up to the microphone.

"Well, God bless you all for coming," I say. There is a ripple of greeting through the group. Fister hoots. Lucia has a Kleenex crumpled into her hand in case of tears. "I'm going to be reading from my first book. It's due out next month," I say and am surprised — I always am — at how big my little voice sounds, blowing out over all those heads. I look down at the book, at the picture I had to fight my publisher to put on the cover: Ma and the kitty sitting on a bed. I clear my throat, trying to get over the urge to retch. The pause is longer than the listeners would like — but I take comfort in the tense, quiet beats and let the adrenaline calm my stomach. They all expect beauty, expect me to pull it out of my sleeve like a bouquet of cloth flowers. They are ready to be seduced, to absorb the truths I'm peddling, to be led. Even Ma looks expectant — but proud. I open my mouth and the words fall out measured, sing-song, the way I've prepared them. Even in my small voice they sound mysterious, divine.

Acknowledgements

I would like to offer my immense gratitude to all those who read and edited these stories, especially Ted Gideonse, John Terauds, Frank Smith, Jonathan Dee, Jhumpa Lahiri, Helen Schulman, Randolyn Zinn, Brian Rubin, Greg Torso and Brian Pera. I'd also like to thank my family for their support and love without which this book could not have been written.

MEMBER OF SCABRINI MEDIA

Quebec, Canada
2005